Single White Incubus

SUPERNATURAL
SELECTION

E.J. Russell

Cover art: L.C. Chase https://lcchase.com
Editors: Rachel Haimowitz, Kelly Miller

ISBN: 978-1-947033-74-0

Second edition
March 2024

Contact information:
ejr@ejrussell.com

Single White Incubus

SUPERNATURAL
SELECTION

E.J. Russell

For my readers, who fell in love with the Kendrick brothers and wanted more stories in their world.

SWI ISO LTR WTR

(Single white incubus in search of
lifetime relationship. Willing to relocate.)

The living need not apply.

Supernatural
Selection

Chapter One

"Ted? Did you hear the question?"

Ted Farnsworth blinked, shifting his gaze from his therapist's neck to his movie-star handsome face. "I'm sorry, Dr. Kendrick. What was it again?"

Dr. Kendrick was used to Ted getting distracted, since it happened at every visit at least once. Okay, twice. Three times, tops. But he never frowned with censure the way the head of the bear shifter council always did. Or snort with annoyance like Ted's brother. Or even sigh with impatience like some of his friends. Nope. Dr. Kendrick just calmly repeated himself.

"Why didn't you come to see me as soon as you got the council's letter of reprimand?"

"Oh. The letter." Ted squirmed, the urge to shift prickling along his spine and over his scalp. He gripped his knees, squeezing tight. *Shifting here would be bad. Dr. Kendrick's nice office furniture isn't rated for grizzlies.* "I couldn't come to town until now. My truck's in the shop."

Dr. Kendrick's eyebrows drew together. "But I installed the emergency communication app on your phone for a reason. You could have called me for transport through Faerie. There's a threshold in my backyard and another practically on top of your cabin."

Ted shrugged sheepishly and picked up his cup of Dr. Kendrick's excellent office coffee. "I know. But I didn't want to bother you."

"Arranging an appointment, especially when it's council-ordered and you could be censured for ignoring it, is a perfectly legitimate use." He crossed his legs and settled his hands on the arms of his wingback chair. "I want you to promise me that— Is something wrong?" He tugged on the knot of his tie. "You keep staring at my neck."

"No! Nothing. Nope." *But I'm pretty sure that's a hickey peeking over your collar, and it's* really *distracting.* "I guess I'm just not used to the new look."

"Ah. Is this better?" Between one blink and the next, Dr. Kendrick morphed from young-Hugh-Jackman gorgeous to the comforting face Ted was used to from before Dr. Kendrick had broken his curse: outsized skull, overhanging brow ridges, broad, misshapen nose, the whole nine.

Fae *glamourie.* It was a thing. Although Dr. Kendrick was the only fae Ted knew who would use it to look uglier instead of more beautiful, just to make somebody else feel better.

"Yeah, thanks." *But that hickey is still winking at me.* Ted forced himself to concentrate on Dr. Kendrick's deep-set eyes.

"If your truck is in the shop, how did you get from the coast to Portland today?"

"Oh, I hitched a ride with Matt."

"Matt?" Dr. Kendrick frowned, and with his old face, that was PDS—pretty damn scary. "Matt Steinitz? The tabloid photographer?" The shock in his tone was a good indication of how bad an idea he thought this was. Dr. Kendrick's voice was *never* anything but well-modulated and soothing.

"That's him."

"After the council's *last* warning, I thought you'd broken off contact with him."

"It's not what you think." *Mostly, anyway.* "He lives in Dewton now, down the mountain from my place." Although he wouldn't have moved there if it weren't for Ted's stupid shifter tricks. "We're . . . we're friends."

"But, Ted . . ." Dr. Kendrick did sigh this time, running his hands through his hair. "Your association with him is exactly why Bruno Killingsworth escalated the most recent incident from a bear shifter matter to one for the combined supe council." He pointed to the tabloid newspaper lying on the coffee table between them, Matt's picture of Ted in his partially shifted form on the front page above the fold, with the headline screaming *Bigfoot Sighted in Coast Range!* "Aside from the fact that you're endangering the Secrecy Pact, Sasquatch is *seriously* annoyed at the continued impersonations. They want to file suit against you for identity theft."

"I'm sorry." Ted bit his lip and set his half-empty cup on the table, wishing he hadn't drunk it quite so fast, because his stomach was definitely complaining. Should he confess to Dr. Kendrick that he'd staged another "incident" just two days ago —and that he'd phoned Matt from his motel with an anonymous tip this morning before this appointment?

"The council sent that reprimand because their forbearance is exhausted. They're threatening to *tag* you, Ted."

Ted's heart plummeted to his shoes. "T-t-tag me? But—" He squeezed his hands tighter, his fingers digging into his knees. If they tagged him, he'd have no privacy at all. He wouldn't be able to take a piss without the news being fed to the Supernatural Monitoring Agency. And the sphinxes who ran the SMA were really fussy—they *never* slept and they had *zero* sense of humor. They were worse than Santa.

"And tagging is only one step from form-locking. Two from —" Dr. Kendrick cleared his throat, his gaze sliding away from Ted's face. "Two from termination."

"Termination? You mean . . ." Ted drew his finger across his throat, and Dr. Kendrick nodded.

Nope. Not confessing. Matt might not do anything with the latest photo. And Ted could bail on this morning's tip, not show up this time, even though he hated to disappoint Matt. He was a good guy—and he got so excited about cryptid sightings.

Besides, they were sort of payment for the ride to town and back—not to mention a goodbye present.

Because even if the council hadn't come down on Ted's ass like a ton of manure, after today, he was swearing off Sasquatch impersonations for good.

"You don't have to worry about me anymore, Doctor, and neither does the council. I've got something to show you." Ted hefted his backpack off the floor. But the strap—frayed by too many trips up and down the mountain in his bear's teeth—snapped, knocking his cup over and sending a wave of lukewarm coffee over the table, soaking the newspaper and dripping onto Dr. Kendrick's shoes.

"Shoot!" Ted leaped up, glancing around wildly for something to mop up the spill, but only succeeding in knocking the table with his shins.

Dr. Kendrick waved him back down. "Sit, sit. Please don't worry about it." He got up and walked over to open the door. "David? We've had a bit of a spill. Could you help, please."

"Of course," David, Dr. Kendrick's assistant and husband, said from the lobby. "Be there in a jiffy."

Dr. Kendrick waited at the open door until David appeared, carrying a roll of paper towels and a spritz bottle of some kind of cleanser. David paused, glancing from Dr. Kendrick to Ted. He placed a hand on Dr. Kendrick's neck, leaning in to whisper to him. For an instant, Dr. Kendrick's beast *glamourie* flickered off, and his cheeks flushed dark pink.

Weird.

When David took his hand away, he flashed a brilliant grin at Ted—and that distracting pink spot over Dr. Kendrick's collar was gone. But Ted knew what he'd seen. *It* was *a hickey, and David zapped it.* Dr. Kendrick's husband was an *achubydd*, a magical healer. *Guess that comes in handy when things get a little exciting in the bedroom.*

Ted toyed with the broken strap as David mopped up the spill and Dr. Kendrick resumed his seat. *Guess I need a new pack.*

He carried it in his human or bear form, when he schlepped between his cabin and the cave above Dewton where he kept an extra set of clothes. He hadn't mentioned that to Dr. Kendrick either. When his truck was on the fritz—or sometimes just because he felt like it—he'd shift into bear form to get down the mountain faster, then hike the rest of the way to town after he changed in the cave.

Dr. Kendrick and the supe council probably wouldn't approve of that, and the bear council *definitely* wouldn't approve. Of course, none of them understood why Ted wanted to go to town in the first place. But by now he'd gotten that message loud and clear—he wasn't exactly your average bear.

After David left with the wastebasket full of soggy newspaper and soiled paper towels, Dr. Kendrick smiled at Ted. "Now, you were saying?"

"Oh. Right." Ted pawed through his pack and pulled out two folders, one plain manila and one glossy white. "You know the Walton clan property next to mine?"

"Walton? The marten shifters? Didn't they move up to Canada last year?"

"Yep. They've had the place on the market since then." Ted grinned, flipping open the manila folder, and tapped the grainy photo on the real estate listing inside. "Last month, I bought it."

Dr. Kendrick's eyebrows quirked, but he leaned over to study the picture. "This structure doesn't look very sound. Or complete, for that matter."

"Oh, it not. It's pretty much a shell, actually, but I'm gonna fit it out as a wilderness retreat center."

Dr. Kendrick frowned. "Ted, I don't like to discourage you, but you've had difficulties with follow-through in the past. Do you have a solid plan for the business?"

"Um . . ." Ted dog-eared the corner of the listing, then smoothed it flat again. "Not exactly. But I don't have to." He nudged the other folder, the shiny one, toward the doctor. "I'm married."

Dr. Kendrick blinked, and his face flickered back to beautiful for a second. "Married? Congratulations. I didn't realize . . ." He leaned back in his chair, his beast persona firmly in place. "Who's the lucky supe?"

Ted opened the folder and teased out the picture of his new husband. *My husband!* His heart threatened to prance right out of his chest. "This is him. His name's Rusty Johnson."

Dr. Kendrick glanced up sharply. "Rusty Johnson from the Dawson beaver clan in Eugene?"

"You know him too?"

"Of course. All shifters with inactive shifting genes are required to submit to regular quarterly counseling sessions, although Rusty is the most well-adjusted Inactive it's been my pleasure to treat. But, Ted . . ." Dr. Kendrick laced his fingers together, his expression serious—although it was tough for his beast face to look *un*serious. "The last time I spoke with Rusty, which admittedly was almost three months ago, he was still expecting to mate with Fletcher Dawson, the clan heir. Your courtship must have been quite sudden. When did you two meet?"

"We . . . ah . . . haven't actually met. Yet."

"But you said you were married."

"We are. All signed and sealed. Here." Ted took a three-color brochure out of the pocket of the folder. "You know how in our last session, you suggested I look for other ways to meet friends? I took your advice." He handed the brochure to Dr. Kendrick.

Dr. Kendrick opened it, smoothing it across his knees. "Supernatural Selection?" He glanced up, clearly troubled. "When I suggested you look for other means to meet people, I didn't mean you should *buy* your friends."

"Not a friend. A mate. A husband. I thought you'd understand. You're happier now that you're married, right?"

"Yes, of course, but wouldn't you prefer to meet potential partners in a more . . . organic way?"

"But see, that's the great thing. The agency is run by a witch's collective. They *know* shit. Spells, and . . . and clairvoyance and psychic stuff."

"You think they could know you better than you know yourself? Enough to match you with a compatible partner?"

"They promise a perfect match."

"But, Ted . . ." Dr. Kendrick set the brochure on the table. "They're constrained by their own clientele. They can only connect you with other supes who are on their roster. What if your perfect mate isn't registered? Don't you think interacting with the larger shifter community would be a better bet for you?"

Larger shifter community. That was a laugh, although Ted doubted Dr. Kendrick meant it as a joke. There weren't many shifters larger than a grizzly.

"This is best. It'll be great, Dr. Kendrick, you'll see." He tucked the brochure into the folder and stuffed everything back in his pack. "My perfect match. My lifelong companion. I'll be happy and stay out of trouble from now on."

Guaranteed.

Chapter Two

"Sir. Excuse me. Sir?"

Quentin Bertrand-Harrington cracked open bleary eyes to peer up at the flight attendant in the aisle. The seats next to him were empty, as apparently was the rest of the plane. "I'm sorry. Have we landed?"

"Yes. I must ask you to deplane now so that we can prep the equipment for the next flight. Do you need any assistance?" She reached out to him, but he jerked his arm out of reach.

"No. Thank you, but no." Even with the suppressant still active in his bloodstream, making him woozy and half-disassociated with his body, he shied away from touch. He had been too long without a partner and he was just so *hungry*. Even the casual touch from a stranger was likely to pose a danger to said stranger.

He struggled out from under his blanket—it looked like a space blanket, silver and metallic—but really it was a bespelled cloak that prevented human energy from touching him and tempting him despite the suppressant. He banged his head on the back of the seat in front of him—damn, how did people who flew coach all the time manage?—as he retrieved his carry-on from the floor. He shoved the blanket inside the case and scooted to the aisle.

He hadn't staggered two steps before the flight attendant caught his arm. He whirled on her, jerking himself away with such force he nearly fell over the nearest armrest.

"I beg your pardon, sir, but you forgot your iPad." She held it out to him.

"Yes. Thank you. I'm sorry for . . ." He made a vague gesture with his free hand before taking the tablet from her. "I'm still a bit disoriented, I fear."

"No worries." She pasted on a professional smile. "Welcome to Portland. You'll find your baggage on carousel three."

"Thank you."

Quentin hobbled off the plane and up the jetway. Devil take it, but the large dose of suppressant he'd swallowed in Boston— triple the amount he downed daily to keep his appetites in check—had totally knocked him for a loop. His mouth was dry, his vision blurred, and he felt as if he'd never be able to stand up straight again.

You could if you took a sip—just a sip—from someone big and handsome and—

Stop it!

Quentin was a married man now, for all he'd never met his new husband. Regardless, he'd owed the man fidelity from the moment he'd signed the Supernatural Selection mating contract —in blood, because witches were tradition-bound when it came to binding rituals.

The Portland airport wasn't nearly as crowded as O'Hare, where he'd caught his connecting flight, but it still had far too many people for Quentin's peace of mind. If he were a normal incubus, he'd simply pick one of the couples engaging in a joyous reunion and brush close enough to absorb sufficient ambient sexual energy to remain ambulatory. But Quentin wasn't a normal incubus. Even the regular energy "parties" his grandmother threw with willing human hosts—elegant, oh-so-civilized events with exquisite hors d'oeuvres, themed cocktails, and live chamber music—loaded Quentin with debilitating guilt. Feeding from a stranger, even inadvertently, smacked too much of nonconsent. Hence the heavy dose of suppressant.

But tonight is my wedding night. Tonight, for the first time since he'd nearly killed his last serious boyfriend with nothing more than passionate foreplay, he'd have sex again.

A celibate incubus—it was unheard of. An incubus who cared about consent was even rarer. And after leaving Rory as nothing but a husk, requiring months of treatment both mundane and magical, Quentin hadn't dared go so far again.

Instead, he'd signed a permanent mating agreement with a vampire. There wasn't much damage he could do to a man who was already dead, as long as he kept the sun out of the house and limited his garlic intake.

He took the escalator down to baggage claim. Carousel three was swarming with people, and he shied away, taking refuge at carousel one, which was presently deserted. He could see all three of his suitcases trundling along on the serpentine belt, but didn't dare go close enough to grab them, not when he couldn't avoid coming into contact with the other passengers.

"Mr. Bertrand-Harrington?"

A touch on his shoulder, coupled with his name, made Quentin whirl and stagger back several steps. A young man holding a sign with Quentin's name on it smiled at him hesitantly.

"You are Mr. Bertrand-Harrington, aren't you?"

Quentin clutched the strap of his case with both hands, wanting nothing so much as to grab the man's hand and *feast.* "Yes."

"I'm Jason. Supernatural Sel— I mean, the agency sent me to pick you up. I'm to drop you at your husband's home. Transportation—it's included in your contract?"

"Oh." Between his incessant, nagging hunger and his suppressant-induced disorientation, Quentin had been so out of it when he'd signed the damn thing that he hadn't bothered to read the final version. "Thank you."

"If you could point out your luggage to me, I'll escort you to the car first, then collect your bags afterward. We can be on our way in no time."

"Yes. Thank you—" he checked the driver's name tag "—Jason." *Reprieve.* He wouldn't have to shoulder his way through the crowd, although it was dwindling now. "That would be most welcome."

He followed Jason out the doors and across the roadway to a parking garage. Jason flourished a key fob, and the lights flashed on a nearby Town Car. He opened the rear door for Quentin to slide in. "Make yourself comfortable. There's water in the cooler. I'll be back shortly and we can be on our way."

Quentin settled into the lush leather seats gratefully. To be on the safe side, he pulled out his not-a-space blanket and spread it over himself from shoulders to toes. For any number of reasons, he had no desire to drain any energy from someone who was driving him to his new life. It would be a traffic hazard. It would be the next thing to cheating.

And it would be far too tempting to let it go further.

He leaned his head against the seat back and closed his eyes with a sigh.

"Mr. Bertrand-Harrington? Sir?"

Quentin cracked his eyes open. Jason was peering at him from the front seat. "I'm sorry. Are we ready to get going?"

"Um . . . actually, we're already here. You've been asleep since we left the airport."

"Oh. I'm sorry. I hope you didn't need me to give you directions." Especially since he wasn't sure what they were. They'd been included in the glossy Supernatural Selection folder along with his new husband's dossier and his mating contract copy, but he hadn't read them. He'd barely made it to Logan Airport and onto his flight before the suppressant had kicked in.

"No. Everything was handled by the agency. I've taken your bags to the—" he glanced out the heavily tinted windows "—

the place. Is there anything else you need? I've got to get back to the airport for another pickup."

Quentin shook his head and scooted across the seat to climb out of the car, blinking in the sunlight and shivering a bit in the cold. He'd left his heavy winter coat back in Boston, more as a diversion than with any clear plan in mind. If his grandmother saw his coat hanging in the closet and his boots in the mud room, she wouldn't notice he was missing until she had yet another "eligible" human husband or wife for him.

His decision to contract his own spouse had been an impulse, spurred by a discreet ad in the back of *Supernatural Travel Monthly*. Now, he was forever out of her reach—or rather out of the reach of her scheme for a "normal" 'cubi match for him with a partner who'd live an almost completely separate life, putting up with the occasional necessary sex in exchange for wealth and social influence. But not companionship. Not closeness. Not love. Anyone who wanted *that* wouldn't last ten years married to an incubus.

Or in Quentin's case, judging by past experience, wouldn't last ten minutes.

Still disoriented from the suppressant, he vaguely registered the car pulling away. He turned in a bewildered circle, taking in the vast, autumn-bedraggled meadow, the wide lake, and the trees that ringed the clearing, telltale mounds of snow scattered under their branches. The sun was bright but it wasn't warm, not in the frigid air. *Don't be a drama queen. This is a temperate state. It can't be as cold as it was in Boston.*

He shivered anyway, huddling in his inadequate suit coat. *Wait a minute. Lake? Field? Forest?* His new husband was supposed to live in a spacious modern home in the Portland West Hills. This was a hill, no doubt—or rather a mountain, judging by the peak that rose above the rather derelict building sprawling next to the lake. But where was the city? Where were the neighbors?

Where was his husband?

His hands started to shake from something more than cold. *Calm down, calm down. It's daylight, and sunny at that. Casimir is a vampire.* Perhaps he was still asleep, or at least sequestered somewhere in the dark. Maybe the derelict building was merely a glamour cast over the true mansion—he'd seen the pictures, and the place was impressive—to protect it from prying eyes.

What prying eyes? There's nobody around for miles.

Nevertheless, he stumbled through the rank weeds toward the wide porch where Jason had stacked his luggage. *Any step now I'll break through the veil.* But the farther he crept toward the building, the further his heart dropped. When he climbed the creaking stairs to stand on the wide planks of the porch, and it looked even worse up close than it had from the middle of the clearing, he had to admit that it was exactly what it appeared to be: a rambling, ramshackle shell of a structure, dropped in the middle of nowhere.

But the driver from Supernatural Selection had brought him here. He wouldn't have done that if this wasn't the right place. Somewhere here he'd find his husband. And then he had a few questions for the man—er, vampire. This was hardly the welcome he'd expected.

He clutched the rickety porch rail. The counselor at Supernatural Selection had warned him that Casimir was under council orders to contract an acceptable marriage. In fact, they were the ones who had selected Quentin. Quentin had thought that Casimir had been amenable—he'd signed the contract, after all. Was this some kind of vampire stunt, meant to thumb his nose at the council?

In a way, Quentin could relate. He was doing exactly the same thing to his grandmother and her plans, after all. But he expected to be a partner to Casimir, not an adversary.

Quentin sighed, eyeing his suitcase. Should he dig out a warmer coat? Not yet. First he wanted to find out if he was quite as alone as he thought. He descended the stairs and fought his way through the weeds to circle the building. It had an impressive footprint—like some kind of inn, judging from the number of floors and windows. Although when Quentin peered through some of them—the ones that weren't boarded up—the inside was a forest of bare studs and plywood floors.

The rear of the place had the skeleton of a deck that, if it were complete, would have a stunning view of the lake and the surrounding hills. He stood looking at it, the chill from the damp ground seeping through the thin leather of his Italian oxfords. Some kind of large bird burst from the trees, startling him, and skimmed across the lake with a cry.

The lake lapped quietly at the shore, but he could hear cascading water and . . . was that someone singing? The sounds were coming from the side of the house closest to the trees. Quentin crept forward until he could peek around the corner.

Holy mother of fire.

There was a man. An enormous man. An enormous *naked* man. An enormous naked man, sluicing himself off in an outdoor shower. Quentin should have shivered just from the notion of what cold water in the colder air would do—not that it seemed to have any effect on Enormous Naked Man's . . . er . . . appendage.

Despite the suppressant still floating around in his system, despite his determination to avoid anyone who wasn't his husband, despite the cold air that ought to have cooled him down to almost zero, heat rose in Quentin's core—and so did his cock.

Oh no. Absolutely not. Even if he weren't contractually bound to someone—who could not possibly be this man, since it was broad daylight and his husband would disintegrate under this much sun exposure—Quentin had sworn never again to let his incubus libido endanger another living person.

And then Enormous Naked Man opened his eyes and stared straight at Quentin.

And smiled.

Devil take it. I am so so so fucked.

Chapter
Three

For a second, Ted thought the guy peeking around the corner was Matt—or maybe Larry, the mechanic from Dewton who doubled as the delivery guy for the lumberyard. Then he wiped the water out of his eyes and realized the guy was way too small and frail to be either one. Matt was taller and Larry was stockier—and neither one of them had black hair and a goatee and looked like the least breeze would blow them off the mountain.

A stranger. And I'm naked. Whoops. Good thing he wasn't here ten minutes ago when I shifted. Because shifting in front of a human? Yeah, that was a sure way to bring the council down on his ass, especially after what Dr. Kendrick had told him this morning.

Ordinarily, Ted would have shifted back to his bear form and shaken the water off to get dry—he'd only stopped out here to shower because he'd run afoul of an illegal dump site when he was lumbering back up the mountain after Matt had dropped him off in town. So he didn't have a towel. Or clothes.

Awkward.

Well, it was his place, damn it. Wasn't he entitle to privacy here? He wasn't expecting anyone until Rusty arrived next week, so he should have been able to parade around as naked as a mole rat if he wanted, with no one the wiser.

And even though shifter blood ran hotter than human, and he'd already started to put on the padding around his middle in the run-up to winter hibernation season, it was still damn cold in the wind off the lake.

"Sorry. I—" he gestured to his body "—wasn't expecting company." If he could just get the guy to go around to the front of the lodge, Ted could shift and dry off. Wouldn't help the no-clothes situation, but he had a stash in the lodge, and a cache inside the tree line for emergencies—or when he was running the Bigfoot scam. He sighed. *Can't do that anymore either.*

But the guy just kept staring at Ted, his eyes behind those rectangular hipster glasses getting bigger and bigger. Which had the unfortunate effect of—what did Dr. Kendrick call it? Sympathetic reaction? Because Ted's dick started to keep pace.

I'm a married man now. I need to keep it in my pants. When I have pants. He turned his back. "Could you, you know, go back to your car until I get dressed?"

"I don't have a car." The guy's voice sounded like he was trying to get the words out past someone's fist.

"You too? Yeah, my truck's in the shop, so—" Ted slapped himself on the forehead. *Not relevant.* "If you'd just go around to the porch, I'll be there in a minute and you can let me know what you need."

The guy let out a noise that sounded like *"Awp!"* But since that wasn't a word, it couldn't have been what he'd said. Ted took it for a yes because when he checked over his shoulder, the guy was gone.

"Whew." He shifted back to his bear, heat singing along his bones as the shifter magic reformed his body. He sighed in relief. Ordinarily the itch from the fur sprouting through his skin drove him nuts and he'd search for the nearest tree to rub against, but today he was too damn glad of the heat.

A little thrill raised the fur along his spine. *I'll have a husband to rub up against soon.* Would Rusty like Ted's bear form? Or would it be insensitive to shift since Rusty couldn't? He should have asked Dr. Kendrick about that this morning, dang it. *For Rusty, I can keep it together, control my shifts.* He'd known marriage would take some compromises. If shifting in secret was one of them, at least it would give him practice being "discreet." *That ought to make the council happy.*

He shifted back, the energy drain from the second shift making him a little light-headed. Making a mental note to eat an extra helping at dinner to make up for it, he ducked through the back door of the lodge into the mud room—the only room that held anything but sawdust and building materials. He pulled on a pair of jeans that could use a wash and an old flannel shirt with a stain on the front from when he was changing the oil in his truck. Sheesh. He needed to upgrade his spare wardrobe if he was going to be getting random uninvited visitors.

I need to upgrade it anyway. He glanced at his wedding band, a grin stretching his cheeks. *I'm married now. Time to step up my game.*

He stepped back outside, closing the door behind him. It didn't stay closed, of course. He really ought to fix the latch and put in the locks. Although why bother? Nobody but Larry ever came up here. *Larry and little random hipster dudes.*

Yeah. About that. Ted strode around the lodge and there the guy was, standing on the top step of the porch with his arms wrapped around his middle. He'd be kind of cute if he weren't wearing an expression like he'd just stepped in a steaming pile of bobcat scat.

Still, he was a visitor, and how often did Ted get those? He smiled and held out his hand. "Hey. Sorry about the . . . um . . . casual dress, but I wasn't expecting anybody. Ted Farnsworth."

The visitor glared up at Ted, not offering his hand—or his name—in return. "Well, I certainly wasn't expecting *you.* Where's Casimir?"

Ted blinked. "Who?"

"Casimir Moreau. Are you the caretaker?" He glanced around at the obviously unfinished lodge. "I can't say much for your abilities, if that's the case."

Ted scowled. "Here now. There's no call to get nasty. The lodge is under construction, and it's not like I invited you up here."

"I'm here to meet Casimir. I don't understand . . ." The guy suddenly seemed so lost and confused and *cold* that Ted's anger vanished.

"I'm not sure who this Casimir guy is, but who are you?"

He looked up—even standing on the top step of three, he had to look up at Ted. Jeez, the guy was little. "I'm sorry. I'm just so . . ." He still didn't hold out his hand, but he bobbed his head in a weird little bow. "Quentin Bertrand-Harrington."

Ted nodded in return, since hand-shaking was apparently off the table. "Nice to meet you. That's some double-barreled name you've got there."

Quentin shrugged, and a faint smile lifted the corners of his mouth. "It's tradition in my family. Blame it on stubborn ancestors."

"Huh. Interesting." The only tradition in Ted's family was for everyone to get as far away from each other as possible. But that was a bear-shifter thing.

Quentin gazed around him like somebody who'd just woken from a nap and still hadn't figured out he wasn't in a dream anymore. Ted could relate. He felt the same way pretty much all winter. "Where *is* this place? I can't see any part of Portland."

Ted laughed. "Of course not. Portland's nearly a hundred miles east of here."

Quentin's eyes got big again. "A hundred miles? But . . . but the Supernatural Selection driver said he—"

"Wait. Supernatural Selection?"

Quentin's expression closed down, turning wary. "Yes. Do you recognize the name?"

"Do I?" Ted beamed, holding up his left hand and waggling his ring finger. "They found me my husband."

Relief flickered across Quentin's face. "Oh thank the gods. You're a supe, then?"

"Yep. Bear shifter."

"And your name is Ted? Half the bear shifters I know are named Ted."

Ted scowled at him. "That's an exaggeration. Half the bear shifters are female. Though now that I think of it . . ." Ted scratched the back of his head. "Some of them are called Ted too, although more of them are Winnies. But you've got a good mix of Smokey, Yogi, Baloo, and now and then a Fozzie, if the poor guy's parents had a weird sense of humor."

"You can't be more original than that?"

Ted sniffed. "It's *tradition*."

Quentin cracked a smile. "Fair enough, bear shifter Ted. No wonder you didn't mind the cold."

"If I'd known you were part of the community, I wouldn't have made you run away. Although"—he waggled his finger again—"married, so probably shouldn't be flashing my junk to random guys."

"Yes. Yes, of course." Quentin swallowed and looked down at his feet, faint pink staining his cheeks. "As it happens, I'm married too. I've just come from Boston to meet my husband, and I thought the driver was supposed to drop me at his home. But they left me here." He glanced around. "I don't understand. Unless . . . do you have a vampire retreat hidden somewhere nearby?"

"Vampires? Here? No way. Those jokers wouldn't come so far from the city. No food supplies." He studied Quentin more carefully. He didn't have any obvious supe markers—but then, most supes didn't. It was how they were able to pass for human, and why the Secrecy Pact worked. "You're married to a vampire? Really? That's . . ."

Quentin raised his chin defiantly. "Weird? Perverse? Stupid?"

"I was going to say 'brave,' but I guess you have some feelings about it. How long have you guys been together?"

"We haven't. That is, we've signed the contracts, but we haven't met. That's why I'm somewhat at a loss here."

Ted rubbed his thumb and forefinger together, remembering the feel of the enchanted needle piercing his flesh, and the three witches intoning the binding spell. "Yeah, the signing in blood thing was intense. I just signed mine yesterday."

"Yesterday?" Quentin's gaze sharpened. "Where's *your* husband, then?"

"Oh, he's not arriving until next week. Some kind of big to-do with his old clan. The chief's heir is getting engaged or something."

"But you were together to sign the contracts, right?"

"No." Ted drew out the word, not entirely sure where Quentin was going with these questions. He sounded almost accusatory. "It was by proxy, in the Supernatural Selection office."

Quentin grew paler, if that was possible. *He'd probably pass for a vampire, if he wasn't standing in the sunlight.* "I signed at the supe notary. Yesterday."

"So?"

Quentin whirled and tottered, nearly falling off the step. Ted reached out and steadied him. "Careful. Not too steady on your pins."

He jerked away with a gasp. "Never mind that." He dug through a leather messenger bag, embossed with his initials in gold. Jeez, this guy probably had gold-plated everything. He pulled out a glossy folder with the Supernatural Selection logo. Ted recognized it—he had one himself, with Rusty's dossier and his copy of the mating contract. "They messengered this to the notary's office, but with the suppressant, I barely registered . . ." He opened the folder, rifling through pages until he must have found the one he wanted, because he froze, staring down at it, all remaining color leaving his face. "I don't understand. How could this happen?"

"What?"

Quentin held up the contract, pointing to the stupid "party of the first part" clause at the top that Ted always skimmed over.

The first party, of course, was Quentin Bertrand-Harrington. But the party of the second part . . .

Ted Farnsworth.

Chapter Four

Quentin stared at the huge man in front of him—*Ted. His name is Ted Farnsworth.* And enormous, formerly naked Ted Farnsworth was bent nearly double, peering at the contract as if it were written in ancient Babylonian, his wide brow furrowed.

He poked the paper with a thick finger. "That's me."

"Yes, that's you. And that's a giant problem. It's supposed to say Casimir Moreau. That's who it's said in every other version of the contract since negotiations began last week. How the *devil* did it suddenly become *you*?"

"Why are you asking me?"

"Because it's *your name!*"

Ted blinked. "Shit on a biscuit. Does that mean I'm a *bigamist*?"

"Where's your contract?"

"What business is that of yours?"

"I'm magically mated to you! *That's* what business it is of mine. Where's your bloody contract?"

Ted straightened, tugging at the hem of his shirt. "Chill out, Q-Bert."

"*Q-Bert?*" Quentin's hair threatened to catch fire. "How dare you—"

"I've got the contract here. I just got back from a trip to Portland myself." He took off around the lodge with his giant stride, leaving Quentin to run to catch up.

Since Quentin's breath was already coming in gasps, he was nearly hyperventilating by the time he caught up at the back of the lodge. He leaned against the rough shingles, trying not to pass out, while Ted dug through an oversized backpack with a broken strap.

He pulled out an identical Supernatural Selection folder. "Here it is." He opened the folder, thumbing through the papers at a pace that rivaled a retreating glacier. Somehow, Quentin managed not to snatch it out of his hand, because this was a fucking *disaster*.

"Ah. Here we go. 'Party of the first part, Ted Farnsworth. Party of the second part . . .'" His mouth fell open and he raised wide eyes to Quentin's face. "'Quentin Bertrand-Harrington.'"

Quentin sank down, heedless of the rough shingles snagging on his suit coat or the damp weeds under his ass. "How can this be? They *guarantee* a perfect match. There are spells. Safeguards. *Proofreaders!*"

"I don't get it. This should say Rusty Johnson." Ted rummaged in the pack again, and pulled out a folded bundle of papers, wrinkled and dog-eared. "It *did* say Rusty Johnson. See?" He held up a page with the *Draft* watermark blazoned under the text.

"That hardly matters. The one you signed *in blood* says Quentin Bertrand-Harrington. Didn't you *read* it before you signed it?"

"Didn't *you?*"

Quentin pushed his glasses up and rubbed his eyes. "I was . . . distracted." *Heavily sedated.* "I sent the draft to my lawyers after I reviewed it myself—"

"Yeah, well, I reviewed the fricking draft too. I signed off on the damn thing. What was the point of reading it *again?*"

"Apparently," Quentin said acidly, "to prevent clerical errors. Unless the error wasn't unintentional at all."

Ted pointed that enormous finger at Quentin this time. "Don't put this all on me. You think I *want* some clueless guy who doesn't know any better than to wear a business suit in the wilderness? Who looks like the heaviest thing he's ever carried is a briefcase? Who probably doesn't know one end of a hammer from the other?"

"I know enough to know which end to hit you with," Quentin muttered.

Ted ran both hands through his hair, sending it skyward. "I can't believe this. I sank all my money into this property and the contract. Rusty was going to help me finish it. Get it set up as a money-making retreat. Now—"

"If you think *my* family's money will bail you out, think again. They don't even know I'm here."

"I've never *heard* of your family *or* your fucking money. I don't give a shit about that. I want—" Ted's voice caught. "I want *my* husband. I don't want *you!*"

Before Quentin could say another word, either of apology or accusation, Ted ripped off his shirt, dropped his pants— exposing that truly *stellar* ass—and shifted into the biggest grizzly Quentin had ever seen. Ted took off into the woods at a lumbering gallop, leaving Quentin alone as the sun sank toward the lake.

He let his head thunk against the shingles, lacing his fingers together to stop them from shaking. "Well. That could have gone better."

Ted crashed through the trees, heedless of the branches lashing his face and catching at his fur. *Rusty, damn it. I want Rusty. And now I'm stuck with Quentin Bertrand-Fuckington.* How could this have happened? Well, he knew how it had happened. He'd been so damned *moony* over the idea of a partner, a mate, a *lover,* that he'd rushed through the last ritual with barely a glance at the contract. In fact, he'd been so focused, he'd seen nothing but his name printed below the signature line as the lead witch pricked his finger and dipped the quill in his blood.

He waded into the stream and splashed along downhill. He should have paid more attention—to the ceremony, to whether random dudes were lurking around his property, even to what he'd spilled to Matt. Had he actually *mentioned* who—or rather what—his husband was? He barely remembered anything he and Matt had discussed, either on the way to Portland or on the way home. Something about the lodge. Something about his marriage. *Something something something.* That was the problem when Ted got too excited. He didn't pay attention to details or guard his tongue. Dr. Kendrick was always warning him to think about potential consequences, especially when interacting with non-supes. But it was so hard to remember sometimes.

He climbed out of the stream and shook himself. He really needed to talk to someone. He could call his brother, he supposed, but Ben was a true bear shifter: living alone in the mountains of Montana and liking it just fine. Ted still called him once a week—when the cell signal allowed—but counted himself lucky if he got three sentences out of Ben.

He needed more than that today. Should he call Dr. Kendrick? He froze, staring at his paw on the stream bank. *I can't call Dr. Kendrick or Ben or the dude at Supernatural Selection or anybody. My stupid phone is in my pants back at the lodge.*

He growled low in his throat, startling a crow out of a nearby tree. *Great. As if I needed another example of my impulse control problem.* On the other hand, it was probably a good thing he couldn't call Dr. Kendrick right now. Just the idea of what he'd say about Ted's monumental mistake made the fur on Ted's spine stand straight up.

No, he couldn't confess the disaster he'd made of his life to any other supe. Supes—the kind that didn't get sanctioned by the council—knew how to behave, how to keep a low profile, how to blend in.

It's really hard to blend in anywhere when you're six foot eight.

He needed someone that he could just kick back with. Someone who wouldn't ask him about his supernatural missteps. Someone who thought he was just a regular guy.

Matt.

Yeah, Matt made his living selling photographs to sketchy publications, but he was a good guy. Easy to talk to, unlike some people Ted could name.

Ted took off down the mountain. When he got to the cave where he kept his clothes, it was nearly dusk. Matt had dropped him off less than six hours ago, and the one thing Ted *could* remember from their conversation was that Matt had a dinner appointment with somebody else, some guy he thought might be a new source for him. So Matt wouldn't be around.

But Ted couldn't face going back up to the lodge. Quentin would be there or he wouldn't, and either way, Ted didn't want to deal with it. So he crawled into the cave and curled up next to the wall. He'd sleep—never tough to do at this time of year. Matt always ate breakfast at Wanda's Diner in Dewton, so Ted could catch him in the morning.

As he drifted off, he felt a twinge of worry for Quentin. Yeah, the guy was an asshole, and obviously thought Ted was a waste of space—so far beneath him that he wouldn't even shake Ted's hand—but the lodge wasn't exactly a five-star hotel. Ted's cabin was farther along the lake shore, so Q-Bert would have to hike half a mile in his fancy-ass shoes to get there, assuming he noticed it at all. *Whatever.* He could just shift to his animal form, whatever it was, and stay warm overnight that way, just like Ted was doing.

It's not like I invited him. It's not like I want him. And he certainly doesn't want me.

Q-Bert could damn well fend for himself.

Chapter Five

After his pulse settled and his breathing returned to normal, Quentin stood up and stalked around to the porch. His anger was simmering just below the surface, partly at Farnsworth for running out before they could figure out their next steps, and partly at himself for behaving like an entitled asshole.

Grandmother would have my guts for her viola strings. Pauline Bertrand-Harrington was a firm believer in maintaining the social hierarchy, but she was also a stickler for proper etiquette. And Quentin shouldn't have allowed his own panic to goad him into being rude—or rather, downright nasty—to Farnsworth. He might be an unsophisticated, unconnected bear shifter, but he seemed like a reasonably nice man. Like any decent person, he deserved no less than common courtesy and consideration, and certainly didn't deserve to have his unexpected husband kill him with sex.

However, a generous part of Quentin's anger was directed at Supernatural Selection. How the *devil* had they made such an enormous mistake? The error was theirs, so remediation should be theirs as well, or Quentin's lawyers would have a bloody field day.

Except I can't tell the lawyers where I am yet. They'd tell Grandmother, and she'd use this to push through her own agenda. The whole point of Quentin's decision to use Supernatural Selection was to avoid that agenda. He was a three-hundred-year-old incubus. Surely he could figure this out on his own.

First, he'd contact Supernatural Selection, demand that they send the driver back to pick him up and take him to a cushy hotel in downtown Portland at their expense. Then he'd figure out his next move far, *far* away from the temptation of Ted Farnsworth's ridiculously large body.

He dug his cell phone out of his bag and peered at the screen in the failing light. The battery had a seventy-five percent charge—which was good—but he had no bars, of course. He climbed down off the porch and eyed the roof. He'd been on the suppressant for so long that his wings had drawn back into his body, possibly never to see the light of day again. They'd probably atrophied by now—he hadn't used them since 1973, when he'd flown Rory to the supe ICU. And considering his weakened physical state, he could hardly climb up. He flexed his hands, but his claws didn't extend. Just as he thought—useless.

He quartered the meadow and skirted the lake shore, angling his phone toward a gap in the mountains and finally, *finally* managed to pick up a signal.

Over the last two weeks, he'd spoken to the Supernatural Selection staff enough that the office was at the top of his contact favorites. He started a FaceTime session—he needed to be able to look the counselor in the eye, to make certain *they* knew exactly how they'd fucked up.

The call connected, but the person on the other end wasn't anyone Quentin recognized: a young-appearing man with dark curly hair, round spectacles, and a vague air of desperation. *That's about to get worse, my friend.*

"Supernatural Selection, this is Zeke. How may I help you, Mr."—his eyes flicked down to the bottom of his screen—"Bertrand-Harrington? Didn't our driver pick you up in a timely fashion?"

"Yes. That's not why I'm calling. Who was responsible for preparing my final marriage contracts?"

"Um . . . that would be me. I prepare all the contracts."

Quentin narrowed his eyes. "Indeed. In that case, would you mind telling me how, instead of being married to vampire Casimir Moreau, I find myself mated to bear shifter Ted Farnsworth?"

Zeke blinked rapidly, gold flashing in his dark eyes. "Ted— But that's impossible. Mr. Farnsworth is to be married to Mr. Johnson. Mr. Farnsworth signed his contract yesterday evening, although Mr. Johnson had to delay until next week."

"Check your copies please. I'll hold."

Zeke nodded, his curls bobbing wildly, and Quentin caught the telltale glint of a vision spell overlaying his glasses. *A demon? Outside of Sheol? How—*

Zeke looked up at someone out of sight of the call. "Could you please pull the contracts for Farnsworth–Johnson and Moreau–Bertrand-Harrington?" He smiled uncertainly at the screen. "It will be just a moment. The AI is collecting the documents for me."

"AI?" Quentin pushed his demon logistics questions aside for the moment. "You have an angel interface—and they deign to work with a demon? In a *matchmaking* agency?"

Zeke licked his lips, darting a glance to the side where apparently the AI lurked. "It's a . . . requirement of the Sheol work-release program. No demon can remain in the Upper World without guaranteed employment and an AI observer."

"In that case, how the *devil* could such an error occur? Aren't AIs there to ensure that protocol is followed to the letter? They're doubly vigilant with demons, so I can't imagine one allowing you to cut any corners."

Zeke flinched. "No, of course not, but I checked those contracts myself thrice, as required. They were perfectly executed."

"Check. Again," Quentin said through clenched teeth.

Zeke extended his hand above the screen and retrieved a sheaf of paper. "Thank you, AI." He set the papers in front of him, separating them into two piles. "Here's your contract, Mr.

Bertrand-Harrington, and as I expect, it says here that you're . . . Wait . . . that can't be."

"Let me guess. My 'party of the second part' is Ted Farnsworth."

"Yes, but there's no way that could have happened. Your match and Mr. Farnsworth's match didn't overlap in any way whatsoever. The only thing you had in common was that you both signed your contracts on the same day, and your prospective spouses—your *intended* prospective spouses—did not."

"So it's a clerical error on the part of Supernatural Selection. How soon will you correct it?"

Zeke's eyes widened and his air of panic increased. "I . . . uh . . . can't."

"What do you mean? You made the mistake. Fix it."

"You signed it, sir. In blood. Didn't you read it at the signing?"

"No. I read each of the draft copies of course." *Because it would have been stupid not to.* "But there were . . . extenuating circumstances during the ceremony itself." He rubbed his eyes under his glasses. *I was a supe advocate, for years, for pity's sake. I'm trained to evaluate contracts. Why did I have to let my stupid flag fly at that particular moment?*

"I'm sorry, Mr. Bertrand-Harrington, but that's why we recommend that all our clients attend the signing with a witness. Did you?"

"No. There were—"

"Extenuating circumstances? But surely Mr. Farnsworth—" He glanced up, presumably at where the AI was hovering out of sight. "He didn't either? Oh my stars. Well. This is unfortunate."

"I want to terminate this contract. Immediately. There must be a way."

"I'm afraid there's not much I can do personally." Zeke riffled through his papers, a worried frown pleating his forehead. "I *know* I checked these," he muttered. "Even though it was executed by proxy, it's a magically enforced mating contract. You agreed to the terms when the witch officiant outlined them, didn't you?"

"Yes, yes, of course."

"So when you signed in blood—"

"I wish you would stop saying that."

"Sorry. But it's a good idea to be *really* careful about anything you sign in blood." His face took on a haunted expression. "Believe me. I know."

"You aren't telling me anything new. All this is moot because the deed is done, and the past can't be changed. Unless . . ." A tiny seed of hope took root in Quentin's chest. "You don't happen to have a time-surfer on staff, do you?"

"No. I'm afraid the witches who run the agency are strong believers in natural consequences. There's actually a clause in the contract preventing interference from third parties."

Quentin sighed, pinching the bridge of his nose. "You have to understand. I am an incubus. Do you know what that means?"

"Of course, sir. You're a parasitic demonic entity who feeds on the sexual energies of—"

"Stop." He breathed slowly until his cresting anger receded. Everyone assumed all 'cubi were still relegated to the demon realm by the outdated laws of the Upper World supe councils. His family was one of the exceptions, and the surest way to call down their wrath was to refer to them as *parasites*. "I belong to a dynastic 'cubi family. The oldest one in North America."

Zeke blinked. "Oh."

"Do you *do* your homework? My family name isn't exactly obscure."

"I'm only a counselor-in-training. I don't have access to the private data about any of our clients. Only their public profiles." He glanced at the corner of the screen again. "You're a single white incubus in his fourth century, seeking a permanent partner who—"

"Who can't be killed by meta-demonic sex. I'm aware."

"But incubi can kill anyone."

"Except someone who's already dead. My perfect match—guaranteed by your agency—is a vampire."

"Yes, I know. But the spells that govern the guarantee are global, not simply match-by-match specific. They shouldn't have allowed a clerical error that violates a perfect match. They can't. It's impossible."

Quentin counted backward from ten. "All the more reason for me to be really fucking angry, don't you think?"

"Yes, of course, but—"

"I wish to lodge a complaint. Let me speak to your supervisor."

Zeke's Sheol-pale skin turned gray. "My . . . supervisor? Which one?"

"How can you work in an office environment and be unaware of corporate bureaucracy? The person who writes your evaluations, who docks your pay when you're late, who can *fire* you for bloody incompetence. *That* supervisor."

Zeke's shoulders slumped in what looked like relief, and he regained some of his color. "Oh, *that* supervisor."

"Yes, *that* supervisor. If I have my way, you'll never get past counselor-in-training. You're barely qualified for filing clerk, if this performance is any indication. Now, let me speak with your supervisor."

"Of course. I can transfer you now, but—" his eyes flicked to the left "—she's on a conference exorcism. I can give you to her assistant, or you could hold. Or leave a voice mail and she could call you back."

Quentin pulled his phone away from his ear and saw the battery indicator had dropped below fifty percent. *So fast?* "No. I don't have the time for that."

"I can email you a link to our survey if you like. You should have gotten one of those anyway after you signed your contract."

"Yes. Fine. Whatever. Now tell me how to fix this." Quentin's panic was starting to overcome his anger. "I can't stay married to a living man. Surely you understand that."

"Of course. But you signed—"

"If you say 'in blood' one more time . . ."

"Sorry. There's a counterspell, but I doubt you'd want to sacrifice the necessary body part. Or . . . um . . . parts."

"No one is sacrificing any body parts." Although Quentin wouldn't mind hacking a few pieces off Zeke if he didn't become more cooperative tout de suite. "Isn't there some other way? This is a *contract*. Surely there are provisions for its termination."

Zeke's eyes widened. "That's, um, kind of the thing. A blood contract is a terminal agreement. There is no way out other than, well, the termination of one or both parties."

Quentin ground his teeth together. "If death is the only escape option, then I'd expect Supernatural Selection to *guarantee* that their paperwork is accurate. Don't you?"

"You have to understand, witches view death a bit differently. For them, it's merely another transition. If you—"

"Zeke. It is Zeke, isn't it?" At the man's nod, Quentin forced himself not to shout. "I am not a witch. For me, as for Mr. Farnsworth, death is the end of the line. And I am at the end of my *rope* right now. I am *seriously* unhappy. We're talking my family will take down you and your progeny to the tenth *generation* unhappy. We're talking *zero-star review* unhappy. Do you understand?"

Zeke's tongue darted out, and he licked his lips. "Under the circumstances, perhaps we can invoke the emergency escape clause. Ordinarily, a blood contract wouldn't be eligible, but since it seems to be the result of a clerical error—" he glanced at a flickering golden *something* at his shoulder "—we can make an exception in this case."

Finally. "Very well. Invoke it."

"You must understand, it's an iron-clad, nonnegotiable, irreversible process."

"Excellent. Do it."

Zeke's gaze dropped to the bottom of the screen, his eyes obviously scanning another document. "There are a number of requirements and consequences. First, both of you must agree to the ritual."

"Yes, yes. I agree." Quentin made a get-on-with-it motion with one hand. "I'm sure Mr. Farnsworth will as well."

"You must be absolutely sure, and we'll need to record his acceptance of the terms too. Once the escape sequence is completed, the two of you will be returned to the candidate pool and forbidden from face-to-face contact for . . . let's see . . . Ah, here it is. For all eternity."

Quentin tried not to roll his eyes. He failed. "Since we never intended to have face-to-face contact in the first place, that's hardly a deterrent." *In fact, it's an incentive on both our parts.* "Go on."

"You must indemnify Supernatural Selection of all harm and waive the right to arbitration or legal action."

"Consider yourself indemnified. Next?"

Zeke gnawed on his bottom lip. "Are you *sure* you want to initiate the escape sequence? Once Mr. Farnsworth agrees and it's begun, it can't be aborted. And it must be completed within one solar year or . . ." Zeke's eyes grew round behind his spectacles and his already-pale face drained of all color.

"Or what?"

"You . . . ah . . . don't want to know."

"It hardly matters, since we both want this over with as soon as possible." Quentin took his fountain pen from the inside pocket of his blazer and uncapped it, preparing to take notes on the back of the useless contract. "What are the particulars of the ritual? It's not one of those ridiculous Celtic things, is it? I don't have to stand with one foot on a goat, at dusk, wearing nothing but a fishnet while Ted throws a spear through a hole in a rock, do I?"

"No. It's pretty straightforward." Zeke pulled a manila folder off his desk and sorted through it, pulling out a paper that had remarkably little writing on it. "You have to present a lock of each other's hair, taken with a silver-bladed knife under a moonless sky, tied with a cord of braided grass." He looked up. "You have to braid the cord together, of course."

"Naturally," Quentin said dryly.

"You each have to provide a silver coin." He glanced up again. "Denomination doesn't matter. And a mosquito."

"A mosquito? It's November. There's snow on the ground. Where are we supposed to find a mosquito, let alone two?"

"Oh. Let me check the equivalency chart." Zeke rummaged through a drawer at his elbow and pulled out a color-coded chart. "You can substitute a flea."

"A flea."

"Yes. Or . . ." He squinted at the chart, turning it sideways. "Or a tick. Insects that carry disease." He shrugged apologetically. "It's symbolic, you understand. All of these things are. The mosquito represents pestilence—you vowed to support each other through sickness and health. The coin—"

"Symbolic of wealth. And the hair a metaphor for our bodies. I get it."

"You simply have to bring those to the agency during normal business hours—"

"Which are what?"

"Well, we're kind of a 24/7 thing, because we're global, you know."

"We're in Oregon. Give me the fucking time."

"Oh. The Portland office. That's where I'm based. In that case, it would be between noon and midnight on . . ."

"On what?" Quentin's grip tightened on his phone. "On *what*, gods and devils take it?"

When Zeke didn't respond, Quentin glanced at his phone, ready to fling it into the lake. Gah! The bloody battery was dead. How had that happened so quickly? He smacked himself in the forehead, just as Ted had done. *Why didn't I ask for the bloody car? How am I going to get out of here?*

He stared out across the lake. The sun had dropped behind the hills and the shell of the abandoned lodge at his back. How likely was it that the place had electricity? *Slim to when Satan slurps a snow cone.*

Nevertheless, assumptions had gotten him into this mess: assuming Supernatural Selection's staff was marginally competent, assuming the driver was taking him to downtown Portland, assuming he could manage his own affairs without relying on his family's money and influence.

I hate *the way Grandmother throws her weight around, yet here I am, acting like the privileged entitled incubus I've always tried* not *to be.*

He took off his glasses and tucked them in his pocket. The suppressant dulled his night vision, but once free of the filtering lenses and bespelled frames that protected his Sheol-evolved eyes from the sunlight, he could see well enough to make his way up the path to the lodge.

He found the door where Ted had retrieved his backpack. It wasn't locked—why would it be? There was nobody around for miles. There was barely a road. And besides, there was nothing inside. As he picked his way through the forest of wall studs and around piles of drywall and buckets of nails, his fears were confirmed: no wires or outlets, not even rudimentary ones.

"Wonderful."

Now that his anger had dissipated along with the sunlight, he realized exactly how cold it was. This might be the Maritime Northwest—more or less—but he was in the mountains. There was snow under the trees. He couldn't check the temperature on his phone thermometer, but the plume of his breath told him enough.

I'm going to freeze. He could try to walk down the mountain to the nearest town, but he had no idea where that was, or how far away. He had no winter coat. No blankets. His stupid space blanket wannabe was solely to block others' sexual energy from reaching him, not for keeping him warm.

However, it would do for a start. It had to. Surely Ted would cool down enough—*don't think about* cool. *Or* warm *for that matter*—to return, and he could build a fire or whatever he did. Quentin shivered, his teeth chattering. *He does* live *here, doesn't he?* What if he didn't come back tonight? What if he didn't come back at all?

You can hardly blame him for abandoning you. You acted like a total asshole.

Quentin dragged his luggage in from the porch. The lodge wasn't insulated and had no heat or electricity, but at least it had walls and a roof. He found a corner that was further blocked in by a stack of plywood and opened his suitcase. He took off his jacket and put on two more shirts. He couldn't button the third one because they were too closely tailored to his shrunken body, so he put it on backward. He pulled his jacket back on and added a second one, then just dumped everything on the floor, mentally apologizing to his tailor for the disrespect to his bespoke suits, including his three custom tuxes. *Can't be well-dressed if I'm dead.*

He settled himself into his nest, the floor still hard beneath him despite the padding of all his socks and underwear, and draped the space blanket overhead like a tent. He cursed both his demon and dragon blood—both of which required heat to survive—and settled down to wait for Ted, morning, or loss of consciousness.

At this point, he'd settle for any of them.

Chapter Six

The next morning, Ted took a dip in the stream while still in bear form, then shook the water out of his fur. The night on his own hadn't helped—it never helped. Why did he have to be the only bear shifter in history who not only preferred company, but actively *hated* solitude? His brother laughed himself sick over that on a regular basis.

Ted shifted back to human—resisting the urge to stop halfway, just for old times' sake—and, shivering, pulled on his clothes. *Bet Q-Bert would have felt the chill in his fancy suit if he'd stuck around long enough.*

Guilt pricked Ted's conscience as he hiked the last couple of miles into town. The guy was clearly not the outdoorsy type. Maybe Ted should have at least hung around long enough for him to get off the mountain.

Who am I kidding? I don't need to worry about him. Judging by his clothes, shoes—and oh, yeah, the not-so-subtle hints about his money, family, blah blah blah—Q-Bert probably just called his limo or helicopter or private fricking jet to pick him up. Unlike Ted, he damn sure hadn't spent his last dime on his marriage contract. In fact, he probably had money to spare for a magical divorce and to give it another try or ten.

Ted frowned as he pushed open the diner door. Come to think of it, he didn't know how you got magically divorced. It wasn't supposed to be necessary, after all, but there must be some hocus-pocus that would do the trick. There always was.

Witches never spelled themselves into a corner. *Although they sure made it tough for the spell-ees.*

Ted nodded at Wanda, who was pouring coffee for a couple of truckers, then ducked to peer through the pass-through and wave at Javier, who was flipping bacon at the grill. He sat down at his usual seat at the corner of the counter—Wanda had reinforced the stool just for him—and pulled one of the menus from between the napkin dispenser and the salt shaker.

"I don't know why you bother to look at that," Matt said as he took the stool kitty-corner from Ted. "You always order the lumberjack special, eggs up, extra sausage on the side."

Heat crept up Ted's throat and he shrugged. "Maybe I'm in the mood for something different. Ever think of that?"

"Tell me another one."

"I'm serious."

"I'll believe you after you order." Matt grinned up at Wanda. "Morning, Wanda. I'll have coffee and the short stack."

She eyed him, pencil poised above her pad. "You sure about that? Looks like you'd better stick to the egg-white omelet with a side of collard greens. And decaf."

Matt clutched his chest. "You wound me. Are you insinuating I'm not keeping my girlish figure?"

"I'm insinuating that Doc Adams told you not two days ago at this very counter that you needed to cut back on the carbs and caffeine."

"Doc Adams is an old fussbudget. What happened to doctor-patient privilege?"

"I suppose it's still alive and well, but not if you talk about it in the middle of my diner. You're getting the omelet." She poured him his coffee, then turned away from him. "The usual for you, Ted?"

Ted glanced at Matt, who was scowling into his coffee. "Not this time, Wanda. Gimme the corned beef hash, double order. Eggs poached. Coffee, please."

She frowned at him. "No side of sausage?"

"Hey!" Matt slapped the counter. "How come he gets to have all the things?" He poked Ted's side, where his usual winter love handle was already bulging over his waistband. "He's got some extra upholstery too, if you hadn't noticed."

She grinned and stuck her pencil behind her ear. "Oh I noticed, believe you me. But on him, it looks good. Besides, he'll lose it again come spring, same as always. You? Not so much."

"But—"

"Listen, sweetheart. I like you. We all like you, even though you're kinda squirrelly and you still haven't told us what you do for a living. We'd like you to keep on doing it, whatever it is —and that means you got to keep on living. So follow Doc's orders."

"Yeah, yeah."

Wanda disappeared behind the swinging door into the kitchen. Ted nudged his own coffee toward Matt. "You want mine? I don't mind decaf."

Matt smiled crookedly. "Nah. She's right. I need to eat better and stop sitting around on my ass. It's bad for me and it sucks for my bank account. What's new with you?"

"Me? Not a thing." *I just sank all my dough into a lodge that won't be finished in forever and I'm married to a guy who can't stand the sight of me.* Although maybe he should try to do something about that last one. "Hey, could I borrow your cell? I, uh, left mine at home."

"Sure." Matt handed over his phone.

"Thanks. Won't be a minute."

Ted pushed through the doors and ducked around the corner so he wasn't visible through the diner's window, then punched in Supernatural Selection's number. *How pathetic is it that I've got it memorized?*

"Supernatural Selection."

"Yeah, this is—"

"You have reached the AI. At this time, all our counselors are assisting other supes. Your call is important to us. Please hold and the next available—"

"Crap," Ted muttered, disconnecting the call. He couldn't stand around out here on Matt's phone until somebody at Supernatural Selection decided to pick up. If they were helping a sloth shifter, he could be waiting for hours. Days. *Weeks*.

He deleted the number from the recent call list, then walked back into the diner and returned the phone. "Thanks, man. I owe you."

"No problem." Matt glanced through the side window at the parking lot. "I didn't expect to find you in here today. Your truck's not in the lot."

"It's still in the shop."

"Still? What's Larry doing? Knitting you a fuel pump with his own lily-white hands?"

"It's not his fault. It's an old truck. He's having trouble finding the parts."

"Uh-huh." Matt took a sip of his decaf and winced. "Damn. It's just not the same."

Wanda returned with their plates and plunked them down on the counter. "Here you go, boys."

They both tucked in, Ted because it was November and he always ate like a starving platoon, and Matt because he always focused on anything like his life depended on it. Ted slowed down about halfway through his hash, thinking back on what Wanda said about Matt's work.

"Doesn't Wanda know you're a photographer?"

He glanced at Ted sidelong, shaking his head, his mouth full of eggs. After he swallowed, he grasped Ted's arm. "Don't tell her, okay? You're the only one around here who knows about it, other than Larry, since the two of you had to rescue me from that tree after my first bona fide Sasquatch sighting."

Ted snorted into his coffee. "That was pretty funny."

"Funny, nothing! Skunks can really *move* when they're pissed." He wrinkled his nose, lifting the edge of his half-eaten omelet as if he expected to discover a hidden cache of hash browns. "But Wanda has a point. When I decided to quit *Scoop Weekly* and go freelance, I didn't expect my main source to flake out on me. He's been so reliable up until now, but that tip I told you about in the car?" Matt turned his thumbs down. "*Nada.* Guy stood me up."

Ted nudged a morsel of potato with his fork. He felt bad about that, but after Dr. Kendrick's warning about *tagging* . . . "I saw one of your pictures on the cover of the *New World News* just this week though."

"That was an old shot they pulled from the morgue. I had to call and give them shit about the royalties too. They only had the rights to print it once, and they've run it three times. Guess news is as slow for them as it is for me."

"Yeah. We're not real exciting around here. Can't compare to a big city, I expect."

"Don't you believe it. I love Dewton, the hills, the woods— even without another Sasquatch sighting. That fishing spot you showed me outside of town? Awesome." Matt sighed and pushed his plate away. "I just wish I could find a way to make some cash so I can afford to stay here."

"I'm sure you'll find something."

"Yeah. I've got a couple of ideas. A lead or two to follow up. It'll work out."

"I'm sure it will." Ted stood and slapped Matt on the shoulder. "See you around."

"See you." Matt looked out the window again. "Hey, if you don't have your truck, how are you getting home?"

"Same as yesterday. I'll hike up."

"Need a ride? I don't mind. Not like I've got anything else to do, and I'd love to see your place."

The last thing Ted needed was the council finding out he'd let a tabloid photographer onto his property. "Nah. The walk does me good." He patted his belly. "How else can I work off breakfast?"

"If you're sure . . ."

"Sure as sure. Thanks, though, buddy."

Ted paid for his meal and left, but as he headed out of town toward the path up the mountain, his hair lifted on the back of his neck. He glanced behind him. *Nobody there.* But he had to force himself to walk at his usual pace. Maybe it was the conversation with Matt that had set him on edge. Had there been a little too much interest in Matt's eyes? Did Matt suspect that Ted had something to do with his anonymous tips—and their disappearance? Worse, did Matt suspect Ted was the "Bigfoot" that had shambled out of the woods briefly whenever Matt bushwhacked his way up the mountain?

Matt was a smart guy—Ted had never gotten the impression that he actually *believed* any of the shit the tabloids published. Wouldn't it be just Ted's luck if he'd turned Matt into a believer with the actual truth? Or a version of it anyway.

Just to be on the safe side, he hunkered down in front of the cave for half an hour or so to make sure nobody was on his trail. When he was convinced he was alone in the woods, he stowed his clothes inside and shifted, taking the path through the woods at a steady lope.

When he got to the edge of the clearing by the lake, he stopped and checked out the place. It was as still and quiet as usual. The birds had flapped a bit when he had pushed through the underbrush, but they always squawked at his bear. Stupid birds. It's not like he ever actually ate any of them.

Although a hint of fancy cologne lingered in the air, there was no movement in the clearing, and the luggage was gone from the porch. Good. Q-Bert must have abandoned ship and gone back to wherever he'd come from to keep his money company. Ted headed for the back door and shifted, then collected the shirt and pants he'd abandoned yesterday. He dressed quickly, his clothes damp from lying outside overnight, but he didn't want to take the time to fetch dry things from inside because he had that feeling again—someone was watching. Or maybe not watching, exactly, but like he wasn't alone. The hair on his neck stood at attention and he crouched down, sniffing the air, cursing his less sensitive human nose.

He crept into the vast unfinished main room, freezing when he saw a black leather briefcase and a matching overnight bag next to the front door. *What the heck?* Ted didn't in a million years believe that Q-Bert was the kind of guy to leave his fancy monogrammed baggage behind, so he had to be here somewhere.

"Q-Ber— Quentin? Are you here?"

Nothing. But the sawdust was disturbed as if someone had shuffled through it and the parallel double tracks looked a hell of a lot like the tread of suitcase casters. Ted followed the path and found one of those silver space blanket thingies draped over the end of a stack of plywood.

"Quentin?" Again, no answer. Jeez, was the guy *still* pissed because he'd gotten stuck with a big lumbering bear instead of whatever fancy-ass partner he'd expected? It's not like he wasn't at least half responsible.

Ted heaved a sigh and stomped across the floor, but there was no movement under the silver tent. "Come out, come out wherever you are." He leaned over and peeked into the shadowed hideout. "Holy shit."

He yanked the blanket off and tossed it aside. Underneath a pile of clothes, Quentin was curled up tighter than a hedgehog shifter. His lips were blue. "Quentin! Quentin, can you hear me? Are you okay?" Jesus, was he breathing?

Ted scrabbled the pile of clothes off Quentin—who seemed to be wearing another pile of clothes—and was his shirt on backwards? Underneath all that stuff, Ted couldn't tell if Quentin was breathing or not, but he knew how to take a pulse and he could barely feel anything beneath the cold, dry skin. *I bet this is how a vampire feels. Is he a vampire? No, he couldn't be. He was in the sun.*

He piled the clothes back on top of the unresponsive man. *What good is that gonna do?* Clearly they hadn't kept him warm overnight. Equally clearly, Ted wouldn't be able to fix this on his own. He didn't even have his truck to get Quentin down the mountain to the hospital. And if he was a vampire or one of the other kinds of supes whose vitals were so weird that they couldn't be treated in human hospitals, Ted would catch unbelievable shit from the council for Secrecy Pact violations— not counting what a well-meaning but clueless human doctor could do trying to treat a supe.

He needed help. He needed a supe practitioner—and further, one who could get here immediately.

Dr. Kendrick and David. David was an *achubydd*, a magical healer. He'd be able to help. And Dr. Kendrick was fae. They could gate through Faerie and show up here in a matter of minutes—there was a threshold in the woods near Ted's cabin.

Ted's hands trembled as he pulled his cell phone out of his clammy pocket. It didn't have any juice—or any bars for that matter—but he didn't need either to contact Dr. Kendrick. He had the doctor's special supe communications app, powered by druid spellcraft.

He had to push the button twice before he could get the damn thing to connect. *Oh right. The magic words.* "Please and thank you." The phone started to ring, its sound like the call of a hunting horn. What if Dr. Kendrick wasn't there? What if the spell didn't work? What if—

"Ted? What's wrong?"

Thank Ursa. "Dr. Kendrick, there's this guy. He's hardly breathing and his lips are blue."

"What guy? Where?"

"Here, at the lodge. His name's Quentin Bertrand-Harrington —"

"Quentin Bertrand-Harrington, the incubus?"

Incubus. Holy shit, I'm married to a sex demon. "He didn't go into that, but his family's a big deal, I guess. Never mind that. I can't get him to respond. I need help. Could you and David—"

"We're on our way. Don't move him, but try to keep him warm." He disconnected the call.

Ted tossed his cell on top of the plywood stack. *Keep him warm, he says. Right. With what?* If they were in the cabin, Ted would stand a half a chance, but here? He didn't have a heater, or a blanket that was worth a damn, or any way to build a fire without burning the place down.

But I have me.

Ted stripped off his clothes. "Sorry about this, Q-Bert. I'm not sure how your fancy suits'll handle a run-in with a bear, but better suit-death than you-death."

He shifted and lay on his side, somehow wedging himself into Quentin's little clothes nest. Careful with his claws—at least as much as possible—he drew Quentin against his belly and wrapped his arms around him.

I'm sorry. I'm so sorry. I shouldn't have assumed you were a shifter. I shouldn't have left you alone. Please don't die. Please don't die.

Ted didn't have time to chant his desperate mantra more than a hundred times before he heard the door burst open.

"Ted? It's us."

Ted let out a grunt—he didn't roar and rattle the windows, but that's what he felt like doing.

Dr. Kendrick appeared next to the plywood, David at his elbow. "Good thinking, Ted, but if you could shift back and let David get to him now?"

Ted nodded, his head heavy, oddly reluctant to let go. Quentin felt awfully good against his chest. But he shifted back as instructed. Which meant he was naked in front of people for the second time in as many days. *That might be a record for me.* "Sorry about the . . . you know . . ." He splayed his hands over his groin. "Clothing's not exactly an option during a shift."

Dr. Kendrick *harrumphed*, turning it into a cough. David cast him a sidelong eyebrow-raised glance, then smiled at Ted. "Don't worry about it. Dr. Jealous can cool his jets because I would *never* peek. And anyway, we're here in a *professional* capacity."

Ted backed away, allowing David, who was much smaller than either Ted or the doctor, to get closer to Quentin. David knelt next to him, his brow wrinkled in concentration, and placed his hands on either side of Quentin's face.

"Be careful, Dafydd," Dr. Kendrick murmured. "He can't give you any positive feedback."

"I know. I'm just assessing. Not much energy required." He glanced up at the two of them. "Is there someplace else we can take him? Somewhere with heat and a softer surface than—" He peered down at the floor around his knees. "Holy cats. Am I treating someone on a bed of briefs?"

Ted cleared his throat. "I think he was trying to keep warm overnight. I might have sort of abandoned him after we had a little argument."

"Well, thank goodness you found him when you did. The exposure practically did him in, although I don't think that's the primary problem. So? A warmer and less impromptu bed?"

"Oh. Right. My cabin is about half a mile around the lake. It's not a five-star hotel, but it's got a decent woodstove next to the couch."

"Excellent. Alun, could you carry him?"

"I can do that," Ted said quickly. For some reason, it was suddenly important that *he* be the one to do it.

Dr. Kendrick raised an eyebrow. "Are you planning to do so naked?"

Ted glanced down at himself. "Oh. Right. Clothes. They're here somewhere." He scrabbled around on the floor and found them, pulling them on as David folded Quentin's hands over his chest. Then David stepped aside, allowing Ted to pick Quentin up and cradle him in his arms. He nodded toward the back door. "My place is that way. It's so easy to miss if you don't know where to look. If I had just told him about it—"

Dr. Kendrick gripped Ted's shoulder. "Don't blame yourself. Let's just take care of him now, okay?"

Ted nodded, and Dr. Kendrick held the door open. Then he and David followed Ted along the lakeshore path. Quentin was barely a feather in Ted's arms, fragile as glass, stirring a feeling under his heart that he'd never experienced before. *Don't get attached. He hates you.*

Ted's home, a cross between log cabin and craftsman bungalow, was set back from the lake shore in a little glade of fir, maple, and aspen. Ted mounted the three steps to the porch and let Dr. Kendrick open this door for him too.

Ted strode across the living room and laid Quentin down on the couch. "There's a bed upstairs, but it's chillier up there since I don't need so much heat when I'm sleeping. Here, he'll be closer to the fire. I'll get it started right away, and bring some blankets."

"This is lovely, Ted, thank you." David sat on the coffee table in front of the couch and took Quentin's hand. He smoothed Quentin's hair back from his forehead. "What's he doing here anyway?"

"He's . . . ah . . . *weeellll* . . ." Ted grimaced, not meeting Dr. Kendrick's eyes. "He's my husband."

Chapter
Seven

Quentin was floating on a sea of warm and soft and safe. As he swam up to full consciousness, he realized that something was seriously wrong with that picture. He could *feel* people around him—not many, but more than one, their life energy buzzing along his skin and in his nerves, buoying him up. He flexed his fingers, which, last time he remembered feeling them, had been stiff with cold. A slightly scratchy woolen blanket, redolent of cedar, was tucked under his chin—*not my blanket at home.* His grandmother wouldn't tolerate anything less than cashmere. *Where am I?*

He cracked open his eyes to see a strange man at his side, peering down at him.

"Hey." The man smiled, his brown-gold hair flopping over his forehead as he bent forward. "You're awake. Excellent."

Quentin blinked, then squinted against the light pouring in through a nearby window.

"Oh." The man turned aside for a moment. "You'll probably be wanting these, I expect." He held something in his palm. *My glasses.*

Quentin took them and fumbled them onto his face, breathing easier when the spell filtered out the glare. He stared at the exposed rough-hewn beams above him. He appeared to be lying on a sofa in front of an old-fashioned pot-bellied woodstove. To his recollection, he'd never been anywhere this *rustic* before, at least not since those nights camping under the stars during his post-puberty Change March. The unpainted wood-paneled walls, battered oak floor, and faded curtains spoke of comfort rather than style, something totally foreign to his grandmother's pristine mansion or even his own meticulously restored Beacon Hill brownstone. After all, incubi and succubi were all about the appearance of perfection—creating an image and an environment to incite envy and desire, regardless of how uncomfortable the environment actually was.

That's how they enticed their partners. And that's why the partners they attracted were as beautiful, brittle, and avaricious as the 'cubi themselves.

Quentin blinked again, the notion seeping into his consciousness that he shouldn't *be* this conscious. The suppressant, at the dosage he'd been taking lately, kept him slightly muddled at all times.

The suppressant. It's not blocking— Why can I sense— He fumbled with the blanket, freeing his arms from beneath it because it was useless, doing nothing to deaden his awareness of *others*.

He could *feel* them, their energy pulsing, calling, *seducing* him, making his mouth *water* and his cock harden as it hadn't done in years. His breath sawing in his throat, he pressed his hand against his chest, as if that could mask the sensations.

"Hey hey hey. It's okay. You're okay." The man reached out as if to take Quentin's hand, but Quentin snatched it away, cowering against the sofa cushions.

"Don't touch me."

The man blinked kind blue-gray eyes and straightened—he was seated on a wooden coffee table—holding his palms up. "I won't. I promise. Only if you say it's okay."

"It's not okay," Quentin muttered. "It's never okay. You shouldn't be this close. Nobody should be anywhere *near* me."

The man's eyes narrowed and his full lips pressed together in a distinctly mulish expression. "That's enough of that, Mr.

Bertrand-Harrington. I'm David Evans-Kendrick, by the way, and you nearly died."

"I did?" *Maybe that would have been better for everyone.* Quentin shook his head. *No.* No matter how frustrating his life was, he had no desire to end it. "It was cold."

"Yes, it was cold, but that wasn't the problem. Or at least not the main one." David shifted on the table, a guilty expression flickering over his face. "I... um... usually never touch *anybody* without their consent because otherwise it's too draining, but I had to treat you while you were unconscious, otherwise ..." He spread his hands and shrugged.

"You treated me? Are you a doctor?" Quentin couldn't keep the disbelief out of his tone. David looked as if he'd be more at home dancing in a club than in an operating theater.

"Me?" David chuckled. "No. I'm almost a nurse, though. But that's not—" He blew out a breath. "I'm an *achubydd*."

Quentin frowned. "But they're—"

"Extinct?" A smile quivered on David's mouth. "Apparently not. However, I can't be as effective as I need to be unless my patient cooperates with their treatment, so what I was able to do for you was more in the nature of triage, and a little garbage collection."

"'Garbage collection'?"

When David propped his fists on his hips, he appeared surprisingly fierce for someone no bigger than Quentin was himself. "I don't know where you got that ... that ... *poison* that was coursing through you, but whoever gave it to you should be *shot*."

"Actually, I think they were. Or rather burned. The originator of the formula, that is," Quentin hastened to add, "not the current potion-maker, but that was several centuries ago."

David's eyebrows shot up. "Oh. I didn't mean that *literally*. But that stuff, whatever it was, has seriously compromised your system. Your DNA is deteriorating in a really alarming way. One night, reasonably protected and wrapped in some seriously expensive couture shouldn't have made you blink twice. Any supe would be able to handle it. You were susceptible to the cold because you've practically destroyed your body's defenses. What on earth were you thinking?"

Quentin turned away, facing the geometric pattern of the sofa cushions. "I was thinking that I didn't want to kill anybody else."

"'Anybody else'? You mean you've killed somebody before?"

"Nearly."

"My husband says that you're an . . . an incubus?"

Quentin nodded.

"I've never met one before, but I've only been aware of the supe communities since last summer."

"There aren't many 'cubi families outside of Sheol."

"'Sheol'?"

"The demon realm."

"Oh. I've been to Faerie. Is it like that?"

Quentin snorted. "Hardly. I've heard that people actually *like* living in Faerie. Nobody could like living in Sheol. Several ancient incubi and succubi managed to escape by . . . judicious choice of partner, and founded dynasties in the Upper World."

"Upper World? You mean here?" He gestured vaguely to the room and the sun streaming in through the window. "Like the fae call it the Outer World?"

"Yes," Quentin said dryly. "That should tell you something about where Sheol is located." He nearly laughed at David's wide-eyed astonishment. "The 'cubi dynasties are descended from the first succubus/dragon shifter mating in Britain, although some of us later migrated to Europe or the east coast of the New World. Personally, I'm from Boston."

"Interesting. I'm still learning about supes so I'd like to talk to you more about it sometime." He scooted forward. "But right now I'm going to take your hand. Okay?"

"I'd really rather you didn't. It's . . . it's not a good idea." Quentin tucked his hands under his armpits.

"I promise, you won't drain me. I want you to *feel* something. Something important."

"That's what I'm afraid of," Quentin muttered.

David's warm chuckle was soothing, not—oddly enough—arousing. "Trust me. I'm an *achubydd*." He leaned forward. "Maybe saying that will get old someday, but not yet! Now, take my hand. It'll be okay, I promise." He held his right hand out.

Hesitantly, Quentin placed his hand on David's open palm.

And felt— "Nothing. I feel nothing."

"Isn't that a line from a song?"

"I wouldn't know, unless it's from Wagner. My grandmother is an opera fiend."

"Well, never mind. Now what do you feel?"

A trickle of warmth flowed out from David's hand and threaded its way up Quentin's arm to coil around his heart. "Are you doing that? I'm not . . . not *taking* it from you?"

"Nope. Not a bit. Lately I've been working on controlling my power—throttling things down to an appropriate level for any given healing. No point swatting a mosquito with an *achubydd* howitzer, right?"

"Why can't I feel your life energy though?" Quentin could *see* David's life energy—the man almost glowed with it. But it was contained, as if Quentin were viewing it from outside a window, or David were inside a snow globe.

"Because it doesn't belong to you."

"But I can feel *other* people."

"Can you? Try."

Quentin closed his eyes and extended his despised incubus shadow senses. "There are two other people here. But one of them is like you. Contained."

"That's Alun, my husband. And you're right. He's contained. By me."

The other life force, now that Quentin was paying attention, was so brilliant that he had to squint his mental eyes. "Is that Ted?"

"He's the only other person here."

The warmth, the brilliance, the joy—Quentin wanted to wrap himself around it, bathe in it, *bury* himself in it. There was so much that he could feast, absolutely glut himself— *No!*

Quentin dropped David's hand. "I can't. He's so—"

"Big?"

Yes, but David was probably referring to Ted's physical size, and Quentin . . . wasn't. "Tempting. To an incubus anyway."

David leaned forward, his elbows on his knees. "Listen. I can do a little bit of cleanup on what that nasty potion did to you, but I've never worked much on a *cellular* level, you know? Most of the work is going to be done by your own body. And that will take time."

"How much time?"

David scrunched up his face, yet managed to look adorable nonetheless. "I'm still new at this, but I'd say a minimum of six months."

"Six *months*?" Six months without the suppressant. How the devil was he supposed to *manage* unless he hid in a cave somewhere? The life energy bombardment would tempt him beyond bearing. He wanted to punch something, but he couldn't very well hit David, and the sofa was too soft and yielding to make a satisfactory target.

"That's just to repair the damage. But you can *never* take that stuff again."

"But—but I *need* it. Without it, everyone around me is in danger. Ted . . . I mean, our . . . marriage was a mistake, but that doesn't mean I want him *dead*."

David nodded thoughtfully. "If you want, you could stay in Alun's old place. We have a house, now that he doesn't have to hide from everybody, so the apartment over his office is vacant. We keep it as kind of a supe safe house."

"Office?"

"Didn't I mention? Alun is a psychologist." He grinned brightly. "Serving the supe community in the greater Pacific Northwest!"

"I suppose it's too much to hope for that the office is fifty miles or so from the nearest population center."

David winced. "Sorry. It's in a Portland suburb."

Quentin shook his head. "That would be worse than this. Here, I only have to resist one person. There, it would be thousands."

"Millions, actually. Portland's kind of a big place."

Quentin let his head fall back on the cushion. "Millions. Wonderful."

"If it helps, I can give you a little self-control boost. Actually, I think you'd be able to handle it yourself if you were completely healthy. I mean, how long has it been since you've *been* completely healthy?"

"I don't remember." *Before Rory.* "Puberty, maybe."

"Holy cats." David blinked rapidly. "No wonder you're disintegrating from the inside out. Listen, one of the things I've learned from working with supes—and my husband and his brothers are some of the worst offenders—is that traditions and lore can get so ingrained in your thick supe heads that you start to believe them even if they're not true. I'd recommend testing your assumptions. I bet you're stronger than you think you are."

Quentin nodded, taking a deep breath. "All right. Boost me." He braced himself, one hand clutching the sofa back and the other fisted in the blanket. "What do I have to do?"

David laughed. "It's not *that* painful—or at all, really. You just have to be willing to accept the help. That sets up the right feedback loop for me. I *like* helping people, so if you want to be helped, it doesn't deplete my energy. It actually gives *me* a boost."

"So," Quentin said with an eyebrow quirk, "*I'm* really helping you."

"Exactly." David held out his hand with a grin, and after a moment's hesitation, Quentin took it.

That warmth again, stronger this time, flowed out of David and into Quentin, but it wasn't like absorbing someone's sexual energy or life force. It didn't make him hard, for one thing—and considering the size of the gorgeous fae who stalked in and stood behind David, one hand resting possessively on his shoulder, that was better for Quentin's long-term life expectancy.

No, this just made him feel . . . complete. Energized. Alert. Even colors were brighter. How hadn't he realized that he no longer saw colors? The blue of David's sweater. The red of the blanket. The green of the trees visible outside the window. Everything was *more*.

David sighed and let go of Quentin's hand.

The big fae leaned down and pressed a kiss to the top of David's head. "All right, *cariad*?"

David tipped his head back so the two could exchange a second kiss. "Yes. Don't fuss." He looked at Quentin. "How are you feeling?"

Quentin sat up, not struggling to do so for the first time in forever. "Really good. Thank you."

"Quentin, this is my husband, Dr. Alun Kendrick. Aka, Lord Cynwrig, Queen's Champion."

"Queen's Champion?" Quentin croaked. "Really?"

Dr. Kendrick shot David an affectionate glare. "Give over, Dafydd." He nodded at Quentin. "It's just Alun, if you please."

"Honored, Lord Cyn— Alun."

Alun rested both hands on David's shoulders. "If you could give Quentin and me a moment alone, *cariad*?"

"Sure." David bounced up with a smile at Quentin. "Remember what I said. Don't let hoary old supe-superstitions keep you down."

"I'm stronger than I think. Yes. Of course." *Not likely.* "Thank you."

David trotted across the room and disappeared around a corner. Quentin heard his light tenor and Ted's rumbling bass, but couldn't make out the words.

"Quentin." Alun settled himself in David's spot. Since he was much larger than his husband, Quentin expected the Mission-style table to creak under his weight, but it didn't so much as flex. *It's stronger than it looks too.* "I need to speak to you about a few things."

Quentin nodded and sat forward, his spine straight. Something about facing the Faerie Queen's Champion—whom everyone in the supe communities knew by reputation if nothing else—made slouching out of the question. "Of course."

"First, do you want us to contact your grandmother to let her know that you're all right?"

"No. Thank you, but no." Quentin had bunched the blanket in his fists again at the mention of his grandmother, so he forced himself to let go and smooth out the creases. "She doesn't know I'm here. She may still believe I'm at the chalet in Vermont."

"If you don't mind my asking, why are you keeping your whereabouts—and, one would assume, your activities—a secret from your nearest kin?"

"Because my nearest kin wants me to follow in the grand tradition of our family and marry a person of their choosing, someone who sees no further than tomorrow, and cares for nothing but wealth and luxury."

"That could describe a large number of people, you know. Those born to wealth and privilege are not eager to relinquish it, and those born without often dream of achieving it."

"So much so that they're willing to die early so that the Bertrand-Harrington scions can continue blithely on, living to suck another partner dry? And another? And another after that?"

Alun's eyebrows rose. "Perhaps not. I take it, however, that your grandmother had identified one such person."

"More than one," Quentin muttered, picking at a loose thread in the blanket.

"Is that why you married Ted? To . . . what does David call it? To head her off at the pass?"

"I didn't marry Ted. I mean, I did. I am. We are. Married. But it was a mistake. I was supposed to marry Casimir Moreau."

This time, Alun's eyebrows disappeared under his wavy dark hair. "The vampire?"

"Yes." Quentin shrugged. "I can't very well kill someone who's already dead."

"An interesting theory, but you might find that choosing a partner based strictly on . . . er . . . dietary requirements has its flaws. You might not find the relationship as fulfilling and trouble-free as you hope."

"You don't need to worry about that. I'll deal with any issues that arise, whatever they are, with my future marriage or this one." The less said about how badly Quentin had screwed up by *not reading his fucking contract* and what he had to do to fix it —especially to the Queen's bloody Champion—the better. "I'm confident we'll have this little problem resolved by the weekend, at which time we'll be able to execute the contracts with our *real* matches."

"Good. That's good. Because Ted was very excited about his fiancé, and from what I know of Rusty, he would be the best thing that could happen to Ted. I was skeptical about the matchmaking service, but in this case, I think they delivered on their promise. The two complement each other perfectly."

Quentin swallowed, his throat suddenly tight. "That's encouraging. I can assume then that they've done an equally admirable job for me."

"I suppose." Alun studied Quentin, his head tilted to one side, until Quentin wanted to squirm. "How do you feel about interacting with the supe councils?"

"I'd rather not. There's still quite a bit of bias against the 'cubi because of our demon roots. However, I'm trained as an advocate." He was trained in a number of professions. That happened when you were three hundred years old and still hadn't found a place to fit in.

"Really? That could come in handy." He glanced over his shoulder. "I must warn you. The council is watching Ted closely. There have been . . . incidents in the past where he's endangered the Secrecy Pact, and their patience is wearing thin."

"Ted? He doesn't seem the type."

"He's not. He's not a vindictive or cruel person. He's quite good-hearted. But he's an extroverted bear shifter, and he's been lonely."

"I didn't know bear shifters could be extroverts." On the other hand, he was the only introverted 'cubi he'd ever heard of —something his grandmother preferred to ignore.

"Ordinarily, no. But as long as you're here, I'd take it as a personal favor if you could keep an eye on him. I'm afraid this . . . disappointment may incite him to more reckless behavior."

"Of course."

Alun stood, a smile quivering on his perfect lips. "And your advocacy training may come in handy with your fiancé as well."

"Casimir? Why?"

"Let's say that he's fond of testing limits and leave it at that, shall we?" He held out his hand. When Quentin hesitated, his smile grew. "Don't worry. You won't feel a thing. No 'cubi can affect another unless that person feels at least a vestige of sexual attraction."

"Yes, but that's what 'cubi thrall guarantees."

"Not for me. I want no one but David. You're safe."

"And so are you." Quentin shook his hand.

He chuckled. "You've never seen my husband dance. If you need to reach me, Ted has my number on enhanced speed-dial."

"'Enhanced'?"

"Magic. It's got its uses. David and I can gate through Faerie and be here within minutes. So please—if anything should happen that compromises Ted's safety or your own, don't hesitate to call. I have a fondness for Ted and would take it amiss should anything happen to him." He turned and walked away.

That wasn't ominous at all. Quentin calculated how long it would take him to braid a fricking grass cord, because this whole snafu was turning out to be as threatening to his own health as it was to Ted's.

Chapter Eight

When Dr. Kendrick joined Ted and David in the kitchen, David immediately wrapped an arm around Dr. Kendrick's waist and was tucked close to his side.

That's what I want. The certainty of closeness, of affection, of love. Supernatural Selection didn't guarantee love per se, but a perfect match was bound to get there in the end, wasn't it? Once Ted got shed of his *im*perfect match, he could get right on that.

"Is Quentin okay?" he asked.

Dr. Kendrick nodded. "He seems to be, although David knows far more about that than I."

"He should be fine. He just needs to take it easy for a few days. Rest. Eat regularly. Drink lots of fluids. And keep away from that awful medication he was taking to damp down his nature."

"Do I need to do anything? About the meds or whatever?"

"I think he needs to do that part. But if that soup tastes as good as it smells, you can definitely help him on the eating regularly front."

Ted patted his belly. "We're heading into winter, remember? He'll have as much to eat as he wants, and what he doesn't want, I'll take care of."

David laughed and stood on his toes to kiss Dr. Kendrick on the cheek. "I'm going to check on Quentin again. Will you be ready to go soon? We need to be back in Portland for office hours unless you'd like me to cancel your afternoon appointments."

"No. We can go as soon as you're ready."

David vanished around the corner into the great room.

"Are you sure you two don't want to stay for lunch? There's plenty."

"Thank you, Ted, but we really must get back. I told Quentin, and I'll tell you too—please don't hesitate to call again should anything occur that concerns you about his health or your own safety."

"You're sure?" Ted shuffled his feet, straightening the kitchen towel that was already neatly folded over the oven door handle, not meeting Dr. Kendrick's eyes. "I don't want to bother you."

"It was no bother. In fact, I was quite pleased and proud that you called me in this case rather than—"

"Rather than doing something stupid, you mean?"

"I was going to say rather than acting before due consideration."

Ted snorted a laugh. "That's a nice way to put it."

Dr. Kendrick gripped Ted's shoulder. "I'm serious. You acted thoughtfully and appropriately. I know this has been a letdown for you, that you had your heart set on welcoming Rusty. Please don't let this temporary disappointment prompt you to do anything the council might construe as an infraction."

Ted shrugged. "I'll try. But Quentin's nothing like Rusty. I'm not sure we really fit."

"Yes. However, he told me he's certain the two of you will be able to work out this little difficulty, so I trust it won't be long before you're matched with the correct mate." Dr. Kendrick's expression turned somber. "But if for some reason Quentin's certainty is unfounded, if you're locked into this marriage whether you want to be or not—"

"Don't worry, Doctor. I didn't expect love, you know. Not the kind you have with David. I just wanted someone to share my life with." He thought of Quentin with his fancy shoes and fancier suits. How could Ted fit into the Bertrand-Harrington world? And would Quentin *want* to share a life? They hadn't really talked about much before Ted had bolted—the memory of *that* still made heat rush up his throat under his beard.

The Supernatural Selection contract didn't require them to live in the same place either. Jeez, what a pisser if he managed to trap himself in the same kind of marriage as any other bear shifter. Most bears thrived on long-distance relationships. In fact, they thrived on long-distance. The relationship was optional.

"Quentin has a very different background, you know."

"Yeah, I got that. The whiz-bang monogrammed luggage and the fancy clothes kind of clued me in. So did the bombs he dropped about his family's money and position and me being a gold digger."

"I think that might have been the shock. From what I just spoke to him about, he was trying to escape that life, or at least certain aspects of it. He's an incubus, however, so you need to take care."

"What does that even mean? I've never met one before. He's a sex demon, right?" He sure didn't look or act like one—or what Ted imagined a sex demon would act like. Wouldn't a sex demon want . . . well . . . sex? Quentin seemed almost prudish.

"Incubi and succubi—or the 'cubi as they're known collectively—feed on the life energy of others, and the energy that's most intense and therefore nourishing for them is the energy released during sex. Many in the supernatural community consider them parasites because they take but don't give back. Their partners invariably die young, although they look quite old."

"That's . . . kinda creepy."

"A number of supernatural attributes could be considered 'creepy,' don't you agree?"

Like shifting so you didn't have to remember to bring a towel to the outdoor shower, for instance? "I guess we all have our issues."

"Yes, but it doesn't follow that those are necessarily bad. Give him a chance, but do a reality check on your own feelings if you believe he might be influencing you. 'Cubi can only feed if their partner finds them sexually attractive."

"Don't worry. He's definitely not my type." *And I'm obviously not his.*

"Then you should be fine."

But what if Ted was stuck with a husband who wasn't his type forever? He'd counted on compatibility leading to affection and growing eventually into love. But he and Quentin weren't starting with compatibility. They seemed to be starting with mutual loathing—and Ted wouldn't blame Quentin if he couldn't get over that, considering that Ted had already abandoned him once, leaving him to almost die.

What were the odds that Quentin would return the favor at the first opportunity? Not the dying part, maybe, but definitely the bolting part.

After all, what could a guy with gold-monogrammed suitcases and zero flannel shirts—Ted had checked—do on a remote mountaintop with nobody but an awkward bear shifter for company? Not like they could stage a cocktail party in the unfinished lodge and invite all the local squirrels.

He forced himself to smile and nod as he showed Dr. Kendrick and David out the door and walked them to the Faerie threshold.

He shoved his hands in his jacket pockets and trudged down the path to the cabin. A gray squirrel, its cheeks bulging, darted into the path in front of him and froze, staring at him with wide startled eyes, then dashed back the way it had come.

And there you have it. The damn squirrels would turn down the invitation, just like everyone else, leaving Ted to party alone.

After Ted escorted David and Alun out the front door—without glancing Quentin's way—Quentin lay back on the sofa, sinking into its soft cushions, and stared at the flames dancing in oddly slow motion behind the woodstove's glass door.

Being alert might be better in a universal sense, and the improved perception certainly was nice, but had its drawbacks too.

For one thing, Quentin's belly knotted when he realized exactly how much of an asshole he'd been to Ted, to the Supernatural Selection counselor-in-training, even to his grandmother. *I used to be a nice person. Didn't I?* The whole point of signing on with a matchmaking agency was to *avoid* selfish behavior, yet he'd acted exactly like his entitled cousin, Woodward, currently on his seventeenth wife.

That was the problem with being an incubus—you outlived your human partner, again and again and again. Deep down, by choosing a mate with an unlimited life (or rather death) span, Quentin had wanted to avoid that too. Woodward didn't seem that broken up when one wife faded and he had to find another one. But he'd had centuries of serial monogamy, interspersed with decades of reckless promiscuous abandon. Maybe he'd felt differently at the beginning.

The door creaked open, and Quentin quickly turned over, pretending to be asleep. He wasn't ready to face Ted yet, not after his behavior and then nearly dying. That was just too embarrassing. *No, what's embarrassing is having to thank him for saving my ass when I was nothing but a dick to him.*

He heard the *clish* of dishes and the *tink* of cutlery. Ted must be getting ready to eat whatever that was that smelled so good. *How long has it been since I've smelled something that mouthwatering? How long has it been since I've smelled anything at all?* The suppressant had blunted all his senses, and he'd never even noticed it, the dulling taking place gradually over so many years that he had accepted it as normal.

Why did I think the quality of my life was worth preserving like that? Well, obviously he hadn't. Escaping the need for the sense-depriving suppressant was why he'd made certain to specify a nonliving partner (although he'd drawn at least one hard line: the candidates had to be capable of self-sustained existence, without the third-party maintenance spells required by zombies or golems).

The sound of Ted's heavy tread approached from the direction of where Quentin assumed the kitchen was located. The heavenly aromas grew stronger too. Quentin sighed in time with the rumble of his stomach. Embarrassment or hunger? Which was harder to face?

His stomach growled again. *Hunger wins this round.*

He rolled to his back to find Ted hovering uncertainly next to the coffee table, a laden tray in his hands.

Whoa. Ted's aura was *incredible*.

Quentin's ability to detect auras had faded along with his other senses until he'd all but forgotten about them. David and Alun hadn't appeared to have any aura at all, which might have been the result of them being so focused on each other. Or perhaps it was fae shielding magic. Alun struck Quentin as being very protective of his husband.

Ted's aura, though, was golden, threaded with tendrils of red and pink, with sly flashes of turquoise. Quentin tried to remember his long-ago lessons on interpreting aura color and strength. So much of it was concerned with identifying a compatible sex partner that he'd paid little attention.

Quentin must have been goggling like a codfish, because Ted glanced over his shoulder, as if he expected to see a slavering hellhound lurking in the shadows.

"I apologize. I shouldn't stare. I normally have much better manners, I assure you."

Ted shrugged, causing the dishes on his tray to clink. "It's okay. I don't blame you for the WTF glare. After all, I ran out on you. You nearly died. On my watch."

"It wasn't entirely your fault."

"No?" He set the tray on the table. "You were a guest on my property. You didn't ask to be abandoned here. I didn't ask how you were going to get away or anything. The thing is . . ." Ted sat in a wooden rocker on the other side of the table, leaning forward with his hands clasped between his knees. "I assumed you were a shifter. And that, like me, you'd be able to transform to keep warm or find food or whatever. I never expected . . . well . . . you."

"An incubus, you mean?"

"Well, yeah. I've *heard* of 'cubi. Sort of. But I've never *met* one."

Quentin sighed and sat up, the blanket pooling in his lap. "If you ask my cousins, you still haven't met one. I'm kind of an anomaly in my family."

Ted flashed a crooked grin. "Me too. I think I may be the only extroverted bear shifter in the history of bears."

"Well, I'm the only introverted incubus, and I'm cursed with empathy too."

Ted's eyes widened. "Really? You're cursed? Dr. Kendrick was cursed until last summer too."

Quentin laughed. "No, not an actual curse. Just an unfortunate tendency. My grandmother constantly bewails the fact. It makes her life so difficult."

"Not as difficult as it makes yours, I bet."

Quentin blinked. "I . . . You know, you may be the first person who's gotten that. My grandmother certainly doesn't."

"I'm sorry if I made things worse. I didn't mean to. Dr. Kendrick says I have an impulse-control problem. He used to think I had an exhibitionist kink because I'd . . . well . . ." Ted rubbed the back of his neck. "Phone in Bigfoot sighting tips, then do a partial shift to lure people up here, just to have someone to talk to."

Quentin laughed again. "Really?" When he saw that Ted looked uncomfortable, maybe even hurt, he scooted to the edge of the sofa. "Sorry. It wasn't my intention to distress you. I'm laughing because I think it's kind of a brilliant way to exploit your abilities to get what you want. I've never tried to do anything but squash my abilities, or ignore them, as impossible as that is." Quentin swallowed hard. Could he really confess this to a virtual stranger? *A virtual stranger who saved my life.* A virtual stranger who, at least on paper, was his husband. "You see, I've been taking a potion for years. Decades." He couldn't remember how long exactly, which meant it was probably a good thing he'd been forced to stop. "It suppresses my incubus . . . appetites, makes it possible for me to be around other people's energies without wanting to . . . to—"

"To binge?"

"Yes. I suppose that would be a good description. The thing is, when 'cubi binge, their partners die. I couldn't face that." *Not again.* "Hence the potion. But David essentially told me I've been poisoning myself. I can't take the suppressant anymore, therefore I'm a danger to others."

"A danger? Because you're a sex demon?"

Quentin clenched his eyes shut. "I really don't like to think of myself that way. But yes. The point is, I'm a danger to *you.*"

"Me?" Ted chuckled, a basso rumble. "No offense, Q-Bert, but I don't think you could do much harm to me. I'm about twice your size."

"Size is irrelevant when it comes to sucking the life force out of someone. Besides, I'm stronger than I look."

Ted cast a skeptical glance at Quentin's unimpressive form. "If you say so."

"I do. I also need to apologize to you. Twice. Once for being a jerk to you when I showed up yesterday."

Ted shrugged. "It's okay."

"No, it's not. One of the things my family is *insistent* on is good manners and courtesy." When you had no inherent empathy, you had to put strict rules in place so you didn't behave like an asshole. *Because assholes don't attract willing partners.* "I failed miserably when I was so rude to you."

"I wasn't much better. And I was the one that ran out and left you stranded."

"I guess we can agree we're even there?"

"Works for me."

"All right, then. The other thing I have to apologize for is that David offered me another place to stay—a flat above Alun's office—and I turned him down. Until I get used to living without the suppressant, I can't be around the energies of so many people, so I've rather invited myself to stay here. With you."

A smile flashed again, all the more adorable within the beard. "You know I won't turn down company. That's why I signed up with Supernatural Selection in the first place."

"But weren't you listening? I'm a *danger* to you."

Ted grinned. "Because you want to jump my bones?"

Quentin gritted his teeth. "Because I'm trying *not* to jump *anybody's* bones, and I haven't had any nonmedicated practice resisting that in nearly fifty years."

"I don't see the problem. Everyone has a choice of how they behave. If you don't want to be a sleazy sex predator, then don't."

Quentin rubbed the edge of the blanket between his fingers. "But what if I can't help myself?" He hated how small his voice sounded.

"Does David think you can?"

"Yes."

"Then you're good."

"But he doesn't *know* me."

"Sounds like nobody knows you—including you. Look at it this way. Like you said, there aren't a lot of people around here to tempt you. If I think you're getting that gleam in your eye, I'll just take off again, or call Dr. Kendrick. We'll be fine. Case closed. So." He slapped his knees. "How about some lunch?"

Chapter Nine

The look on Q-Bert's face when he took the first spoonful of soup—*holy smokes*. And his moan? Ted had to excuse himself and go to the kitchen so he could adjust his suddenly tight jeans. This was not good. No matter what the contract said, Quentin was *not* his husband. Ted was still promised to Rusty. Besides, Quentin had made it clear that sex freaked him out. The last thing Ted wanted to do was make him fight that battle with himself.

Chill out, Farnsworth. Pretend he's just a visitor, like Matt. Someone to keep the loneliness at bay. Someone to talk to.

He grabbed the salt shaker and returned, brandishing it as the excuse for his exit. "Thought you might want some salt."

"No." There was that moan again. Damn it. "This is perfect. I don't think I've ever tasted anything this good in my life."

"It's just fish chowder. Nothing special."

"Nothing *special*? Are you kidding? It's divine."

Ted shrugged and sat, picking up his own bowl and digging in. "If you're this easy to please, we'll get along fine. I cook a lot of food at this time of year, but it's not fancy."

"Why cook so much? Expecting neighbors to drop by unexpectedly at mealtimes?"

"Hardly. There's nobody within miles. Besides, I only bought the property last month, although I've rented this cabin for years."

"So you didn't build the lodge—or rather, *start* building the lodge then?"

"Nope. Not the cabin either. The whole spread used to be owned by a marten shifter clan. They had some trouble with the F word."

Red washed up Quentin's throat. "The F word?"

"Yeah. 'Finish.'" He grinned. "They started stuff, but never followed through." He shrugged. "I kind of have the same problem. I mean, I'd love to finish, but I get distracted by *everything* that needs doing. So I never make it very far with anything. That's what Rusty was supposed to help me with."

Quentin's blush spread to his cheeks, and he seemed to shrink against the sofa cushions. "Rusty? Is he your husband?"

"No. That would be you, remember? But he was *supposed* to be."

"Right, right. Sorry. Um . . . tell me about him?"

"Sure. He's a beaver shifter, but he's Inactive. He didn't let that stop him, though. He went to college. Got his master's in construction engineering. Runs his own company."

Quentin was suddenly very interested in the dregs of his chowder. "He sounds terrific."

"Yeah. Dr. Kendrick knows him, says he's a great guy too. I thought that with his help, we could get the lodge set up as the mess hall for a wilderness retreat. Then maybe have yurts out in the trees. Camping spots along the lake and farther up into the hills. Maybe run hikes or other adventures. You know, for people who want to get away from it all and rough it for a while. As long as we keep the place simple, we don't have to worry about electricity or fancy amenities, and it should be quicker to finish, don't you think?"

Quentin frowned and set his bowl on the coffee table. "Yes. I suppose so. But is that all you'd want to do? *Can* you run electricity up here?"

"There's a substation about five miles away, but when I checked, it would cost a bundle to get the service run up here.

That's another thing the martens didn't finish. In fact, I suspect it's one of the reasons they decided to sell."

"What about alternative energy sources?"

"A solar array big enough to power this place would kinda destroy the wilderness experience, don't you think?"

"I suppose."

Ted sighed. "Anyway, it's not the kind of place you'd be interested in."

"Why do you think so?"

"I saw your suits, your shoes. You—" Ted coughed into his fist "—may have mentioned family and money once or twice, while you were busy being horrified by the distance to town and, well, me."

Quentin winced. "I said I was sorry. Do you have to remind me what a jerk I was?"

Ted set his own bowl aside. Normally, he'd have gone for second helpings, even thirds, but his appetite had deserted him. "I can't help it. All my plans are toast. I sank all my money into this place and the Supernatural Selection contract. My plan was to find a husband with the right expertise. But since I don't have him . . ." Ted lifted his palms in a shrug. "I'm kind of screwed."

"Maybe not."

"How do you figure? We're contracted. Not much we can do about it now except figure out how to make the best of it." He held up a hand. "And don't worry. I don't expect you to throw any of your family money at me."

"Good, because I don't have any anyway. They don't know I'm here, and they definitely don't know about the Supernatural Selection contract. My grandmother still expects me to marry her choice of sacrificial partner."

"Then we're both screwed. And when Rusty and your vampire find out, they might be upset too. I mean, they both agreed to the contract. It was only a last-minute clerical error that messed everything up."

Quentin sat forward, his eyes intent. "Before my plunge into temporary coma, I called Supernatural Selection."

"You too? I tried but I got put on hold. Wait a sec. That's right." His heart soared. Maybe he still had a chance for his perfect life after all. "Dr. Kendrick said you'd told him we'd have this sorted out in a jiffy. Did Supernatural Selection say they'd fix it?"

Quentin bit his lip. "Not exactly. There's what's called an escape clause—a way to get out of the contract, provided we follow certain rules and requirements."

Ted leaped up. "Then let's do them. Now."

"We can't do everything now." Quentin filled him in on some of the details—something about no face-to-face contact, maybe something else, but who cared?

"Whatever. The sooner the better though, right?"

"As long as you're sure . . ."

"We've covered this, Q-Bert. Let's move it along."

Quentin huffed. "Fine. You have to call them and give them your official approval first, and some things have a timing component. Others, I'm not so sure of. I don't suppose you know where we can catch a couple of mosquitos?"

"Here? In November? Not likely."

"How about fleas?"

Ted scowled. "Now you're just being insulting."

"I don't mean *you* have fleas. But failing mosquitos, we need either fleas or ticks."

Ted shuddered. "No ticks. Those are just revolting."

"So do you know where to get fleas?"

"I know who *has* fleas around here. Squirrels, rabbits, and rats. Whether we can catch one long enough to encourage a couple of fleas to hop off on command is another question. Do the fleas have to be alive?"

Quentin blinked. "I didn't ask. And my phone died before I could get any additional details."

"Mine's almost dead too, and I don't have anything to charge it with right now."

"Isn't the point of having a cell phone so that you can call people? How do you normally charge it?"

"I use my truck. But it's in the shop. I could have charged it when I was in town, but I forgot to bring the dang thing with me."

"You were in town." It wasn't a question. "That's where you went yesterday."

"Well, this morning, actually. I spent the night in a cave."

"I drove you out of your home into a cave?" Quentin looked like he was going to wad the blanket into the next dimension. "Why didn't you say anything?"

"It's not a big deal. I use that cave all the time, so I keep a spare set of clothes there. I used to use it for the Bigfoot scam, but it's come in handy since my truck's been in the shop. I can travel a lot faster as a bear. Can sleep there comfortably in fur. Then hike the last couple miles into town like any other guy."

"You slept in a cave. I can't believe you slept in a cave."

"I'm a bear, Q-Bert. Get over it." Ted drummed his fingers on his knees. "I'm expecting a lumber delivery later on." Not that he could do much with it yet, not without Rusty's help. "The driver's an independent trucker. Owns his own rig and contracts with a bunch of lumberyards for remote deliveries like up here." He shook his head with a chuckle. "That's not enough for Larry, though. He owns the town auto shop too, so I can ask him about my truck when he gets here. Once we've got phone juice back, we can find out whether we need live fleas or not. I hope not." Just the thought of fleas made his beard itch. "What else?"

"We each need a silver coin."

"Pure silver? I suppose a regular old dime or quarter wouldn't do?"

"It's a witch's ritual. What do you think?"

Ted winced. "Definitely pure silver."

"There's a thing we have to do in the dark of night with a silver-bladed knife, but it's tedious more than difficult."

"You gonna tell me what it is?"

"Let's just say don't get a haircut in the next couple of days. The point is, we've got a way out. Yesterday, we were both reacting out of shock and disappointment because we had these fantasies about how our lives would be better once we'd married our perfect mate. Faced with . . ."

"Imperfect mates?"

"Let's say 'misaligned.' We're perfect for someone, just not each other."

Ted cocked his head, studying Quentin with his designer clothes and hipster glasses. "What is it you do anyway?"

"I'm trained as an advocate. Or at least I was. I'm an art historian now."

"An art historian? What does an art historian *do* all day?"

"I consult. With museums and galleries. Write articles for journals. That kind of thing."

"You consult?" Ted laughed, long and loud, slapping his knee, until Quentin scowled.

"What's so damn funny?"

"You've gotta admit," Ted wheezed when he could speak again, "if Supernatural Selection thought *we* were a perfect match, they are the worst matchmaking service in history."

When Ted finally stopped laughing—and really, it wasn't *that* funny to think Quentin wouldn't be a good match for somebody —he stood up and headed for the row of hooks next to the front door. "There's more chowder in the kitchen if you're still hungry. David said you needed to rest up and build your strength." He took down his jacket.

"Oh. Thanks. Are you going out?"

"Larry should be here with that lumber order soon. I need to clear a place for it in the lodge basement." He sighed. "Sure wish I could have called it off and gotten my money back, but it was too late."

"Don't worry," Quentin said, although he hadn't managed to stamp out his own nerves. "We'll get this straightened out before long, and you and Rusty can make this place into your dream. Have you spoken to him? Let him know this is just a temporary glitch?"

Ted paused with his hand on the doorknob. "I . . . um . . . haven't actually met him yet. We've texted each other on the Supernatural Selection message app, but just general stuff, you know? 'Hi, how are you, looking forward to meeting you,' that kind of stuff. But his profile is blocked now because—" Ted gestured between the two of them and shrugged "—not my husband."

Casimir never messaged me. But then, Quentin had never initiated a conversation either. He cleared his throat. "So you're assuming this would be his dream too?"

Ted scowled, a lock of hair falling forward across his forehead, and a spear of *want* shot through Quentin's chest. *Why would a wayward lock of hair ignite my dormant lust?* Quentin would have sworn he didn't have a secret yen for scruff, but apparently he didn't know himself as well as he'd thought.

Not an option. Not only was Ted committed to somebody else, but Quentin was too. At this point, neither one of them knew what their *real* mates might want, or what they'd think about their contracted partners shacking up together (in a literal shack) before their official wedding nights. Was this like one of those stories where the wedding attendant sleeps with the groom the night before the ceremony?

Ugh. The last thing Quentin needed was to become even more of a cliché. But Ted's golden aura practically shouted that he'd never do anything dishonorable. And the contract might say Quentin was Ted's husband, but in Ted's mind, it was obvious that Rusty was already in residence.

"I'm sorry," Quentin said, hugging the blanket to his chest. "I shouldn't— I mean, you must have mentioned this plan in the Supernatural Selection profile. I know I had to spill my guts about everything I wanted—and declare everything I didn't mind giving up."

Ted rubbed the back of his neck, which sent that wayward lock farther down, brushing his eyebrows. Quentin swallowed, making sure the blanket covered his groin, because *really*. Hadn't he been humiliated enough?

"Thing is, I didn't actually mention it. I wanted it to be a surprise. Kind of a wedding gift."

"So for a wedding gift, you were going to say, 'Guess what, honey! I'm taking you up into the wilderness and making you build a giant lodge!'?"

"Well, when you put it like *that* . . ." He pushed his hair back. *Damn it.* "But he has his own place. His own business. So he wouldn't have to stay here. But he's been having some issues with his clan, so I thought he'd appreciate someplace far away. Someplace that doesn't have any associations, you know?"

No no no. Don't be thoughtful too. It's just not fair. "I do. And that's really nice of you."

Ted's brow cleared. "You think so? Really?"

"I really do. You're a good man, Ted. I can tell by looking at you."

This time, his frown was laced with suspicion. "Nobody can tell that by looking."

"I can. It's your aura."

"You can see auras? Like druids can?"

"I can't speak for druids, but 'cubi can definitely see auras. It's how we— Never mind." Quentin didn't know what difference it would make, telling Ted that 'cubi were the original sexual predators, but for some reason he didn't want Ted to think poorly of him. *I wonder what my aura looks like? I'm betting it isn't a sunburst of gold.* "I don't want you to be late for your appointment." He turned his head, detecting the distant rumble of an engine. "In fact, I think I hear a vehicle approaching."

"You can hear that?" Ted pulled on a ball cap. "Thanks for the warning. Guess I'd better do some research on incubus abilities, huh?" He opened the door, but paused at the threshold, a chilly breeze sneaking in to eddy around Quentin's feet. "If you want to clean up, the bathroom's down the hall. There's hot water— I've got a propane tank for that, same as the stove, so you can shower. I brought your luggage in from the lodge too, so you can change if you want."

"Thank you."

"Well. Better run."

"Don't forget to call Supernatural Selection and give them your approval for the escape clause."

"Right. On it as soon as I help Larry unload." He ducked out the door before Quentin could lift a hand in farewell.

Quentin sighed and pushed the blanket off his lap. He looked down, where his erection was making a mockery of his tailoring. "Don't get any ideas. He's off-limits." Everybody was off-limits, for that matter. *I really hope David knows what he's talking about. I'd hate for Ted to be the first victim of my lack of self-control.*

Quentin stood, wobbling just a little and barking his shin on the coffee table when he tried to correct his balance. It was as if the world were reorienting itself around him, a new spatial awareness to go along with his recovered sight and taste and smell.

He circled the sofa and surveyed the rest of the room. It was similar to his little corner—unfinished wood paneling, pine floors scattered with faded throw rugs in earth tones. A far cry from his Boston town house with its old-world elegance. *You knew what you were giving up when you signed the contract.* He sighed. *But I thought I was getting Casimir's mid-century modern estate in return.*

The kitchen wasn't quite as rustic as he'd expected it to be. Red Formica countertops and a giant soapstone sink. A refrigerator that looked like something from the fifties. A refrigerator? Without electricity? A propane refrigerator. *Who knew?* The stove was a huge six-burner monstrosity, and a wheeled cart with a butcher block top stood in the middle of the space. *I guess rustic doesn't have to be primitive. Don't be a snob.*

He wandered down the hall, still feeling as if his legs were too short for his body, or that the floor was in the wrong place. When he got to the bathroom, he stopped in the doorway and stared.

A wide window backlit an enormous claw-foot bathtub with a rainfall showerhead suspended above it. *A tub big enough for a bear and a companion. Or two.* At this time of day, the room was bright with sun, but oil lamps stood on the vanity and a Mission-style table against the wall. The table's lower shelves were stacked with fluffy brown towels. The toilet and sink gleamed white, not a stain or a scratch, and the floor was cork, the same kind he had in his kitchen at home.

Bemused, Quentin stepped back into the hall. "Rustic unfinished walls. Battered pine floors—also unfinished. Scarred countertops." Then he ducked back into the bathroom. "And an *Architectural Digest* bathroom. What the devil?"

He eyed the tub covetously, but before he could plunge in, he needed to find his luggage. A staircase stood opposite the bathroom door, so he took it. After a dogleg turn at the landing, it opened into a room that ran the length of the house—Ted's bedroom, obviously, judging by the size of the mattress on the floor. The room was almost as bright as the outdoors, with windows on either end and three pairs of dormers marching along the long sides. Quentin wandered over to the middle dormer on the west wall. It overlooked the lake, with a view of the lodge along the shore.

When I'm married, I won't have a room like this. On the other hand, he'd probably have a closet, a bed frame, and a bureau or two rather than pine shelves stretched across cinder blocks. The jeans and shirts and underwear on the shelves were all neatly folded, but Ted obviously didn't spend a lot of time or effort on the niceties. And as for the tiny bathroom opposite the bed, *serviceable* was a charitable term for it. *Can he even fit in a shower stall that narrow?*

Quentin's luggage wasn't up here—he wasn't sure whether to feel relieved or insulted that Ted didn't expect Quentin to sleep with him. *Relieved. Definitely relieved. Safer for everyone if I stay as far away as possible.* He descended the stairs and turned down the hall, pushing open a door at the end.

And did another double-take.

This room had a similar footprint to Ted's room upstairs, but instead of dormers, it had banks of double-hung windows, and a set of French doors opening onto a deck with that same lake view. The floors weren't pine—they were burnished oak. A huge cherrywood armoire loomed next to the door, flanked by built-in shelves. A smaller woodstove was tucked in the corner, a Mission-style love seat in front of it. But the showpiece of the room was the cherrywood bed frame—Mission-style again, its supporting slats sturdy enough to hold an army. *Or maybe sturdy enough to hold a bear shifter and his equally giant mate.* The frame didn't have a mattress yet, which, along with the empty shelves and unlit stove, gave the room a *waiting* feeling.

That's exactly what it's doing. It's waiting for Rusty. The bathroom, this bedroom. Ted wasn't wasting any effort on his own comfort. *He's building a den for his mate.*

And somehow, Quentin had ruined that for him.

His breath caught in his chest, and he pinched the bridge of his nose *hard* to keep the tears at bay. Was Casimir anticipating Quentin's arrival with the same joy and care? Was Rusty worrying about Ted, maybe preparing a special spot in his house for Ted to feel welcome?

"Screw this." His suitcase was next to the door, so he grabbed it and towed it into the bathroom.

He had planned to loll in the tub, but the evidence of exactly why he wasn't welcome here had spoiled his taste for it. Instead, he stripped off his clothes, his newly recovered sense of smell informing him that he was doing everyone within a ten-foot radius a huge favor. When he stepped into the shower, he got another sharp reminder that he'd been released from the deadening suppressant: the water, warm and silky, overloaded his senses as it sluiced against his skin. He lifted his hands, mesmerized by the way it trickled through his fingers and down his arms; tilted his head back to revel in the tender beat of it against his scalp. He could—

No! He'd disciplined himself against sensual indulgence for years. But what if he'd only been able to resist because he'd overmedicated? What if he had no will at all? *What if I'm not stronger than I think?* Or worse, what if he was exactly as weak as he feared?

So he scrubbed his skin mercilessly, even though he wasn't particularly grimy. He had an impulse to down the rest of the suppressant in his bag, just so he wouldn't feel so damned hollow.

He dried off—those towels were as fluffy as they'd looked—and yanked on clean briefs and an undershirt. The only marginally casual clothes he had were his workout clothes—and since he'd expected to work out in Casimir's home gym, not outdoors, they were shorts. He had to put on a pair of wool slacks and an Oxford with a blazer. He left off the tie—his one possible concession to wilderness attire.

He wandered back into the living room and sat down on the sofa. The fire crackled cheerily in the woodstove. Quentin stared at it morosely. The bright open bedrooms, upstairs and down, the sun spilling in the window by the sofa, weren't things he had any reason to expect. Vampire dwellings perforce were sunless during the day.

Sure, Quentin could go out in daylight if he wanted, but that would show a lack of respect for his husband that was unacceptable. If Casimir lived in the dark, then Quentin would too. In theory, it wouldn't harm him physically—after all, his roots were in Sheol, where the sun never shone. But emotionally? He wasn't so sure.

He remembered when his grandmother broke ground on her third vacation home in the wooded Vermont mountains. Quentin had been lethargic and depressed after Rory's near death, but he had found something close to peace in the solitude and beauty of the place.

He'd avoided the building site while the crews were at work, but he'd sat on top of a dirt mound next to the concrete well of the basement the day before the first-floor deck was to be installed. The sun had shone down into it, filling him with melancholy, because the basement walls had no windows. That day was the last time that floor, those walls, would ever see sunlight.

He wondered whether vampires thought of that—and whether they mourned the daylight—before they made the decision to leave their humanity behind.

Chapter Ten

"Hey, Larry? Can you back the truck up to the bulkhead doors? I need to haul this down into the workshop."

Larry tipped his ball cap up with one finger. "Thought you was gonna build yourself a pole barn to hold the lumber."

Ted opened the metal doors that led into the lodge basement. "I was, but I ran a little short, you know? And plans changed."

"I hear ya. Nothin's the same but change, am I right?"

Larry ambled to the cab of his truck, climbed aboard, and backed it up to within ten feet of the doors. Ted winced a little as the tires sank into the earth, but it was cold enough—and had been dry enough—that it didn't look like it would get stuck.

Larry helped cart the load of oak flooring down the half flight of stairs and stack it on the sawhorses Ted had set up next to the wall.

"Thanks, man. Say, how's my truck doing? It's been a couple of weeks now."

Larry took off his cap and wiped his forehead with a red bandana. "Still waiting for the fuel pump. 'S hard to get parts for that model. You oughta upgrade to a new one. I could get you a deal."

"Nah. No spare cash for that. Besides, I like my old truck."

Larry shrugged. "Guess you'll have to wait, then."

Ted closed the bulkhead doors, gazing across the lake at the cabin. He needed to lay in some more supplies. A guy like Quentin wouldn't want the simple meals Ted had planned for the next few days. Maybe he could step up the menu, at least pretend to be a decent host. Yeah, he wanted Rusty, but Quentin was a guest too—one with a common goal. No reason why they couldn't be friends, right? "Say, Larry? Would you give me and my, uh, friend a ride into town?"

Larry scuffed his foot in the weeds, uprooting a clump of grass. "I s'pose. How you planning to get back?"

Hmmm. Good point. "I'll see if Matt can give us a ride partway."

Larry shrugged. "No skin off my nose. But you gotta be ready in ten. I've got a full afternoon ahead."

"No problem. I'll be right back."

Ted legged it down the path beside the lake. He wasn't as fast in human form as he was as a bear, but his legs were long enough that he made good time. *Time... time... wasn't I supposed to do something else? Something that had to be done in time?* Ah, shoot. Supernatural Selection. He'd promised to call 'em, and it had gone clean out of his head.

He pulled out his phone as he jogged. It didn't have much of a charge, but that wasn't a problem with Dr. Kendrick's magic app.

"Supernatural Selection. This is Zeke. How may I help you?"

Zeke. He'd given Ted the contract to sign the day he'd gone into the Portland office. Cute guy with curly black hair and glasses. *Wonder what he'd look like with a goatee like Quentin's.* "Hey, yeah. This is Ted Farnsworth. I'm supposed to let you know I approve of the escape clause thingie."

"Oh. Yes. Mr. Farnsworth. One moment please."

Ted reached the porch and mounted the steps while the sound of rustling papers and a muttered curse came over the line. "Mr. Farnsworth?"

"Yeah?"

"Are you absolutely certain you want to proceed? Mr. Bertrand-Harrington informed you of the consequences, correct?"

Had he? They'd talked about something over lunch, but the details were a little hazy. Something about hair? Not that it mattered. They needed to get this taken care of and get back with the right husbands, whatever it took. "Yep. It's all good."

"Very well. The AI is recording, so if you could repeat after me. I, Ted Farnsworth."

Ted sighed. "I, Ted Farnsworth." *Awkward, idiotic bear shifter.*

"Do hereby request."

"Do hereby request." *That we get on with it already. Q-Bert didn't say he had to go through this crap.*

"The initiation of the escape sequence."

"The initiation of the"—*what now?*—"escape sequence."

"Of the contract between—"

"How much longer does this go on? I'm kinda in a hurry here."

"Please, Mr. Farnsworth. This is ritual language. The consequences of any errors are quite dire."

Ted snorted. "As dire as the consequences of putting the wrong fricking names on the contracts in the first place?" The silence on the line was deafening. "Sorry. Go on."

"Of the contract between." Zeke's voice shook, which made Ted feel kinda bad for the guy.

Guess I should give him a break and be more cooperative. "Of the contract between."

"Quentin Bertrand-Harrington and me."

"Q-Ber— Quentin Bertrand-Harrington and me."

As soon as the last words left Ted's mouth, a sound like an enormous brass gong clanged over the phone and, weirdly, in the air around him, as if it were reverberating off the mountains.

"Thank you, Mr. Farnsworth. The escape sequence has officially begun. Please be sure you complete the required ritual by the deadline, or . . ."

"Or what?"

"Well, let's say that when witches use the word 'deadline,' their meaning is rather more literal than you might expect."

Ted gulped. Maybe he should have paid more attention to Q-Bert after all. "Good to know."

"If you—"

"Hello?" Ted pulled the phone away from his ear. The screen was black. *Not like I didn't expect it.*

When he strode into the cabin, Quentin was standing next to the couch, his face pale and his hand at his throat. "Wh-what was that sound?"

"I just called Supernatural Selection and okayed our escape clause. Guess it came with sound effects."

"Mother of fire, it nearly scared me out of my pants."

That'd be something to see. Ted banged his fist into his thigh. *Stop that.* "Good. You're ready."

"Ready for what?"

"I got us a ride into town in Larry's rig. We can do a little shopping, get whatever stuff we need for the escape thing." He eyed Quentin's outfit, which avoided being a suit only because his jacket was tweed and his trousers were plain gray. "We can get you some clothes that won't get trashed when we're out searching for fleas or doing our dance by the light of the moon."

"We don't have to dance."

"Yeah, yeah. Haircuts. Whatever. But we still need the coins and the silver-bladed knife. And something to keep the fleas in. Shoot. The fleas. I forgot to ask about them."

"We can call again later, but do you really think we can find all we need in—what's the name of the nearest town?"

Ted grinned. "Dewton. And you'd be surprised what you can find at Stuff 'n' Things."

Quentin stared at him, one eyebrow quirking up. "Seriously?"

"Don't knock it. It's an awesome place."

Quentin glanced around the room, uncertainty written all over his narrow face. "I'm not sure—"

"You think I don't know a good thing?"

"What? No. I mean, that's not it. It's just . . ." Quentin swallowed, color draining from his face. "I may not be ready to face a town full of people."

Damn. Ted had forgotten that Quentin was dealing with some kind of incubus drug withdrawal. "Q-Bert, I may not know much about you, but I know this: you're no pushover. Anytime it feels like it's too much? You give me the high sign. There are plenty of places down there that are private, where you can catch a breather. But Larry's still waiting for a part for my truck, so this is the best chance we've got to collect what we need."

Quentin rocked back and forth a little bit—probably didn't even realize he was doing it, but it was pretty obvious he was waffling.

"Tell you what. Bring your phone and charger too. We can stop by the library or the diner and juice it up."

As Ted had suspected, that did the trick. Quentin dug his charging cord out of his case and shoved it into his jacket pocket. "All right. Let's go."

"Don't you have another coat? That jacket's not going to keep you warm."

He shrugged. "I didn't expect to be venturing out on the frozen tundra, you know."

Ted barked a laugh. "It's not *that* bad, but you do need another coat. Shirl's bound to have something that'll do at Stuff 'n' Things."

"They carry men's clothing?"

"They carry everything. Let's go."

Ted tried not to rush Quentin as they headed back to the lodge. A couple of times, Ted thought he'd have to haul the guy out of the trees or the lake. Seemed like he couldn't walk in a straight line. Maybe that was part of his recovery.

Larry was waiting by his rig, staring at his watch, when they stepped into the lodge clearing.

"Hey, Larry. This is my friend Quentin. Quentin, Larry."

Larry gave Quentin the once-over—not like he was checking him out, but like all of the locals did with strangers. He didn't offer his hand, just nodded. "Nice to meet you."

"A pleasure." Quentin's voice had a little bit of an edge to it. "I trust we haven't kept you waiting unduly?"

"Nah." He climbed into the cab. "All aboard."

Ted led the way to the other side of the truck. "Sorry, but you'll have to sit in the middle. My legs are too long."

"That's . . . that's all right."

"Doesn't sound like you really think so."

"You're doing me a favor. The least I can do is not make you ride down the mountain with your knees up to your ears." Then he blushed. "I mean—"

"Just get in, Q-Bert," Ted said, chuckling. "Although you might keep the sex jokes on the down-low for the ride. I'm not sure Larry's the kind of guy who'd appreciate them."

Quentin hadn't realized exactly how far away from everything Ted's property was. *I must have been completely out when the driver brought me up here.*

Squeezed onto the narrow jump seat between Larry and Ted, Quentin did his best to become even smaller than he was so he wouldn't brush against either of them—which was harder than he expected. Although the cab's bucket seats were wide enough to accommodate someone Ted's *physical* size with room to spare, the auras were another matter.

Quentin had forgotten that psychic energy wasn't just visual, it was tactile too. Every time the truck hit a pothole too fast or cut around a sharp curve, the other men's auras would brush against him—although there couldn't be a bigger difference between them.

When the truck skewed right, Ted's golden energy brushed Quentin's skin like the welcome warmth from a cozy fire. When it skewed left, causing everyone to lean to the right, Larry's dark, crabbed aura slithered against him like an eyeless worm.

Quentin began watching the road intently, anticipating the turns. When it looked like a left was coming up, he scooted discreetly (he hoped) toward Ted. He barely registered what Ted and Larry were talking about—something to do with the tourist season, and a new resident who was trying to make a go of a business nobody wanted, and if Ted had noticed anything funny up in the woods, because there were rumors again.

The only funny thing in the woods is the idiot from Boston, who, despite being nearly three hundred years old and a trained advocate with five college degrees, is still stupid enough not to read the first fecking paragraph of a blood contract.

By the time they'd wound down the mountain and taken the last leg into a tiny town with the sea glimmering at its back, Quentin was sitting on the edge of his seat, all but in Ted's lap.

"You all right there, Q-Bert?"

"What? Oh. Absolutely."

"Larry, you can drop us at Wanda's. I'll check in with you later about what to do with that last lumber order."

"No problem, Ted."

The truck slowed and pulled to the side of the road in front of a retro restaurant, a long counter with red-topped stools visible behind its plate glass windows. Ted jumped down. "Thanks, man."

Quentin scooted across Ted's still-warm seat. "Yes. Thank you for the lift."

"Was coming this way anyhow. You sticking around at Ted's place for a while?"

Quentin glanced over his shoulder at Larry. Did he sound a little too interested in that answer? Apparently not, since he was fiddling with his side mirror.

"No. Just a brief stay. I'm ... evaluating the place. As an investment." Quentin winced internally. *Don't give out information that isn't specifically requested — especially not if it makes you invent the whole thing.*

"Good deal. Later."

Well. That was apparently that. Quentin slid down out of the truck, the ground a long way away.

"Careful." Ted caught his arm, steadying his landing. "Don't want to call David on you again."

"Shhh." Quentin glanced over his shoulder. The truck door was still open, but Larry didn't seem to be paying any attention to them.

"You know, Q-Bert," Ted said as he slammed the door, "nothing says 'Hey, listen to this sketchy info' like shushing someone over nothing more than the mention of a name."

Quentin's face heated because Ted was perfectly right. "I'm sure he'll chalk it up to the weird stranger in town."

"I don't think he'll chalk it up to anything. Larry doesn't really give a shit about anything but fishing and Seahawks football." He nodded toward the diner. "Need a snack or cup of coffee before we take the grand tour? You still look like you need feeding up."

Quentin peered through the windows. The diner was three-quarters full, and the clash of colors from all the auras was like a B-grade psychedelic movie from the sixties. He shuddered. "No, thank you. I'm fine. Let's get this over with."

"Suit yourself. You mind if I get a to-go coffee though? Won't be a minute."

"I'll stay out here, if that's all right." Quentin sidled up to the brick wall next to the window, wrapping his arms across his chest.

"You sure? It'll warm you up."

"Trust me. I'm sure."

"Back in a minute."

Ted disappeared into the diner in a warm puff of steamy air. Quentin scanned the town. It didn't take long, since there wasn't much of it. A number of businesses lined the main highway, presumably to take advantage of the coastal traffic, although none of it appeared to be stopping. Most of the activity on the main drag seemed to be funneled from the scattering of houses that climbed the foothills on the east side of the highway. The west side didn't have room for anything between the businesses and a line of grassy sand dunes that—judging by the dull, rhythmic roar—masked the ocean.

The ocean. He'd spent time at the family's summer cottage on the Cape, of course, but for some reason, the Pacific smelled wilder and less civilized than the Atlantic. Which was ridiculous. There was only one ocean, connected across the globe, regardless of what label cartographers put on it.

Nevertheless, the salt scent of the waves that crashed on the hidden coastline stirred a longing for something that he hadn't sought since he'd turned Rory from a vibrant young man to a desiccated near-mummy in his arms.

It wasn't *peace,* precisely. It was too wild, too urgent for that.

Freedom. How long had it been since he'd been free? Free of obligations, free of denied desire, free of guilt?

I don't think I remember. I'm not sure there ever was such a time. Every incubus came into the world with the burden of that hunger threaded into their DNA. The weight of their familial obligation fell on their shoulders as soon as they were aware enough to understand the concept of "consequences."

His grandmother's words were practically engraved in his mind. *"We have a responsibility to our ancestor, the one who first climbed out of Sheol and set us free. We continually strive to improve our bloodlines, enhance our status, increase our wealth. Above all, we never endanger the covenants under which we're allowed to remain in the Upper World. Discretion. Restraint. Stewardship. You wouldn't want to be the 'cubi who sends us all tumbling back to Sheol, would you?"*

Of course, in all these eons, plenty of incidents had broken the spirit of those covenants, if not the letter. However, when you had the money and power and influence of his family, those infractions could be covered up, whitewashed, ignored. And as long as humans didn't discover them, the supe councils looked the other way.

Rich incubus privilege. It was definitely a thing.

The door of the diner opened again and Ted reappeared holding two to-go cups. He handed one to Quentin. "Here. I know you said you didn't want anything, but it's chilly and that coat is crap."

Quentin accepted it, simultaneously touched by Ted's thoughtfulness and annoyed at the insult to his Tom Ford blazer. The cup was almost too hot against his palms, but he cradled it against his chest anyway. Besides, Ted had a point about the inappropriateness of Quentin's wardrobe for seaside adventures. "Thank you."

Ted cast a worried glance through the window. "I was hoping I could catch a ride back up the mountain for us, but my friend isn't here."

"Friend?" An unexpected spike of possessive jealousy shot through Quentin's chest. He tried to tamp it down by taking an injudiciously large sip of his "coffee"—only to succeed in burning his tongue and discovering that it was in fact a chai tea latte.

"Yeah. Matt. He, uh, he's given me rides into Portland a few times. He's a good guy. You'll meet him— No, I forgot. You won't meet him because you'll be back in the right place soon. Vampire society dos. What do they call 'em? *Swa-rays?*"

"They probably call them gatherings, affairs, parties," Quentin said woodenly. Attending endless rounds of them, regardless of what they were called, seemed less attractive now than ever, even though all the revelers would be dead.

"Well, they could hardly call them dinners, right? Do vampires even eat?" Ted's eyes rounded. "Will they eat *you?*"

"Ted. Be quiet." Quentin glanced wildly around. The sidewalk wasn't busy, but it wasn't empty, either. There was a steady stream of customers in and out of the diner and the bakery next door. "The Secrecy Pact—"

"Oh, come on. Who's gonna believe we're talking about *real* vampires? Forks isn't that far up the coast, so half the people driving through town are probably on their own sparkly vampire tour." He took off down the sidewalk with his giant stride, forcing Quentin to jog to catch up.

"Alun said you were in trouble with the supe council for pact violations."

Ted stopped so suddenly that Quentin overshot him and had to turn around and retrace his steps. "He told you that?"

"Yes. When you were in the kitchen with David."

Ted glanced down at his cup and then away, although his unfocused gaze and furrowed brow made Quentin think he wasn't all *that* interested in the sparse dune grasses. "He's my therapist, damn it. Isn't shit like that supposed to be confidential?" His voice held unmistakable hurt.

Quentin stepped closer, inside the agitated swirl of Ted's aura, threads of murky brown invading the gold.

"He's also law enforcement for the council. I think he was speaking to me in that capacity. He doesn't want you to get in trouble, Ted."

"He didn't tell you about any, well, *other* stuff?"

Quentin frowned, taking a cautious sip of the nuclear tea. "Other stuff like what?"

"Well, the *reason* the council is on my ass?"

"Only that there had been some pact infractions before."

"Just that? Not the . . . the consequences?"

"No."

Ted gave an exaggerated sigh. "Thank Ursa for that."

"All right, now you've got me curious. Have you done something other than impersonate Sasquatch?" He nudged Ted with an elbow. "Care to share the details?"

"No." He caught Quentin's elbow and hustled him along the sidewalk until they were opposite an unlovely, flat-roofed building. "We cross here."

The sign atop the building screamed *Stuff 'n' Things* in five-foot-tall blood-red letters. Below, a smaller, less lurid font read, *You need it? We got it.*

"I'm not sure whether to be appalled by the lack of specificity of the business name, the grammar infractions, or the universal merchandise claims."

"She doesn't want to limit herself with a stricter name. And it's not false advertising."

"Really?" Quentin allowed Ted to tow him across the street in a break in traffic. "She has *everything* in the entire world in a shop that's only a fifth the size of a Walmart?"

"Not everything. Just what you need."

"I find that hard to believe."

Ted glanced down at Quentin with annoyance. "Yeah, you don't believe in much, do you?"

Quentin scowled. "What's that supposed to mean?"

"Just that. You don't believe in love, or random kindness, or even yourself."

"I believe in things that make sense. Like natural-fiber clothing, and recycling, and the *New York Times* Sunday crossword puzzle. A store that holds everything? It's not a TARDIS, for pity's sake."

Ted paused, his hand on the Stuff 'n' Things' door. "You watch *Dr. Who?*"

"Yes. Everybody has at one time or another."

"Well, well, well, Q-Bert. You might be human after all."

"Don't be insulting," he muttered, making a valiant attempt to ignore the seductive brush of golden energy as he tossed his empty cup in the trash and marched into the store.

Chapter Eleven

Ted was still chuckling after he ditched his coffee and followed Quentin into the store. The guy was hilarious when he got all prickly, especially since Ted could tell it was mostly an act. He'd had plenty of practice detecting that—his brother, Ben, was a master at it, using grumpiness and pretend indifference to keep everyone at a distance.

Although Ted had a feeling that the reasons Quentin wanted distance were way different than Ben's. Ben didn't like people and found them irritating. Quentin? Well, he seemed to be more afraid of getting close, even though he was desperate for it.

Oh yeah. Sex demon. That might have something to do with it.

Quentin was standing in the store vestibule, staring through the second set of doors at the mad jumble on the acres of tables and haphazard arrangement of shelves. "Even if they do have everything, how the devil do they *find* it? Is there *any* kind of organization?"

"Sure there is."

"Oh really? What might that be?"

Ted held the door and nudged Quentin inside, toward the counter where Shirl was perched on a stool, regarding them from behind her cat-eye glasses. "I think it's kind of like the Big Bang."

"That's not an organizational principle. That's a cosmological model."

Ted shrugged. "Whatever. It's all about where everything lands."

Quentin humphed and took a sharp right between two rows of shelves.

"Hold on a sec, Q-Bert. You can't find anything here yourself."

"Stop calling me that." He bent over, poking at a nest of cutlery on the lowest shelf. "I'm able to find what I need because I proceed logically, from evidence and deduction. You should try it."

"Not sure that'll work here. If you want something, you have to *ask*."

For a second, Quentin froze, his fist clenched around a rusty butter knife. "I'm not sure I can—"

"Don't worry. She won't bite. She leaves that to her sister."

Quentin looked up at him, lifting an elegant dark eyebrow. "Does she keep her sister in the back room for just such occasions?"

"Nah. Her sister owns the diner."

"Yes, I imagine there would be far more opportunities for chomping there." He poked at a deflated inner tube with the flat of the knife blade. "And, one would hope, an array of more digestible targets."

"Fine. Wander around if you want. I'm checking in with Shirl."

"Suit yourself."

Ted chuckled. "Now you sound like Larry."

"Please." Quentin shuddered. "Don't even mention us in the same sentence."

Ted cut a quick glance at Quentin. Had he intended to sound that revolted? But Ted let it drop, since Q-Bert was already creeping down the aisle, his elbows clamped to his sides like he was afraid to brush against the shelves. To be fair, some of them were pretty overflowing, but nothing in here was carnivorous or explosive. At least Ted didn't think it was.

He moseyed over to the counter. "Hey, Shirl. How's business?"

She pulled a pencil from behind her ear and filled in something in the crossword puzzle book on her lap. "Can't complain." Instead of replacing the pencil where it had been, she stuck it into her jet-black beehive hairdo, where it joined at least three other pencils and a Sharpie. "Whatcha need today, Ted?"

"A few things. Do you have one of those off-grid phone chargers?"

"Thought you already had one of those."

"I do, but the crank broke a couple of months ago, so I was using my truck. Since it's been in the shop I've been charging up when I come into town. Doesn't put me out that much, but I've got a guest staying at my place now."

She nodded. "Guess you'd need one, then." She reached under the counter and pulled out a red-and-black plastic gizmo about the size of Ted's palm. "Here you go. Solar and hand-crank. Radio, flashlight, phone charger. That'll set you up."

Ted picked it up, turning it over in his hands. "Cool."

"What else?"

"My, uh, guest needs some clothes for the cold weather. He wasn't expecting to rough it so much."

"What kind of fool comes out here expecting a five-star hotel?"

"He wasn't really expecting to be here."

"Nobody expects to be here," she muttered. "Well. Where is he? How do I know what he needs if I can't size him up?"

"Yo, Q-Bert!" Ted called. "Leave off deducing and come here."

Quentin appeared from around an endcap, its table sagging under a pile of cast-iron pans. "I told you. Don't call me that." He stalked toward them, scowling mightily. For some reason, it made Ted want to ruffle his too-smooth dark hair.

"Shirl, this is Quentin."

She blinked at him for a minute. "Hey."

He nodded, barely glancing at her. "I think we should go, Ted."

"Nah, we haven't gotten everything yet. What do you think, Shirl? Got anything that'll fit him?"

Quentin shifted uneasily, edging closer to Ted. "I can afford to buy new clothes. I don't need used ones."

"Trust me, Q-Bert, you don't want to wear new Levi's. They'll chafe your thighs."

"My thighs will be fine."

"Yeah, as long as you don't buy new jeans." Ted turned to Shirl. "Got what he needs?"

She snorted and pushed off her stool, ducking through the curtain into the back room.

Ted rounded on Quentin, poking him in the chest with a finger. "Are you this much of a dick with everyone, or are you just so far above us hicks that you don't think you need to be polite?"

Quentin goggled at him, then clamped his lips together, pushing irritably at Ted's hand. "I didn't mean to be rude. I just don't see how this place could possibly have the specialized equipment we require. We need to go to the goblin market or an arcane supply."

"You call clothes for you 'specialized equipment'?"

"No, but . . ." He glanced at the ground and then away, pink staining his cheeks. "It's hard for me to wear clothing that belonged to someone else. Their energy signature never really fades, and if they ever, you know, got amorous in them, it's worse. It gives me a rash."

Ted wanted to laugh, but Quentin looked far too mortified. "Is this an incubus thing?"

Quentin's gaze flew to Ted's face. "Will you hush?"

"There's nobody here but Shirl, and she's somewhere in the back room. Chill."

"All right, yes, it is. But I can't exactly ask a thrift store clerk, 'By the way, do you happen to know if the former owner ever came in his pants?'"

Ted couldn't control his guffaws. "I don't think folks who get rid of their old clothes have to fill out questionnaires about their behavior."

"Well, they should."

"Yeah, I can see that working out great."

Quentin looked like he was gearing up for more arguing, but Shirl emerged from behind the curtain, a bundle of clothing in her arms. "Jeans." She took a couple of pairs of faded 501s off the top of the stack and dropped them on the counter. "Flannel." At least three, all in assorted plaids, joined the pants. "Thermals." She dumped a bunch of waffle-weave shirts on top of the other stuff. "And a jacket." She draped an all-weather parka over the whole thing. "Socks and boots in your size are right over there. Pick what you want. They're all the same price."

Quentin blinked at the pile of clothes. "I don't think I'll need quite so many pants and shirts though. One of everything should be enough."

"No," she said, "it won't."

"I'll only be here for another day."

"Best to be safe. You can always bring back what you don't need. Or Ted can. Someone'll need it eventually, and no harm done."

Quentin reached out a tentative finger to touch the jacket, then flinched back. "Oh." He touched it again without flinching, a smile flickering on his lips. He glanced up at Shirl from under his brows. "Where can I try them on?"

"Don't need to. You're a twenty-eight waist, twenty-eight inseam. Men's small. Shoe size nine."

"I— How did you know?"

"Experience."

Quentin still looked uncertain, but before he could insult Shirl some more, Ted gave him a gentle hip check. "You got the list of the other stuff we need for the you-know-what, Q?"

"Subtle, Ted, real subtle," he muttered. "I hardly think—"

"Coins, wasn't it?" Ted leaned his elbows on the counter, even though it wasn't exactly at a comfortable height. "We need a couple of pure silver coins, Shirl. You got anything like that?"

She tilted her head, tapping a long red fingernail on her jeans-clad leg. "Do they have to be any particular size?"

Ted glanced at Quentin. He shook his head. "No. Um, denomination isn't an issue."

"Good." She punched a key on her old-fashioned cash register, and the drawer sprang open. She poked around and pulled out a handful of coins, then sorted through them and tossed two on the counter. "Those do?"

The coins were no bigger than Ted's pinky fingernail, each of them bearing the almost invisible outline of some kind of flower. Quentin picked one of them up, placing it in his palm and studying it. "Where did you get these?"

She shrugged. "People from all over stop in here. I don't ask questions."

"Ah. Well. These will do. Thank you." He swallowed visibly. "You don't happen to have a . . . a silver-bladed knife, do you?"

Her eyes narrowed. "Blade like that's too soft for much. You sure it's what you need?"

Quentin nodded. "Yes. It's . . . ceremonial."

"Uh-huh." She stalked into the back room again.

Ted smirked down at Quentin. "Decide to start cooperating?"

"Do you know what those coins are?"

"Silver. That's all that matters, right?"

"They're Faerie silver. From before the Celtic Unification."

Ted shrugged. "So? That should make them perfect for the ritual, right?"

Quentin waved his hand as if to bat Ted's words away. "Yes, yes. But the point is not even why she has them, but who in

Faerie is shopping in Dewton with coins that haven't been seen for centuries."

Ted was still mystified. "I admit that's a poser, but—"

"The point, Ted, is that you're not the only one who's violating the Secrecy Pact. Somebody was extremely careless. At least, I prefer to *think* it was carelessness rather than deliberate exposure."

Ted was about to demand more from Quentin, but Shirl came back with a horn-handled knife about the length of Ted's index finger.

"This is the best I can do."

"That's . . . that's remarkably perfect," Quentin said. "What do we owe you for—

"Fleas," Ted blurted. "Don't forget those."

Quentin glared at him, but turned to Shirl with a smile. "Do you have any kind of receptacle for containing insects?"

"Alive or dead?"

Quentin exchanged a glance with Ted. "Alive. Maybe. We're not sure."

"Humph. People should learn how to be more precise." She pulled a cardboard box from under the counter and rummaged around in it. "These might work." She held out her hand to display a trio of glass vials stoppered with corks. "Depending on the size of the insect and how long you have to keep them alive."

"Yes. Those will do admirably." Quentin selected two of them and laid them on the counter next to the coins. "I believe that's everything."

She squinted at him, then at Ted. "I doubt it. But whatever." She rang them up, and the total made Ted swallow an oath. The coins and the knife must be *really* valuable. Ted started to sweat. He didn't have the money to cover even a quarter of this.

He rubbed the back of his neck. "Uh . . . Shirl, do you think I could—"

"Do you take American Express?" Quentin held out an American Express Black card.

She took it, holding it between her thumb and finger like it might bite. "Have to run this through in the back. That a problem?"

"Not at all."

She nodded curtly and ducked behind the curtain again.

"Thought you said you didn't have any money?" Ted whispered.

"I don't. Not cash, anyway. But that's the beauty of credit. By the time the statement comes due, I'll be married to Casimir and have access to my family funds again."

All righty, then. I guess family money is handy for something, even when you don't have it. Quentin must *really* want to get out of this marriage contract.

But so do I. Don't I?

"You didn't have to pay for everything." Ted's tone of voice combined mortification and accusation. "I could have put it on my account."

Quentin glanced up at the big man from under his lashes as they gained the sidewalk opposite Stuff 'n' Things. "Do you have the money to pay off your account?"

"Well. No. But—"

"It's the least I could do. You said we'd find what we needed there. You were right."

"But the money—"

Quentin sighed and stopped in front of the diner. "Listen, Ted. In my opinion, a partnership works when both—or all, depending on how many partners we're talking about— contribute to the common goal."

"Yeah, but all I contributed was a ride to town and a latte."

"No, you contributed your knowledge and social network, something I don't have. I *do* have money—or at least a monetary equivalent—but it wouldn't have done me any good if I couldn't get to where I could spend it. Upper World society as a whole places a disproportionate value on money in a relationship."

"'Upper World'?"

Quentin flushed. "I'm an incu—" He edged closer to Ted as a couple of townsfolk passed by, nodding at Ted in greeting. "A you-know-what."

Ted grinned down at him. "Subtle, Q-Bert. Real subtle."

Quentin buried his laugh. "Shut up. Sheol is"—he pointed to the ground—"below, so this is 'upper.'"

"There's a reason why people place a value on money. Because it's damn hard to live up here without it."

"Well, that's a very *human* perspective. So forget it. As far as I'm concerned, we're even."

Ted's forehead bunched, and for an instant, Quentin thought he'd argue, but then he grinned ruefully. "I probably should fight you on this, but to tell you the truth, I'm kinda relieved. So thanks."

Quentin pulled his new jacket closer around him, grateful for the way the nylon outer shell cut the wind. "You don't have to thank me. This will benefit me as well as you, remember? That's what I'm talking about—we're working toward a common, mutually beneficial goal."

"Okay, then. Partners?" Ted held out his hand, and although by now Quentin should be getting used to the golden aura, it still pulsed in an enticing way around Ted's fingers, sending out tendrils in Quentin's direction.

But to refuse to shake would be to refute his assertion. He took Ted's hand—and his eyes nearly rolled back in his head from the surge of energy that shot up his arm, making his whole body feel as if it had been expanded. His *whole* body. He was intensely grateful for the jacket for another reason—it covered his groin.

"P-p-partners." Quentin forced himself to let go. Mother of fire, this "partnership" was going to strain his self-control to the limit. What a time to be deprived of the suppressant.

Ted peered at him curiously. "You okay?"

He tucked his hand under his arm, the aftershocks still tingling along his skin. "Certainly. Are—are *you*?"

"Sure. Why wouldn't I be?" Ted blinked, his eyebrows rising as if the light had suddenly dawned. "Ooohhh! I get it." He grinned. "Sex de— I mean you-know-what mojo."

Quentin glared at him. "Very funny. Now what's next on the town tour?"

"Grocery store. I need to stop in and place my order."

"You need *more* groceries? I've seen your pantry, Ted. You've got enough supplies laid in for a battalion."

"No. I've got enough laid in for a bear shifter in November. *Early* November. And now I've got a house guest."

"Not for much longer."

Ted shrugged. "Like I said. It's early November. I'll have to stock up at least three more times before the solstice."

Quentin blinked. "*Three* more times? How much to you *eat*?"

Ted grinned. "Guess you'll find out at dinnertime." He jerked his head to the right. "Come on. It's this way. I might be able to score us a ride home in the market too, as long as Fred isn't already out on delivery."

But after Ted had placed an enormous order—suitable for an entire boarding school full of teenage boys—they discovered that the delivery guy was taking a sick day.

"Damn," Ted said as they stepped into the fitful wind. "I'm running out of options."

Quentin shifted the Stuff 'n' Things bag to his other hand. "How do you usually manage transportation?"

"I use *alternative* means. If you get my drift."

"Oh." *Bear shifter. Sleeping in a cave.* "Right."

"If Larry's not too swamped at the shop, maybe I can convince him to take another trip."

In his unpleasant encounter with Larry's aura, Quentin had detected slyness and avarice. "I'm sure if we cross his palm with sufficient silver—or rather, American Express—he can be persuaded," Quentin said dryly.

"No." Ted scowled and increased his pace, forcing Quentin to jog to catch up.

"But—"

"Look, Quentin." Ted ran a hand through his hair. But it wasn't the haunted look in his eyes or the defeat in his tone that made Quentin stop and pay attention—it was Ted's use of his actual name. "You're only gonna be here until we get this mess cleaned up. If we're lucky with the flea hunt, that may only be another day or so. But I'll be living here the rest of my life. I've got arrangements, okay? If you throw money at these guys, it may not be a big deal to you, but you'll set a precedent that'll wreck stuff for me, maybe forever."

Quentin hugged the bag of clothing to his chest. "I understand."

"Good. Now come on and I'll introduce you to my baby."

"You have a child?"

"No, you dork. My truck."

Ted led Quentin past the diner. Larry's Motors was located at the far edge of town, just off the main drag. It had three service bays, two of which were occupied, although there only seemed to be activity around one.

Ted led Quentin to the vintage red pickup in the inactive bay. Its hood was propped up like a patient saying "Ahh" for the doctor. Ted slapped its fender. "Here she is. Had her for more than forty years."

"Ted," Quentin murmured. "Not here."

"What?" He glanced at the mechanics who were working on a Mercedes in the bay closest to the office door. "Oh. Right."

Quentin sighed. No wonder Alun had warned him about Ted. He was way too trusting. He needed to develop a hard outer shell like Quentin's.

"Hey, Joe," Ted called. "Larry around?"

The mechanic who was lying on a dolly rolled out from under the car. "Hey, Ted. Yeah, he's in the office, talking to a supplier. Go on in and grab a cup of coffee while you wait."

"Sure thing." He ambled across the garage, past the busy mechanics. Quentin kept close to his side, within the nimbus of his energy, well away from the mechanics' intersecting auras. It was obvious none of them were happy with their job. *Who could blame them, if they're working for someone with Larry's negativity?* Whatever the cause, though, Quentin didn't want the brush of defeat on his skin.

Ted held the waiting room door for Quentin. As soon as it closed, he whispered, "Don't touch the coffee. I think they make it with antifreeze."

"Thanks for the tip."

A couple was sitting in the waiting room, the woman reading a magazine and the man frowning at his phone. Ted nodded at them, but got no response. He walked down a short hallway toward a door marked *Office*.

"I don't believe it," Quentin said.

"What?"

"There's actually someone in this town that you're not best friends with?"

"I don't have best friends. Just regular friends. And those folks aren't from around here. Must be passing through and had a problem with their car."

"I see."

Ted peered through the glass in the upper half of the office door. "Good. Larry's off the phone." He tapped on the glass, then opened the door, stepping into the tiny room. "Hey, Larry. Got a sec?"

Larry tilted back in his rolling wooden chair. "If it's about your truck, Ted, I told you. Still waiting for the part."

The office was lined with crowded metal shelves, and with Ted in it, it seemed like the size of a shoebox. A full shoebox.

Quentin retreated down the hallway so he wouldn't interfere with Ted's negotiations. He had no desire to hear more of Larry's excuses, or be anywhere near his slimy aura.

Quentin didn't want to go back to the waiting room, where a black cloud was almost visible over the man's head. Waiting in the service bays was out, since he didn't want to get in the mechanics' way—or find out any more about their unhappiness.

The relentless influx of energies—both positive and negative—threatened to overwhelm him. *I need space. I need quiet.* But where?

There was an unmarked door at the end of the hallway. Quentin staggered to it and tried the doorknob. *Unlocked.* Thank all the gods and devils. He slipped inside and was greeted by the smell of new rubber and pine cleaner. The room wasn't too large, but it was neater than Larry's office. Metal shelving lined the walls, and another set marched down the center of the room.

Quentin took a moment to lean against the door and breathe, insulated from energies, both human and supe, for the first time since he'd left Boston. He strolled down the aisle, idly surveying the new tires and jugs of antifreeze, the cans of motor oil and packages of replacement wiper blades.

As he finished the circuit of the room, about to start a second pass, he noticed the last shelf was full of miscellaneous things, all labeled with computer printouts. He stopped to take a look. A new timing belt for a Roger Turnbull. A rebuilt carburetor for Shirl.

He chuckled. "Guess she doesn't have *everything* in that store of hers." His laughter died in his throat, though, when he saw what was at the back of the shelf. He snatched the printout, not trusting his eyes, but there was no doubt.

Fuel pump for Ted Farnsworth. The received date was ten days ago.

"Why, that sleazy little shit. I *knew* he had the aura of a criminal."

Quentin flung open the door and marched down the hall and into the office. Larry had his feet up on his desk, his fingers laced over his paunch, shaking his head at Ted, who was smiling at him amiably—the way he smiled at everyone except Quentin.

"Oh hey, Q-Bert. Looks like we'll have to try somewhere else for a ride. Larry's booked."

"Yes. He is. He's personally installing your fuel pump."

"But the part's not in yet. Larry said—"

Quentin slapped the printout on the desk. "Perhaps Larry wants to rethink his statement."

Larry's eyes widened as he stared up at Quentin. Quentin wasn't sure exactly why the dickhead looked so freaked out. Hadn't anyone ever called him on his bullshit before? How this asshole could take advantage of someone as nice as Ted and sit there and *smirk* about it, knowing the proof of his lies was not twenty feet away . . . Well, it made Quentin's blood steam. And with 'cubi, that was a literal condition.

"Larry?" Ted sounded hurt, as well he might. "You've already got the part?"

"I . . ." Larry tugged at the collar of his sweatshirt. "My assistant must have received it and not told me."

"Really?" Quentin flicked the printout with a finger. "Is your assistant named Larry too? Perhaps *everyone* out there is named Larry. Shall I give a shout and see who responds? I expect only hiring people with the same name would save on the monogramming costs for your shirts. You could order them by the gross."

"I swear, it must have been an oversight." Larry was sweating now—probably because of the heat Quentin was throwing off.

Quentin smiled, turning faux-affable. "Oh, yes. I'm sure. And you can make amends by installing the part now, so Ted and I can be on our way."

Chapter Twelve

Ted couldn't believe it. Larry had *lied* to him. But why? They were friends. Surely friends didn't do this kind of shit to each other. Ted hunched in the corner, not knowing what to say as Larry gabbled at Quentin like a turkey.

"I can't now. I have a schedule—"

Quentin apparently didn't have a problem finding words. "I'm sorry," he said, his tone silky and scary as hell. "I believe you just said the word 'can't.' Am I mistaken?"

"No. That is, I've got deliveries. Other orders that take priority."

"Really? How long has that couple in your waiting room— the one whose car all three of your mechanics are currently swarming over like locusts—how long have they been in the queue?"

"A long time. Really forever."

"Is that so? Shall I ask them to make certain?" Quentin turned as if to leave the office.

"No! That is, their car broke down outside of town. It was an emergency."

"An emergency. Are they on the way to the hospital for a kidney transplant? Negotiating nuclear disarmament? Fleeing the zombie apocalypse?" The angrier Quentin got, the smoother his voice became—and the harder Ted's cock grew. Because, Ursa bless, who'd have ever thought a little dude like Q-Bert could be so fricking *masterful.*

"Of course not. They're vacationing in—" Larry gulped. "I mean—"

"Say no more, Larry." How could Quentin make his voice soft and sharp at the same time? And the way he said *Larry*, he might as well have said *You're dead*. "I think your schedule has just freed up, don't you? Because nobody in this very close-knit community would want to think you'd fuck over one of their own for the sake of wealth profiling, now, would they?"

"I wouldn't—"

"How long has Shirl been waiting for her carburetor?"

Larry blanched. "You wouldn't—"

"Install the damn fuel pump, Larry. Now. We'll wait."

Larry nearly dumped over backward in his chair, overbalancing when his heel caught on his inbox, sending papers flying across the office. He scurried out, cutting a wide berth around Quentin, who glared at him all the way as if he wanted to set the seat of Larry's jeans on fire.

"I hope all your friends aren't similarly odious, Ted, because if they are . . ." Quentin shook his head. "*Damn.*"

Ted knelt and began gathering the scattered papers off the floor, not really wanting to face Quentin and admit he'd never even suspected Larry wasn't being honest with him. *Could I be a bigger idiot?*

"I don't get it. Why would he do something like that to me? Or to *Shirl*, for Pete's sake? I mean, does he have a death wish?"

Quentin sniffed. "It's obvious. Power. He's an empire-builder, and you threaten him because you're, well, *you*. Shirl threatens him because *she* has power. Plus, she's freaking scary. He *wishes* he had the same influence."

"Thanks for standing up for me." Ted peered at Quentin, who was still glaring after Larry. "It was nice of you."

Quentin shrugged. "I wasn't nice in the least, but that's what the situation called for." He glanced down at Ted, and thankfully, his glare softened. "It drives me absolutely mad when people take advantage of others simply because they can.

That kind of self-important, egotistical, self-aggrandizing *muscle-flexing*. Ugh. It's infuriating. Besides . . ." He flipped the inbox upright. "How else were we supposed to get home?"

Ted didn't hold any illusions that Quentin thought of the lodge as home. His color was still high from his outburst, so he was probably not firing on all cylinders. Ted stood and dropped the papers in the inbox.

"I've got to say, though, Q-Bert. When you're mad, you are one sexy devil."

Quentin shot him an irritated glance. "Dynastic 'cubi may have demon ancestors, but we are *not* devils, thank you."

"Sorry. Didn't mean . . ." Ted caught a whiff of a familiar aroma. He sniffed, leaning closer to Quentin. "It's you."

"What's me?"

"You smell like a perfectly toasted marshmallow." Sweet, but with fiery undertones.

Quentin's lips twitched. "Please. I prefer to think of it as the burnt sugar crust on a crème brûlée."

"You know about it?"

Quentin quirked an eyebrow. "It's been mentioned before," he said, his tone dry. "Is there anything else we need to do in town? Despite Larry's obvious incentive to get us on the road quickly, I expect the actual labor won't be instantaneous."

"No. We're set."

"Excellent. I'd say we should join the vacationers in the waiting room, but they didn't look particularly interesting. We could stand in the service bay and observe Larry's efforts, but —"

"You'd probably make him piss his pants if you did that. Better let him focus on my truck."

"A point." Quentin opened the lapels of his parka and fanned them. "However, 'cubi internalize their anger, and I need to dissipate some of this heat."

"We can take a walk down to the beach if you need to cool off."

"That sounds perfect."

After barely a half-hour stroll along the shore, though, they were in Ted's truck and heading back up the mountain.

"I had no idea you could install a fuel pump that quickly."

"He was inspired," Quentin said, watching the trees flash by as they wound up the road. "Besides, I suspect most of the work was already done. He just had to put on a show so you wouldn't know the whole sordid truth."

"You think?"

"With an aura like that? I'd believe anything. I think it's far too easy for people to take advantage of you, Ted. You need to be more assertive."

"That's not what the council says. They say I need to be less impulsive."

"Assertive and impulsive are not opposites. However, I refuse to spare another thought on Larry. He's irrelevant." Quentin rooted around in the Stuff 'n' Things bag and pulled out the knife. He weighed it in his palm. "I can't believe she had something this perfect just lying about on hand."

"Hey. Truth in advertising, right?"

Quentin chuckled. "Apparently. What time is moonrise tonight?"

"I'm not sure. About ten maybe? Although there won't be much of a moon. We're right at the tail end of the cycle."

"But it'll be dark earlier, yes?"

"Oh yeah. No later than five." Although it was barely past four, Ted had already turned on his headlights. "We're far enough north that after daylight savings time, our days are pretty short. Solstice is only about six weeks away, after all."

"Excellent. We can knock off one of the escape clause requirements tonight."

Ted glanced sidelong at Quentin. He was leaning his head against the window, his eyes closed, the knife held loosely in one fist. "You okay, Q-Bert?"

"A trifle faint. Nothing to be concerned about."

Alarm shot up Ted's spine, causing him to grip the steering wheel harder. "David said you were supposed to take it easy, and I forgot because Larry was already there and—"

"I'll be fine, Ted. Although I may need to nap before we go out tonight. I expended too much energy getting angry at Larry, that's all."

Damn it. Quentin's condition was Ted's fault. Again. "You need to eat. As soon as we get home, I'm making you dinner. In fact, tell me what I have to do for the escape thingie tonight, and I'll take care of it. You can stay inside and rest."

"That's very gallant of you." Quentin's voice, although slightly wavery, was laced with amusement. "However, this is something that we have to do together. Now that I consider it, I think it was good that both of us went into town—truck acquisition aside—because I'm not sure any of this would work if we didn't do it together."

"Why not?"

"Because it's a ritual, and rituals are by their nature symbolic. You know how fixated witches are with symbolism and sympathetic magic. They're worse than druids."

"So?"

"So, we're trying to undo a contract, a spell, that's a covenant between two people who have agreed to share a life. The symbolic offerings won't pack as much punch if they don't fully embody that." Quentin dropped the knife into the bag with a flourish. "Sending you out shopping while I lounge about eating bonbons is not what I would call representative of a partnership."

"I don't know about that. Weren't you just on at me about how we should measure our contributions by what we're good at? Maybe I'm better at shopping. And you might be stellar at eating bonbons."

"Nobody could be *that* good at eating bonbons."

Ted snickered as he turned onto the road that led to his place. "I'd pay a lot to see you try." He cut a glance at Quentin. "Not that we have time for that."

"True. The sooner we get the offerings ready to go, the sooner we can move on with our lives. I have to admit . . ." Quentin sounded exhausted. "I'm not sure how long I'll be able to manage without consuming some energy, so the sooner the better. Especially since Casimir's energies are bound to be diminished, or at least different. It may take me some time to adjust."

"'Consuming energy'? Is that an incubus euphemism for fucking?"

Quentin snorted, a ridiculously adorable sound coming from such a buttoned-up guy. "It can be. But I haven't fucked anybody, as you so delicately put it, for decades."

Ted nearly ran the truck off the road. "You're kidding. You're a sex demon, for crying out loud. That doesn't even make any sense."

Quentin glared at him, but it was a pale imitation of the nuclear blast he'd aimed at Larry. "How long is it since *you've* had sex, Mr. Expert?"

Heat rushed up Ted's throat, and he was grateful for the camouflage of his beard and the darkening cab. "A—a while."

"How long is 'a while'?"

"I don't keep a fricking calendar, okay? I don't get a lot of company. That's one of the reasons I registered with Supernatural Selection, remember?"

Quentin sighed. "Yes. I'm sorry."

His quick surrender deflated Ted's annoyance. "No worries. But I don't know that much about your kind, so try to chill if I say something stupid, okay? I'm bound to do that anyway. It's kind of my trademark."

"That's fair. To answer your question—even though you didn't quite ask it as I would like—'cubi consume life energies. It doesn't have to be from sex. It can be from a consensual touch.

But we can also absorb ambient energy from peoples' auras when they're sparking."

"'Sparking'? Is that a euphemism for—"

"It's *not* a euphemism for fucking, no."

Ted flexed his hands on the steering wheel and glared at the road. "I wasn't going to say that."

"Of course you weren't. No, sparking is when people are excited about something. It can be sexual attraction, and 'cubi are definitely drawn to that quite strongly. But it can be other things: a political debate, an evocative play, a party. Nothing sparks so brightly as when people are doing something"—his voice turned wistful—"or are with someone that they love."

"So you can hang out at parties or the mall to get juiced up?"

"Again," Quentin drew out the word, "delicately put. And the mall? Definitely not."

"Why? Bertrand-Harringtons too good to shop with the masses?"

"Of course not!"

Ted chuckled at Quentin's outrage. "Suuurrre."

"I'm serious! There usually has to be a touch, and there are only so many times you can brush up against somebody before it doesn't look accidental anymore. Other 'cubi have no problem with that, but I can't. Not without consent. And because I'm not a social person, I rarely . . . engage. Consequently, I don't get a lot of action."

"Action. That's the goal, right?" Ted braced himself as the truck hit a pothole, one hand reaching instinctively for Quentin. But he drew back before an actual touch. "Sex?"

"Yes. Sex is a tradition for us, I suppose, but it's not the only answer. However, since I'm up here, where there's no ambient energy from anyone but you, I'm not, well, feeling the love."

"So you're starving? Like before?" Damn it, why hadn't Ted read that stupid contract?

"No. Stop feeling guilty."

"How can you tell I'm feeling guilty?"

"You're aura went all brown and squiggly."

His aura wasn't the only thing that was squiggly. The notion that Quentin could tell what Ted was feeling—maybe what he was *thinking*—just by looking made his stomach writhe like a can of bait. "Can you *not* see auras if you want?"

"Yeees. Usually."

"Could you do me a favor, then Q-Bert, and don't look at mine? It's kinda stalker-y."

"I'll try. But yours is rather overwhelming."

"Yeah," Ted muttered, "like everything else about me."

Quentin cleared his throat. "How did we get on this subject anyway?"

Ted shot him a sidelong glance, getting more than a little satisfaction that Quentin looked just as bothered as Ted. His usually smooth dark hair was rumpled, which revealed it wasn't actually smooth—it was crisp and wavy. "Sexless sex demons."

"I don't think so."

"Well, that's what *I* remember."

"I believe we were discussing this evening's task, which is intended to be a joint venture."

"Okay. What is it?"

Quentin patted the Stuff 'n' Things bag, the crinkle nearly drowned by the swish of gravel under the tires. "We have to cut a lock of each other's hair with the silver knife under a moonless sky, and bind it with braided grass. We also have to braid the grass together, apparently."

"Do we have to braid the grass after we give each other a haircut, or can we have it ready beforehand?"

"He didn't say."

"He didn't say a lot of stuff," Ted grumbled.

"I intended to ask for specifics, but my phone died." Quentin punched his thighs with his fists. "Hells and devils take it, I forgot to charge my phone in town."

"No worries. I got a solar charger with hand-crank backup. You're set."

Quentin was quiet for such a long time that Ted finally glanced at him to find him staring at Ted with a very peculiar expression on his face—although maybe it was just the failing light in the cab. "Thank you."

"No problem. I needed to replace mine anyway." Ted laughed and smacked his forehead. "I'm an idiot." He pointed to the adapter plugged in to the old-style cigarette lighter socket. "You could get started now if you want."

"Oh. Of course. I didn't think of that either." Quentin pulled out his cable and hooked it up. "I suggest we wait until dark to braid the grass, but do it before we cut the hair, otherwise it'll blow away and we'll have to do the whole thing again. I'd prefer not to do this more than once. My stylist might forgive me for one lock of hair, but she would probably draw the line at a serial chop job."

"You already have a stylist in Portland?"

"Oh. No. I forgot."

"Seems like there's a lot of things you forgot, Q-Bert. Let's hope these weird directions aren't one of them."

After dinner—another extremely large, highly caloric, and exceptionally tasty meal—Quentin changed rather gingerly into his clothes from Stuff 'n' Things. He pulled one of the thermals on over his own undershirt, unwilling to let the used shirt touch his skin more than necessary. He gritted his teeth, eyes closed, waiting for the itch and burn of the previous owner's residual energies. But after a few minutes—longer than he'd ever lasted sans rash before—nothing had happened. The fabric was soft and warm against his skin.

Maybe I should do all my used clothes shopping at Stuff 'n' Things.

After he'd finished dressing—and he had to admit, the clothes were just as comfortable as his bespoke suits and far more so than his tuxes—he returned to the kitchen where Ted was cleaning up from dinner.

Ted stacked a couple of bowls in the cabinet and shut the door, then glanced at Quentin. He grinned. "Mountain man casual is a good look on you, Q-Bert."

Quentin grimaced at Ted's continued use of that ridiculous nickname, but asking him to desist was clearly useless. "Are you ready?"

"Sure. Let's go braid some grass."

The two of them shrugged into their coats and stepped onto the porch. The sharp wind from earlier in the day had died, leaving behind a fitful breeze.

Quentin shoved his hands in his jacket pockets. "Where should we go to find grass long enough to braid?"

"Down by the lake. It's mostly dead now, so it may be more brittle than if we were doing this in spring, but hopefully our braids don't have to pass too close an inspection."

"I think it's the activity that's important, and making sure it can be tied tightly enough to hold a lock of hair."

"Could be tricky. I, uh, suppose you know how to braid things?"

"Don't you?"

"Can't say it's ever been a priority. Not like I need to know how to do it as a bear."

"Yes. I know how." Quentin was proud that his voice didn't shake, despite the twitch in his back as he tried to keep long-buried sense memories *buried*. "It's not difficult." And the memory surfaced anyway.

"It's not difficult, Quentin, you worthless cretin." The master's voice cut deeper than the lash as he struck Quentin with every flogger he deemed unacceptable. "Try again."

Although producing an acceptable one hadn't stopped the whippings. *Perhaps that's why I haven't braided anything since.*

"Come on, then."

Ted led the way down a barely discernible path. *Oh. Glasses.* Quentin removed his spectacles, and the terrain—not to mention Ted's ass—was instantly visible to his dark-evolved 'cubi vision. He gritted his teeth as he tucked the glasses in his shirt pocket. *This is going to be a long night.*

Ted stopped next to a large, flat-topped boulder, its base crowded with clumps of faded grass. "I figure this'll do for both. We've got the grass for the braiding stuff, and we can use the rock as a seat and a work surface." He slapped the rock. "Although I suppose this isn't the cushy salon chair you're used to."

"I don't believe it's *anyone's* idea of a cushy salon chair, even rugged bear shifters who don't mind sleeping in caves." Quentin yanked a handful of grass out of the ground. Unfortunately, when he laid it on the rock, a gust of wind scattered it onto the surface of the water. "I'm not sure this will work. We need to anchor the ends somehow, and your rock isn't particularly yielding."

"It's not the only thing," Ted muttered, tugging on his inseam as if his pants were binding him. "Here." He grabbed another handful of the wilted blades. "I'll hold them. You do the braiding thing. That'll count as doing it together, right?"

Quentin peered up at Ted, checking for derision in his expression, but there was none. He wasn't quite certain how to deal with someone who said what he meant without layers of sly innuendo, hidden digs, or jockeying for advantage.

'Cubi depended on nuance and careful word choice to manipulate those around them. Even his grandmother rarely told Quentin straight out what she expected of him. Everything was roundabout and embellished, intended to hide her true purpose until he agreed to something he'd never intended. She was good. *Too* good, which was another reason he'd had to get away. He'd been afraid he'd suddenly be engaged to her choice of spouse when all he thought he was doing was offering an opinion on the new drapes.

Ted, though. Ted hid nothing. *Which is probably why he's always in trouble with the supe council.* When your existence—the existence of entire societies—depended on secrecy, someone so open was a liability to all. The 'cubi would have eliminated him years ago.

The thought of Ted's overwhelming, uncomplicated, *good* existence being wiped out to preserve the 'cubi's brittle immortality made Quentin's eyes prick with unshed tears.

What is wrong with me? He was almost crying over a threat that didn't even exist, to a man he barely knew. *A man who's shown me more kindness and consideration in twenty-four hours than my family has in centuries.*

"Q-Bert? You okay?" Ted peered down at him, his brows bunched in concern.

"Yes. I'm perfectly well, thanks."

"Hey, you're not wearing your glasses." Ted leaned closer. "Wow. You have really pretty eyes. They kind of glow."

Quentin's breath sped up, at Ted's closeness, at his scrutiny. "Incubus. We're evolved to see in the dark of Sheol. The glasses allow me to see in the sunlight."

Thankfully, Ted straightened and stopped staring so intently at Quentin's face. "Oh. I guess that's one thing you've got in common with your vampire, huh?"

Vampire. Casimir. My intended husband. "Yes. I suppose you're right." Quentin selected three long strands from Ted's fist, teasing them out and focusing his attention strictly on the grass. "These should do. Hold them out."

"How about this?" Ted took the blades and slapped them against himself below his beard. Then he grinned. "Oh, guess I should make it a little lower. Wouldn't want you to have to stand on your toes." He inched his hand down. And down. And down farther, until it reached his waist, the grass dangling in front of his fly.

"That's enough. This isn't an X-rated ritual," Quentin muttered, his lips twitching with the urge to smile. He nudged

Ted's wrist upward until it was out of the danger zone. "There. Hold that steady. It'll be easier if the grass isn't flapping in midair."

Quentin took a deep breath, wondering why he found Ted's rather ample midsection so endearing. He stared at the three strands of grass fluttering in the breeze and was suddenly unable to make his fingers move. *The last time I did this, it was for a far different purpose.*

"Q-Bert? What's the problem? I thought you knew how to do this."

"It's not like I sit about braiding my hair all day. I learned years ago. Or rather I was supposed to. At . . . at camp."

"'Cubi have summer camp? Did you canoe on the lake? Take nature hikes? Sing songs around the campfire?"

The breeze tossed Quentin's hair into his eyes and he pushed it back, his hand trembling. "No, you infuriating bear. It wasn't that kind of camp."

"Then what was it?"

"A forced march that all 'cubi have to endure when they hit the Change."

"What's 'the Change'?"

"When our metabolism changes from needing solid food to consuming energies. It's the 'cubi version of puberty."

Ted grinned. "A bunch of teenage 'cubi in the woods. I'd give something to see that."

"You wouldn't have. Seen it, that is. All of us were at least a hundred years old at the time."

"If you were a hundred years old, couldn't you handle learning a couple of new things from the comfort of your home? That's what I'd lobby for."

Quentin shot Ted an impatient glance, and yanked on the grass too sharply, breaking one of the blades. "Shit." He yanked up another handful and passed it to Ted. "It's not that simple. We're not . . . not in control. It's not safe for anyone, especially anyone whose auras we find appealing, when our hungers change. We have to learn how not to gorge. Not to binge." *Not to kill our partner.* "The disincentives administered by the masters of the march are, shall we say, stressful for your standard audience. Slasher films have nothing on a 'cubi Change March."

"How long do they last?"

"As long as it takes."

"All right. I'll bite. How long did *yours* last?"

Quentin's hands jerked and he broke the grass again. "Twenty-two years."

"Jeez." This time, Ted plucked the grass, arranging it against his belly again.

"We were expected to construct the implements of our own torture. I was supposed to braid studded leather for the master's scourge. You'll have to forgive me if I've lost the knack."

"Hey." Ted's big hand closed over Quentin's fist, sending a jolt of warmth up his arm. "I'm sorry if I hit a nerve. I didn't mean to be an asshole."

"You didn't. You're not. I'm . . . I need to get over it." Quentin tried for a smile, but given the way his lips trembled, he'd probably failed. "It's been almost two hundred years, after all."

"There's no expiration date on suffering, Quentin. It's not your job to pretend you're happy just to make other people feel better."

Quentin laughed on a shaky breath. "You're pretty smart for a guy who pretends to be dim."

Ted shrugged. "There's nothing people hate more than having their expectations upended. Sometimes it's easier to let them believe what they want. But sometimes"—his eyebrow quirked—"it's not."

Quentin jerked a nod. "Yes. You're right." He smiled up at Ted. "Shall we try this again?"

"Sure." He patted the grass he still held against himself. "Go for it, Q-Bert. You got this."

It was the nickname that settled Quentin's nerves. Snark he could handle. Snark he knew all about—it was his stock in trade, after all. Kindness, compassion, caring—those would gut him faster than an executioner's blade.

Quentin's fingers were clumsy with cold, and he had to try three times before he grasped the first strand.

Muttering a curse, Ted tossed the grass aside. "You must have used up all your heat when you were flaming at Larry." He captured Quentin's hands between both of his.

"Don't. You shouldn't touch me."

"I'm just warming you up, Q-Bert, not trying to jump your bones. How do you expect to do the braiding stuff if your fingers are too frozen to move? Besides, you're trembling like a leaf."

Quentin clenched his chattering teeth. "Even a touch is dangerous. I could drain you. I could—"

"You trying to suck me dry?"

"No! Of course not!"

"Then stop bitching." Ted rubbed his hands together, Quentin's trapped between them, and Quentin had to admit there was nothing amorous about it.

He's not succumbing to the 'cubi thrall. Of course, Quentin probably didn't know how to engage it anyway, after burying it under the suppressant for so long.

"Better?"

Quentin withdrew his hands reluctantly. The stroke of Ted's palms, rough with calluses in a way that would appall his grandmother and her set, was more pleasant than he wanted to admit. "Yes. Thank you. If you could . . ." He nodded at the grass at the foot of the boulder.

"Right." Ted plucked three more strands and held them against his belly.

This time, Quentin was able to braid them easily, top to bottom, his fingers still tingling from Ted's touch. "There's one."

Ted held it up. "Hey. Not bad." He tucked it in his pocket and winked. "Wouldn't want it to blow away after all that work, would we?" He grabbed three more blades. "Round two?"

Quentin nodded, and finished the second braid even faster than the first. "I guess you really never lose the knack. Assuming you don't freak yourself out with morbid memories."

"Or try to do it in the middle of the night in close-to-freezing temperatures. Give yourself a break."

"Being overly critical of oneself is hardly a 'cubi failing."

"Maybe not most incubi. But you've got overly critical nailed." Ted pulled the tiny knife out of his other pocket. "So. Haircuts next?"

"Yes."

"'Kay. You can do me first. That way I can get an idea of how much hair we're talking about and I won't ruin your do."

Ted dropped to his knees, which put the top of his head even with the middle of Quentin's chest. Mother of fire, the man was big. And warm. And vital. Quentin swayed forward, but caught himself before he came in contact with Ted's skin again. *Because that would be a bad idea.*

Quentin took a firm hold on his inappropriate urges, and studied Ted's hair dispassionately. *Dispassionately. Ha!*

Ted wore it shorn on the sides, long on the top, and combed back unless the wayward breeze tossed a lock over his forehead. *Like now. Gah!* Quentin edged around him, straddling Ted's legs so he could get a better angle to the back of Ted's head. "It will show less if I take it from behind."

Ted chuckled. "Getting a little risqué there, Q-Bert?"

"Shut up and give me the knife, you infuriating bear."

Ted passed the tiny knife over his shoulder with a deep rumbling chuckle. "Just rattling your chain a little. Lighten up. You're not about to behead me." He glance over his shoulder, his eyes wide in mock terror. "Are you?"

"Don't tempt me." Quentin ran his fingers through the longer hair at Ted's crown, eliciting a shiver from both of them.

Ted's lips parted in a quick inhale. He swallowed and faced front again. "Wouldn't dream of it."

Before Quentin could get lost in the sensation of the soft hair between his fingers, he twisted a hank of it together and sliced it neatly halfway to Ted's scalp. "There." He ruffled the hair into its usual disarray. "It barely shows."

"Not like I can tell. I don't spend a lot of time checking out the top of my head in a mirror." He glanced over his shoulder again. "Want to step aside so I can get up?"

"Oh. Sorry." Quentin scuttled sideways. "Let's tie this up before we do mine, to make sure the braids won't break."

Ted pulled one of the braids out of his pocket. "Hold my hair up, and I'll do the honors. That way, we're doing it together, right? Wouldn't want to be disqualified on a technicality."

"Good thinking." Quentin held up the twisted lock, and Ted wound the braided grass around it twice and tied it off with surprisingly deft fingers, considering their size.

"Okay." He took the bound hair out of Quentin's grasp and tucked it carefully in the breast pocket of his flannel shirt. "Now hand over the knife, Q-Bert, and prepare to be scalped."

"You're not filling me with confidence here."

Ted grinned. "Just fucking with you. Turn around."

I wish you were fucking. With me. But Quentin did as he was told, gritting his teeth when Ted's fingers brushed the nape of his neck.

"You don't have much length here, Q-Bert."

"My length is just fine, thank you."

Ted chuckled, the vibration in his fingers tickling Quentin's neck. "Do all 'cubi turn everything into a comment about sex, or is it just you?"

I think it's you. "Just get on with it, please. I'm freezing."

"Sorry." Ted bent down until his breath ghosted across Quentin's skin. "Wish I had your fancy eyesight. My night vision's not bad, but I don't want to mess this up. You want to look good when you meet your vampire."

"Don't worry about it." Quentin clenched his fists, as if that would allow him to hold on to his self-control. "We need to get this done before moonrise, or we'll have the whole thing to do again tomorrow."

"Ah. Right. Okay. Hold still. Your hair is really soft." Ted twirled a lock of Quentin's hair in his fingers, then the silver blade flashed in Quentin's peripheral vision. "There. Hope I didn't mess it up too badly."

Quentin stepped away, putting some distance between them. "I'm sure it will be fine. If necessary, I can ask the stylist to cut it all closer back there."

"That'd be a shame. It's nice hair. If your vampire doesn't like it, he's an idiot."

Something warm burgeoned in Quentin's chest. *Ah, no. Don't get maudlin over a simple compliment.* "Thank you. Now, if you could hand me the grass braid?"

Ted passed it over and held Quentin's lock of hair up between them. Quentin matched Ted's binding method, although his tie-off wasn't nearly as neat, and he nearly broke the braid with his trembling fingers.

"Shit, you *are* cold. Let's get you back inside and I'll make some tea or cocoa or whatever you want for a nightcap."

"Brandy?"

Ted scrunched up his face. "Nah. Sorry. I don't have very fancy tastes when it comes to booze."

Quentin allowed himself to pat Ted's arm. They were one step closer to dissolving their inconvenient marriage, and he felt he'd earned the right. "Don't worry. I was only teasing. Cocoa sounds perfect."

"Yeah?" Ted's grin flashed in the starlight. "To me too."

Inside the cabin, Quentin hung his parka on the hook next to Ted's. The warmth of the cabin after the chill outside made his fingers tingle with returning circulation. At least he hoped that was what the tingle meant. *I should never have relied on the suppressant for so long. I have no idea what's* normal *for myself anymore.*

As Ted hummed and thumped around the kitchen, Quentin settled on the sofa, nearest the stove, and took off his boots. He wiggled his toes inside the red-striped socks from Stuff 'n' Things, relishing the warmth soaking into them. Maybe he should invest in some more flamboyant socks after his marriage. He didn't *have* to stick to the strict wardrobe color palette that his grandmother insisted on—for preserving his dignity, she claimed. Besides, if he was relegated to the dark forever, he needed something bright in his life, even if it was only on his feet.

Ted passed a huge ceramic mug of steaming cocoa over Quentin's shoulder. "Heating up?"

Quentin raised an eyebrow. "Now who's making suggestive comments?" Ted chuckled as Quentin took the mug, appreciating how it further warmed his hands. He took a sip. "This is excellent."

"Don't sound so surprised. I may not cook fancy, but that doesn't mean I put up with crap food."

"Sorry. Of course not. Everything you've prepared for me has been wonderful."

"Thanks."

The two of them stared into the flames dancing leisurely in the stove as they sipped their drinks.

"Why do the flames look as if they're in slow motion?" Quentin asked, almost dreamily. The combination of the comforting cocoa, Ted's soothing presence, and the sinuous dance of the flames mesmerized him.

"That's how it looks when the air intake is throttled down. Once the fire's established, it doesn't need a lot of air to keep it going. Less air, the wood burns slower, the fire lasts longer without having to be stoked again."

"Oh. I didn't know that."

Ted chuckled. "I'm guessing you don't have to build up the fire in a woodstove at home."

"No. Central heating is a wonderful thing."

Silence settled over them until Ted set his mug on the coffee table with a thunk.

"So. Vampire. I'm guessing 'cubi blood isn't poisonous to them like shifter blood is, or he wouldn't have married you. Er, wanted to marry you."

"That's correct. Our blood doesn't contain the same hostile factors."

"Will he . . . you know . . . suck you in more ways than one?"

A strangled laugh escaped Quentin's throat. "You do have a way with words, Mr. Farnsworth." The telltale heat began in Quentin's blood, although it was more embarrassment than arousal. "I would expect so. That's the point, isn't it? He should get as much benefit from the marriage as I do."

"But if vampires can't feed on just anybody, I'm guessing 'cubi can't either?"

"Vampire energy isn't as strong as humans or shifters or fae— or any of the living races, for that matter. It can't be, since they're not technically alive. But it's . . . adequate."

"You're gonna settle for an 'adequate' marriage?"

Quentin stared into the fire, unwilling to meet Ted's gaze, especially if the expression on his face matched the sympathy in his voice. "It's the best I can hope for. More than I have a right to expect."

"Bullshit, Q-Bert. You have a right to expect an awesome marriage. Everyone does."

Quentin flashed a wry smile at Ted. "You do, anyway. Dr. Kendrick was right. You're a great guy."

"I'm a screwup. I know it. The bear council knows it. It won't be long until Rusty knows it too." Ted leaned his elbows on his knees. "Shit, he knows it already. I mean, I signed a blood contract with the wrong fricking *name* on it. What idiot does that?"

"That would be me."

"You had a reason, though, right? Those meds you were on."

"Don't excuse me for that reason. One would argue that overuse of the suppressant—to the extent that it was altering my DNA—was absolute proof of idiocy."

Ted chuckled. "We're quite the pair, aren't we?"

Quentin leaned back on the cushions. "A matched set." He grinned at Ted. "Even to our haircuts."

"Nah. Yours is way cooler." He nodded at the empty mug still cradled in Quentin's hands. "You done?"

"Yes. Thank you." He handed the mug over. "It was lovely."

Ted smiled crookedly. "So are you." He leaned over and brushed his lips against Quentin's cheek, then stood up and disappeared into the kitchen while Quentin sat frozen. The slam of a cabinet door broke him out of his stupor, and his hand crept to his cheek.

"Good night, Q-Bert. Hope the sofa's comfy enough for you to get a good night's sleep, because tomorrow's the great flea hunt." Whistling, Ted tromped up the stairs, the ceiling over Quentin's head creaking as Ted moved around in his Spartan quarters.

For a long time, Quentin sat staring at the flames, hand cupping his cheek where the ghost of Ted's lips seemed hotter than the fire dancing behind the grate. He tracked Ted's movements overhead, both alarmed and guilty that his incubus senses allowed him to know exactly where Ted was: when he brushed his teeth, used the toilet, undressed. Quentin heard the sigh and the change in breathing when Ted tipped over the edge into sleep, apparently not as shattered as Quentin was by the kiss.

Of course he's not. It was innocent. He meant nothing by it other than exactly what he said.

As if in a trance, Quentin rose and stole down the hallway. He stood at the foot of the staircase, Ted's quiet, even breathing sounding louder and louder in his ears.

I could go upstairs. Slip in next to him. I wouldn't have to wake him. I could just lie there next to him, listening to his heartbeat, absorbing his presence, taking comfort—

Quentin staggered backward, pressing against the rough paneling of the hallway. *Absorb? Take?* What the devil was he thinking? Ted wasn't his, and he was far too nice a man—a man who still dreamed of his perfect mate—for Quentin to take this kind of advantage of him.

You think you're so different from your grandmother, your cousins, your aunts and uncles. But you're just the same, just as despicable. Go to sleep and dream of your own life. A life in the dark. It's what you deserve, after all.

Chapter Thirteen

"Ted. Ted! Ted Farnsworth, get your ass down here! We have fleas to catch."

Ted groaned and rolled over, clamping his pillow over his head. *Who invited the lousy steel drum band into my cabin?* Then he realized it wasn't drums but pots and pans. Quentin was making enough ruckus in the kitchen to wake the dead.

"Guess he's practicing for his marriage," Ted grumbled as he levered himself off the mattress. "Keep your pants on, Q-Bert," he called down the stairwell, "I'll be there in a minute."

"Sixty seconds. I'll start the timer."

Jeez, what had Quentin's boxers in a bunch this morning? He'd been a lot more relaxed last night. Almost friendly. Which had prompted Ted to kiss his cheek. He winced. *Oops. Probably should have asked first.* Figuring out how to act with a sex demon was trickier than it seemed.

Ted yawned, scratching his belly as he stumbled for the bathroom. Today they'd get the last task buttoned up and head into Portland to get this whole mess straightened out once and for all. A sharp pang speared Ted's chest. *It'll be lonely here without the little dude.* But Rusty would be here soon. Then everything would be good. Normal. Exactly the life he'd wished for.

He splashed water on his face. *I wonder if I'd have wished for a different life if I'd met someone like Quentin before.* No point in thinking about that. He wasn't a time-surfer, able to go back and change things. He wasn't sure such people even existed. Thinking about them only made him lose focus. That's how he got distracted. How he had so many unfinished projects lying around. Good thing Rusty would be here soon to keep him on track.

He had a momentary qualm, remembering Quentin's tart remarks about how Rusty might not be a fan of becoming Ted's supervisor. Maybe he'd mention it to Rusty before he signed their contract. At least give him a heads-up. Maybe they should put off the ceremony for a while anyway. They could get to know each other. He'd ask Rusty to visit. Make him some soup and cocoa.

Give him a secret haircut by the lake.

Okay, that was just his loneliness talking, but Ursa's eyeballs, it had been so fricking *hot*. Who'd have thought he could get that hard just by cutting some guy's hair?

He pulled on his boxers, his jeans, and a Henley. Shoved his feet into a pair of wool socks, then trotted downstairs as he stuck his arms through his flannel shirt. Quentin was sitting on his usual corner of the couch, staring into the woodstove—which needed stoking—a mug cradled against his chest.

Ted ambled over to the box in the corner and pulled out a couple of logs. "You had anything to eat yet?"

"I'm not hungry."

He stood up, a log in each paw, and glared at Quentin. "David said you need to eat."

Quentin returned the glare, and Ted could see that the mug held nothing but water. "I also need to get out of this contract."

"If you're comatose when you get out of the contract, you won't do anybody any good. Vampires may sleep like the dead sometimes, considering that's what they are, but they do wake up now and then. Or so I've been told."

"I'll be fine."

Ted opened the stove door and shoved the logs inside. Shit, the embers of last night's fire were nearly gone. He might need to build the whole thing up again. "Sure you'll be fine." He shoved a handful of twigs under the logs and hoped for the best, then shut the door. "You'll be fine because I'm making breakfast and you're going to eat it."

Quentin jabbed a finger at the window. "It's already after nine. We need to get going."

"We will. After breakfast. Even if you don't eat—and I think you'll be less pissy if you're not hungry—*I* will. It's November, remember?" He grinned. "Hey, poetry. What do you know?"

"So what?"

Ted sighed. "Q-Bert, I know you've had a rough couple of days, but you could at least pretend you're listening to me. I'm a bear shifter. We eat a lot leading up to the solstice."

Quentin's cheeks reddened, and he stared down at his water. "Oh. Yes. I remember now."

"And we sleep a lot too. Since this is the last day you have to worry about that, maybe you could cut me some slack?"

Quentin sighed and scrubbed one hand through his hair, sending it sticking up in all directions. "I'm sorry, Ted. You don't deserve my bad temper. You don't deserve— That is, I'll try to be a more pleasant companion. And if I'm honest—" he peeked up at Ted from under his eyebrows "—I am a bit peckish."

"'Peckish'? Is that another sexual innuendo?"

He frowned and stood up to smack Ted on the arm. "No, you infuriating bear. It means I'm hungry."

"Well then. How do you feel about waffles?"

Quentin squinted one eye, peering up at the ceiling with his lips pursed. "I feel . . . like I could eat a mountain of them."

Ted grinned. "Excellent. Two waffle mountains, coming up."

And Quentin wasn't kidding. Ted set a bear-sized stack for each of them on the breakfast bar, and Quentin pounced, matching Ted waffle for waffle—something not even Ted's brother could manage.

"You eat like this at home, Q-Bert? If you did, you'd be bigger than a minute."

"I'm not *that* small." Quentin took a gulp of milk. "But to answer your question, no. I don't eat this much. 'Cubi meals are different. Since we don't rely on solid food for our nutrition—that comes from life energy consumption—dinner parties are all about outdoing the last host or hostess. Micro meals. Exquisite presentation. Delicate flavor combinations. My grandmother once went an entire year eating nothing but the amuse-bouche that our chef invented every day."

"'Amooz boosh'? What's that?"

"It means 'mouth amuser.' Little tastes of things, no more than a single morsel."

"What would happen if you *did* eat well? Or at least better than a bite a day."

Quentin paused, a forkful of waffle dripping with syrup halfway to his mouth. "I—I'm not sure. It's never happened. Once we've gone through the Change March and are able to consume energy, we usually never look back."

"I don't know if I could handle that. Well obviously I couldn't. A bear would starve without regular meals."

"We have regular meals. They just don't involve proteins and carbohydrates. Or the digestive system."

Ted eyed the way Quentin was putting away waffles. "You're not gonna get, uh, indigestion, are you?"

"Of course not. We're not like vampires. Our digestive systems *work*. It's just considered vulgar to use them since they're not really necessary."

Ted shook his head. "Pretty fricking weird, Q-Bert. Personally, I'd miss the proteins and carbs. Although—" he patted his belly "—I wouldn't look quite so upholstered during the lead up to hibernation season if I could cut back."

"Do you really hibernate?"

"Nah. Just sleep a lot more." He shrugged. "That's one of the reasons bear shifters tend to live alone. Nobody to gripe if you feel like napping instead of talking." He stood up, collecting his plate and Quentin's, which was finally empty. "We can leave cleanup for later, since you're so anxious to go find the fleas."

Quentin smiled, his dark goatee framing a bright flash of teeth that caused Ted's groin to tighten alarmingly. "Thank you. I really think we'll both feel better when we've got everything together for the ceremony, don't you?"

"Yeah." He cleared his throat. "Sure." He dumped the dishes in the sink. "Good thing we got the truck yesterday. As soon as we've caught the fleas, we can head into Portland."

"So soon?" Quentin blinked. "Oh. I intended to call Zeke to find out whether the fleas need to be living. We should probably make an appointment before we show up." Quentin frowned, punching his thigh with a fist. "Hells and devils, I forgot to charge my phone."

"We can hook it up to the solar charger before we go. Although you might need to use mine instead. The reception up here is nonexistent most of the time, but I can use Dr. Kendrick's magic app to bounce a call through his line if you want."

"Thank you. Yes. Let's plan on both."

After they hooked up Quentin's phone to the solar charger and Ted's to his truck battery, they headed into the woods, Quentin with the insect vials in his pockets. Unfortunately, their passage through the underbrush scared all the small animal life away. They searched for an hour without success.

"People who bitch about finding needles in haystacks have never tried to find fleas in the forest," Ted grumbled.

"I realize my experience in the wilderness is limited to certain parts of the Boston Common, but do you typically have success in locating wildlife by crashing through the underbrush?"

Ted shot Quentin a sour glance. "I don't typically try to locate wildlife. But you've got a point. We should probably sit in a hunter's blind and be quiet, wait for a squirrel or a rabbit to wander by."

Quentin tipped his chin up and scanned the tree branches overhead. "It's odd. It's been impossible to *avoid* squirrels in the last couple of days. Yet I don't see a single one anywhere around. It's as if they know we have wicked designs on their flea populations."

"That's the thing with squirrels. They're only around if you don't want them, the annoying little shits."

"Maybe we shouldn't assume fleas would flock to nonanimal hosts." He gestured to his parka and boots. "Especially ones wearing such relatively heavy personal armor."

Ted eyed him suspiciously. "Yeah. What do you suggest, then?"

"Well . . ." Quentin laced his fingers behind his back and smirked. "I believe *one* of us has another option. A form that might potentially attract a flea or two."

"You want me to shift. Here? Now? And *try* to get infested with fleas?"

Quentin gave Ted the Bambi eyes. "All for a good cause. Besides, wouldn't you be able to track rabbits back to their nests —"

"Burrows."

"Fine, *burrows* better with your bear nose than your human one?"

Ted scowled, but stripped off his coat. "If I didn't know better, I'd think you *wanted* to see me naked."

"Would you rather I turned my back?"

"Suit yourself." Ted tossed his coat on a mossy boulder and unbuttoned his shirt. Quentin settled himself on a fallen log nearby. He pretended to study the lichen on its bark, but as Ted stripped down to bare skin, he caught Quentin slyly checking him out. He turned his back to shuck his boxers because those secret glances were giving him a stiffy. Once he'd tossed his underwear with his other clothes, he didn't waste any time shifting.

"Oh," Quentin breathed. "I've never seen a shift this close. It's . . . remarkable. The way the magic illuminates your bones. Did you know that there's a sound too? It's like an extended note from an octobass."

Ted grunted and lowered his nose to the ground, sniffing for rabbit scat, until he located a burrow and excavated it with his claws. The little nest was empty, but he'd screwed up their warren big time. *Sorry, little bunny dudes.*

"You really are a most handsome bear. I never knew grizzlies had that kind of silver ruff. Or is that a shifter thing? The analog for your beard?"

Seriously? He reared up on his back legs and stuck his snout into a knot hole on an oak tree that smelled strongly of recent squirrel activity, but contained no actual squirrels.

Quentin edged closer, riffling the fur along Ted's spine, making him twitch. "It's so thick. I expect any flea would feel privileged to nestle in for a long winter's nap."

Ted growled, prompting Q-Bert to laugh, although it had a nervous edge to it. "Sorry. I don't expect that's a very comforting thought."

He kept up the same running commentary—Ted's bear form, the forest, random facts about insects—and did Ted really need to know that an engorged tick could grow to five times its unengorged size? No, he did not.

Ted tried to ignore the nonstop chatter as he covered the ground in the clearing and the surrounding woods, Quentin practically plastered to his side and occasionally checking Ted's fur for hitchhikers.

Finally, he grew so irritated by his lack of success and Quentin's nattering that he shifted back, nudity be damned. Quentin uttered a startled *Eep!* and scuttled away, his hands behind his back and his face redder than a baboon shifter's butt.

Ted propped his hands on his hips and glared. "I thought we'd agreed to be *quiet*. No rabbit or squirrel would come within a mile of this place with all that racket."

"I'd think it more likely they wouldn't come within a mile of this place because of the bear. Haven't you found anything?"

"No, I haven't. It's a little hard to concentrate with all your chatter. What the heck is an octobass?"

Quentin rubbed his hands along his thighs. "It's this twelve-foot-tall stringed instrument. I'm sorry. I just got nervous. I'm not used to this kind of silence." He glanced over his shoulder. "I thought I heard something rustling in the brush, but it seemed bigger than a rabbit. Are you sure there are any around here?"

"More in the spring and summer." He crouched down on a patch of withered moss and poked the ground. "I know they had burrows around here."

"That's not very precise."

Ted glared at Quentin. "Why can't *you* find them? Rabbits fuck enough. Can't you home in on them with your sex radar?"

"I don't have sex radar. Especially for other species. I have an . . . an affinity for people I find appetizing, but that doesn't mean I can locate them like some NSFW game of Hide the Thimble."

"'Hide the Thimble'? What the heck is that?"

"You know—'You're warm, getting warmer' to indicate proximity when the hider gives the seeker clues."

Ted huddled on the moss. "I wish I was getting warmer." He scratched his beard. "Because this is—"

"Hold still." Quentin darted over, smacking Ted's hand out of the way, and pinched his cheek.

"Ow! What the hell?"

Quentin grinned, holding up his thumb and forefinger. "Got one." He jammed his fingers into a vial and stoppered it. "One more to go."

"Oh man," Ted grumbled. "I'm gonna have to shave my beard off after this."

"Don't be a baby. It's nothing that an industrial-grade shampoo won't take care of. Why I'll bet—"

"Don't move." Ted reached up and captured a flea from under Quentin's ear. "You were saying?"

Quentin's eyes got big. "I am taking *fifty* showers."

Ted chuckled as he stepped into his pants. "I'm not sure the hot water heater is up for that. But you know, an industrial-grade shampoo—"

"Shut up."

"Don't worry, Q-Bert. I'll let you have the downstairs bathroom first."

Quentin couldn't seem to stop rubbing his hair with the towel, certain that he felt tiny feet scampering across his scalp. Which had to be his imagination. Didn't it? He eyed the vials with the fleas leaping randomly inside them. They hadn't escaped, thank all the gods and devils, because he didn't think he could go through that again.

Although the insect incursion hadn't been the most challenging part. Full frontal view of Ted naked? Now *that* was a challenge. A challenge not to rub himself against all that glorious skin, burrow into the warmth of that lovely energy, maybe even taste—

His back burned, phantom lashings more devastating than the real ones because he knew the consequences of his weakness now. *I won't. I can't. Restraint. I'm a Bertrand-Harrington. I'm more than my impulses. I. Can. Resist . . .*

He closed his eyes until his breathing leveled out. *A challenge, yes, but I overcame it. For the moment.* And now they had everything they needed to remove him from temptation permanently.

Before he'd gotten in the shower, Ted had shown Quentin how to use the magic phone connection app. So Quentin marched to the sofa and, backed by the sound of Ted's humming over the cascade of water, muttered the rather peculiar incantation necessary to initiate a video call to Zeke at Supernatural Selection.

"Supernatural Sel— Oh. Mr. Bertrand-Harrington. I've been trying to reach you since our conversation the other day."

"Yes, well, the reception up here is nonexistent, as is the electricity, so I've been unavailable. However, I wanted to let you know that we've collected the required elements for the escape clause ritual."

"You have?" He blinked behind his wire-framed glasses. "That was quick."

"We were motivated," Quentin said dryly. "By the way, are the fleas required to be alive?"

"I don't think—" Zeke scrabbled through the papers on his desk. "It doesn't say. No, wait. Here it is. They *can* be live, but it's not required."

"Good." Quentin had no desire to ride all the way to Portland with live fleas that might escape. The thought made his scalp itch again. "We'd like to make an appointment for the ritual to be completed. Would this afternoon be convenient?"

"Oh, but—" Zeke passed a hand through his curls. "That's right. We didn't finish our conversation. You can't terminate yet. The contract, I mean."

"What do you mean? We have all the required ingredients. Both of us would like to get this nightmare concluded as quickly as possible."

"Yes, I understand, but—"

"Have you notified our *intended* partners of the error?"

"Yeees." Zeke's gaze slid away from the screen.

"I trust you made it clear that we're doing everything we can to expedite the solution."

"Of course. Although . . ."

"Although what?"

"Neither of them is in a particular hurry."

Quentin's belly tightened. Had Casimir changed his mind? Had Rusty? For some reason, the thought of Ted's dreams being dashed was more upsetting than the notion of losing a vampire mate that he'd never even met. "They haven't reneged, I trust?"

"Oh no no. But as I said, they're . . . ah . . . willing to wait." He smiled brightly, although it had a definite edge of desperation. "Which is a good thing, actually. Because the ritual has a timing component too."

"Timing?"

"Yes. It can only be conducted between dusk and midnight on the night of the first full moon following the consummation of your contract. Miss that window, and the contract remains binding forever. In your case, though, because of the escape clause, 'forever' is a maximum of one solar year from—"

Quentin took a deep breath through his nose. "I'm aware of the timeline, thank you." *As well as the associated death and/or untold destruction.*

"Unless you want to sacrifice—"

"Yes, yes. The body parts. I remember. But consummation? Suppose we don't want to consummate."

"Um . . . I don't think there's a provision for that, since you both chose the consummation package."

"Of *course* I chose the consummation package. Devil take it, I'm an *incubus*." *Ted chose it because he wants to be loved, and I chose it because I thought I was marrying someone who was already dead, not someone I could kill with sex.* "Isn't there another option? Something on your equivalency chart?"

Zeke's eyebrows drew together, his mouth pinched in what looked like pain. "I'm sorry. But consummation is clearly specified, and you both signed the contract in—"

"In blood. Trust me, you don't need to mention that again." Gods and devils, the full moon was over two weeks away. Could he maintain his control that long? He took a deep breath, grinding his molars. "Very well. Please set up an appointment for us on the night of the full moon, the earliest you've got."

Zeke fumbled with his mouse, his gaze obviously tracking a program elsewhere on his monitor. "As a matter of fact, we only have one appointment available that evening. The last full moon before the solstice is a busy night, you know."

"No. I didn't." Quentin held onto his patience by a thread. "What time is the appointment?"

"Ten forty-five. You'll need to bring representatives from both your clans as witnesses."

"But—" Quentin pinched the bridge of his nose. If he—and presumably Ted as well—hadn't waived the right to clan representation at the original contract signing, they wouldn't be in this predicament now. Of course, if anyone in Quentin's clan had known about the contract, they'd have hustled him into marriage with some avaricious Boston blue blood before the fatal finger prick. Quentin would have to find some way to avoid that fate this time around. *I'll think about it later.* "Fine. We'll see you at 10:45 two weeks from Tuesday."

"Are you sure? Because if you fail to keep the appointment, there's a penalty."

"I would expect nothing less."

"Great. I'll send you an email reminder so you can put it on your calendars."

"You do that. And if you wouldn't mind letting our prospective husbands know what's happening, I'd appreciate it."

Zeke bit his lip. "I'm not sure . . . I mean, there's a confidentiality agreement."

"Surely you can convey a message to them. They're our contracted mates."

"No. Actually your contracted mate is Mr. Farnsworth. If you recall, you signed—"

"*Don't* say it again. But please, do whatever you are allowed to do to make sure the next contract we sign with you is with our correct, guaranteed perfect match."

"Of course." Zeke smiled hopefully. "Have a nice day."

Quentin disconnected the call without responding, tossed the phone on the coffee table, and dropped his head into his hands.

"Hey, Q-Bert, easy on the phone, huh?"

Quentin jerked upright, skewing his head around to look at Ted. *Eeep!* Ted was standing there wearing nothing but a towel around his waist as he rubbed his hair and beard with another. Ted's towels were big, but Ted was *bigger*. Although his groin was covered (more or less), the left side of his body was bare from his toes up to his very sturdy (and long!) leg, past his hip bone and his rounded belly, up to his massive pecs.

Quentin swallowed, unable to tear his eyes away. *Don't think about consummation. Don't. Don't. Do— Gah!*

He'd thought about it.

Ted peered at him, concern puckering his forehead. "Q-Bert? Something wrong? You been sitting too close to the stove? You look a little red around the edges."

"No. I've been— That is, I've just had a conversation with Zeke at Supernatural Selection."

"Yeah?" Ted went back to toweling his hair. "So, fleas. Alive or dead?"

"Either one."

"Good. Let's drown the little buggers before they get out and infest my house. When's our appointment?"

"It's . . . ah . . . two weeks from Tuesday."

Ted whipped the towel off his head. "Two *weeks*? But . . . but why? We've got everything ready to go now."

"There's apparently another requirement that I wasn't aware of. Since my phone died during my last conversation with Zeke, we didn't get to it."

Ted heaved a sigh, which caused his chest to expand—getting even bigger; *how is that possible?*—and his towel to slip farther down his body. "Well that's just great. What is it this time? It better not be more insect collection or haircuts, because I'm not sure my water heater will survive the first, and your hairdo won't survive the second."

"No. No insects. Or hair. Or even silver."

"Thank Ursa for that. So what is it?" Ted blanched. "We don't have to sacrifice an animal or anything, do we? Because I'm not up for that."

Quentin choked on a half-hysterical laugh. "No animal sacrifice."

"Then what? You're scaring me, Q-Bert." Ted strode over, his peekaboo towel peeking a little bit more, and sat next to Quentin on the sofa. Fortunately—or unfortunately, depending on whether Quentin's wildly vacillating emotions were on the *hells no* downswing or *gimme some of that* upswing—he sat on Quentin's left, so Quentin wasn't directly exposed to quite as much naked skin.

But nothing could mask Ted's energy. Even though Quentin wasn't looking at his aura—as he'd promised—he could still feel it, enveloping him, teasing him, tempting him.

I am so fucked. But Quentin would do whatever he could to make sure that Ted was not.

"Do you remember the little check box on the last page of the Supernatural Selection registration page?"

"There were a lot of check boxes. Which one?"

"The one that asked whether you wanted your contract to include the consummation clause?"

Ted's brows drew together. "Consum— Oh. That. What about it?"

"Apparently the escape clause can only be exercised between dusk and midnight on the first full moon following the consummation of our . . . our union."

"That's a pretty damn narrow window. Do we— Wait." Ted's eyebrows rose slowly, eyes widening, and a smile tugging at his lips. "Oh. I get it. We have to have sex."

"Yes," Quentin said, clipping the word off sharply. "And it's not funny." He turned away so he wouldn't get distracted by the thick mat of curly dark hair on Ted's chest.

"Hey, I'm not laughing. Well, not at the situation. It kinda sucks, actually."

Quentin dared a glance at Ted's face. *He looks ill. And angry. Of course. He doesn't want me. He wants Rusty.* "I know. I'm sorry."

"You're sorry? Why? It's not your doing."

"In a way it is. I'm the one who signed the contract with the wrong name on it."

"So did I. But sex demon or not, you shouldn't have to be with someone you don't ... how did you put it? Find appetizing."

"That's not really the issue," Quentin said dryly, doing his best not to lean into Ted to absorb that lovely golden energy directly from his skin.

"No? Well, I suppose that's a plus." He slapped his thighs and stood, propping his fists on his hips. "Then here's what we're going to do."

"We're going to do something?" Quentin huddled on the sofa, looking way way up at Ted's face, because focusing on what was right in front of him—Ted's groin—was firing far too many formerly dormant synapses in his brain.

"Yep. Who's to say what the definition of 'consummation' is? I mean, everyone has different boundaries, right? If all that 'you have to do this together' stuff from the other tasks holds true, then all we should have to do is jack off together. Mutual orgasms, and booyah." He grinned. "Mission accomplished."

Chapter Fourteen

Ted waited for Quentin to nod or shake his head or something, but all he did was stare at Ted with his mouth agape.

"C'mon, Q-Bert. You want to get this done, right? It doesn't have to mean anything. I mean, who hasn't done that with a buddy in the past?"

"Me! I haven't."

"No?" Ted grinned. "Who knew a sex demon could be so prudish? Spend a lot of time with your right hand, did you?"

"For your information," Quentin said frostily, "I'm left-handed. And 'cubi can't . . . can't . . ."

"Ursa strike me blind. You can't jack off? Man, being a sex demon isn't all it's cracked up to be."

"You have no idea," Quentin muttered.

The towel around Ted's waist kept creeping downward, losing the battle between gravity and his spare tire. His semi wasn't helping any, and the more Quentin glanced at it and away, the harder Ted got. He sighed. "Look, we gotta take care of this. If we don't, and if we don't do it before the deadline . . ." Ted drew his finger across his throat.

Quentin clenched his eyes shut. "Don't."

"Okay, but come on. Since you can't wank yourself, then don't you think it makes sense for us to help each other out?"

Quentin cracked an eye open. "'Help each other'?"

"Jerk each other, Q-Bert." Ted peered down at him, suddenly worried that he'd misunderstood pretty much everything about 'cubi. "You *have* had sex before, haven't you?"

"Of course I have, you infuriating bear. But this is a dreadful idea."

Thank Ursa for that. Well, the Q-Bert's-had-sex-before part, not the dreadful-idea part. "Why? It's not like we're cheating on anybody. We're married to each other. At least for now. And neither one of us has ever met our real husbands."

"That's splitting hairs and you know it. Besides, that's not what I meant."

"Then what?"

"I'm an incubus."

"So?"

"I can— I could kill you with sex."

Ted raised his eyebrows. "You do that on purpose?"

"No! Of course not." Quentin laced his fingers together like he was shooting for a Supe Scout knot badge without the benefit of rope. "But if I lose control, it could happen."

Ted shook his head, chuckling. "Q-Bert, you are the biggest control freak I have *ever* met. No way would you lose it if you didn't want to."

"But—"

"Shhh. What I'm saying is, I trust you. I know I'm not the guy you want—"

"That's not—" Quentin swallowed "—entirely true."

"So you want me?"

"Gods and devils, *yes.* I mean, who wouldn't?"

"Lots of people. Most people." Ted scratched his beard thoughtfully. "Pretty much everyone, actually."

"You're delusional. I saw the way everyone in town—men and women—looked at you. All you'd need to do is crook a finger and you'd have all the company you want."

Ted grinned. "Crook my finger? You mean like this?" He raised one huge hand and beckoned.

"*Ted . . .*" Quentin packed a lot into that word—warning, defeat, maybe a little desire too? Unless that was Ted's wishful thinking.

"It'll be okay. One and done."

"'One and done'?"

Jeez, Quentin looked like a kid with his face pressed against the candy store window. *He sees me as desirable?* That was a first, no matter what Quentin imagined about everyone in town. So Ted determined to make this good for him, no matter what.

He held out his hand. "Have I ever hurt you? Well, other than abandoning you on the mountain five minutes after we met and leaving you to almost freeze to death."

Quentin choked on a laugh. "That wasn't entirely your fault. And I trust you too, Ted. I really do. It's myself I don't trust."

Ted shrugged. "You'll never know if you don't try. One time, Q. Have you ever sexed someone to death in one blow?" Ted grinned. "So to speak?"

As Ted had hoped, Quentin smiled. "No. I don't pack quite that much firepower."

"Well then. We're good. Up you get." He grinned again. "See, I'm getting better at sneaky sex references."

Quentin didn't take Ted's hand, but he stood, then turned away, his shoulders nearly up by his ears, and unbuttoned his flannel shirt. He dropped it on the couch, then skinned his long-sleeved thermal over his head.

Ted's breath caught. Quentin's skin was as pale as milk, but he had two massive scars, red and angry looking, that followed his shoulder blades. Ted wanted to touch them, soothe them, but that wasn't part of this deal. This wasn't about anything but meeting the terms of the escape clause. *Got to remember that.* Because when Quentin dropped his pants, revealing the most perfect ass Ted had ever seen, Ted wanted to *touch* more than anything.

Quentin turned around, his gaze on the floor, but his dick—long, slender, uncut—was hard, curving toward his belly. It was longer than Ted had expected for a little guy like Quentin, reaching past his navel even with the curve. *Maybe that's a sex demon thing.*

Ted cleared his throat and dropped his towel on the floor. "Come closer? Can't reach you way over there."

Quentin jerked a nod and stepped closer until his chest was maybe a hand span from Ted's.

"Gonna touch you now, so don't freak out, okay?" Ted closed his fingers around Quentin's shaft, and Quentin drew in a hissing breath, eyes fluttering closed. When he opened them again, for a moment, red flashed in their depths.

Then Quentin fisted Ted's cock and Ted's eyes nearly rolled back in his head. Quentin's hand wasn't big. He couldn't close his fingers around Ted's dick like Ted could with Quentin's, but Ursa's teeth, it didn't matter.

He groaned. "Oh man. It's like I'm coming without coming."

Because while Quentin's touch was fricking *electric* on Ted's dick, the thrills chasing up his arm from his grip on Quentin's shaft were just as intense, maybe more. Somehow, their strokes were synchronized—pressure, speed, and Ursa's *teeth*, the *heat!*

He shut his eyes as his balls drew up, his ass clenched, his legs trembled. *Too soon. I can't come so soon. What about Quentin?*

But then Quentin gasped and whimpered and it was all over. Ted shot with a moan, and as his dick pulsed, Quentin's jizz hit Ted's chest in the identical rhythm.

Knees wobbly, he opened his eyes to find Quentin panting, staring down at his hand, which was covered in Ted's semen.

"I guess—" Ted croaked, then cleared his throat. "We should clean up." When Quentin didn't respond, Ted touched his shoulder, which caused him to flinch. "You okay?"

Quentin nodded jerkily. Still not meeting Ted's gaze, he collected his clothes and scuttled toward the bathroom.

Great. Now it's gonna get weird. Ted didn't want Quentin to freak out anymore, so the best solution was for Ted to take off. Give Quentin a chance to decompress.

Normally, Ted would want to nap after sex, especially at this time of year. But he felt too antsy for that. *Kill two birds with one stone, I guess.*

He picked up his towel and crept town the hall. "Hey, Q? Take your time in there. I'm gonna head out for a while. There's leftover soup if you want some, and I'll stoke the fire before I leave." No answer. "You okay?"

"Yes." Quentin's voice, even muffled by the door, sounded shaky. "I'll be fine."

"You sure?"

"Of course. Please don't give me another thought."

Yeah, not likely. "See you later, then."

Ted ran upstairs, did a quick cleanup at his crappy sink, and got dressed. Quentin was still in Rusty's bathroom when he got back downstairs. *Will it be weirder if I stay, or if I go? Jeez, I'm so bad at figuring this stuff out.* If it were him in there, he knew what he'd want: for his partner to be there when he got out, ready to cuddle for a while. Naked or not, it didn't matter. But Quentin had different ideas about being close. He'd said he was an introvert, so maybe he'd want some alone time? It wasn't like he could escape the cabin and get away anywhere on his own, so it was up to Ted to take off. At least he had friends in the area and could travel quickly.

He put on his coat and grabbed his phone. When he stepped out onto the porch, he called Dr. Kendrick's magic line.

"Ted? Is everything okay? Is Quentin all right?"

"Yeah, we're fine, but I, uh, have to go into town. I was wondering if you could maybe install the magic phone app on Quentin's phone. I feel funny leaving him here on his own after what happened last time."

"Certainly."

"Really? You don't mind?"

Dr. Kendrick chuckled. "The spell isn't mine anyway. It's something my brothers' boyfriends cooked up between them because they didn't like the inability to communicate between

Faerie and the Outer World. It was a lucky side effect that it works for remote areas with no cell coverage too, as long as there's a supe to boost the signal. Although it works much better in close proximity to a Faerie gate, so your place is optimal. They expect to roll it out to other supes soon, so this can be a beta test for them."

"Oh. Well. Good. Thanks."

"I'll be there within the hour. Will you still be around?"

"No. I've got to take off now." Ted trudged down the steps, oddly reluctant to leave. "But Quentin will be in the cabin."

"I'll see him then. I planned to stop by soon in any case because I have a few things to discuss with him, so it's good that you called."

"Thanks, Doc. I really appreciate it."

"Anytime, Ted."

Ted pocketed his phone and headed up to the lodge. He took off his clothes and tossed them in the mud room, then shifted to take his usual path down to the cave. After he changed, he headed into town, making it to the diner right at the dinner hour. Matt was sitting at his usual seat at the counter, and raised his hand in greeting, gesturing to Ted's empty stool.

"Come join me."

Ted ambled over, waving at Wanda, Javier, and a couple of other friends along the way. "Do you ever eat at home?"

"Nah. I'm a terrible cook. Ramen noodles or Kraft dinners are about my speed."

Ted wrinkled his nose. "Man, that is just wrong."

"I know." He raised his mug. "Luckily, Wanda keeps me fed, even if she makes me drink decaf."

"How's the job search going? Did that gig pan out?"

Matt shrugged. "I'm sort of on trial, but I'm not making much progress, and a deadline is looming." He set his cup down with a clatter. "I wish my old source hadn't dried up."

Sorry I ever strung you along, Matt. Ted covered his discomfort by signaling Wanda for a cup of coffee. "Having a hard time scaring up a new one?"

"That's not the point. I don't like—"

Wanda arrived with two carafes in her hand. "Didn't expect to see you here, Ted. Dinner?"

"No, thanks, Wanda. Just coffee." She poured him a cup with one carafe and topped Matt's up with the other, then bustled away. Ted doctored his coffee with cream and sugar. "Guess she didn't expect me here for dinner because she knows I *do* cook."

"I don't think that's the reason. She's probably as surprised as I am that you showed up. You've got company up at your place, right?"

Ted frowned over the top of his cup. "How'd you know that?"

"Shirl."

Ted shifted uneasily on his stool. It might be sturdy enough to hold him, but it was still smaller than his ass. "So you're pumping Shirl for tips now?"

"Yeah, like that'd work. No, I was in there for a new memory card and she told me. Guess she figured it was something I needed to know."

Ted blinked. "You needed— But why would Shirl think—"

"The guys from Larry's shop were talking about it in here too. They were far too pleased with the way your guest managed to get his way with their boss."

That was *pretty awesome.* Ted sighed. The problem with living in—or rather outside of—a small town was that everybody's business was ... well ... everybody's business. "That's just temporary."

"Is that so?" Matt grinned. "I know you've stocked up on groceries too."

"Don't tell me. Fred?"

"Yup."

"Those were for me."

"Hell, Ted, even a strapping young man like you can't eat *that* much in a few days." He nudged Ted's shoulder with his own. "If you need help, I'd be glad to help you put some of that away. Give you my expert opinion on your cooking skills. It'd be a change from Javier's patty melts."

Ted studied Matt out of the corner of his eye. Was Matt *flirting* with him? Quentin's remarks about the reactions of his friends took on a different meaning. Maybe he needed an outsider to point out what had been right under his nose all along.

Or maybe he's fishing for another tip.

All of Ted's Bigfoot stunts had been in the woods near the lodge. A chill skated down his back. He wasn't especially careful about his shifts up there because it was his home and he'd felt safe and secluded, but maybe it wasn't as safe or secluded as he thought.

He wasn't worried about his ability to take care of himself—nobody around here was as big as he was, even when he wasn't a bear. But he had Quentin to think about now.

Quentin. He was there by himself, and he *wasn't* big. Plus he had no idea how to take care of himself in the wilderness. He was used to cities with 911 and Uber. What if there was an emergency? What if he passed out again? What if somebody saw one of Matt's old pictures and decided to go cryptid hunting? With a gun?

He pulled out his wallet and tossed some bills on the counter for his coffee. "Gotta run, Matt. Sorry. Hope the new gig works out." *Because you're not getting any more from me, not if it puts Quentin in danger.*

Ted rushed out of the diner and was halfway up the path to the cave before he stopped. *Quentin won't get hurt because he won't be here. In two weeks, he'll be gone.*

He steadied himself against a tree when his knees threatened to give out. *Get over it. He's not my perfect match. I want him to go so I can marry Rusty.*

He trudged the rest of the way to the cave and crawled inside. Instead of undressing and shifting right away, though, he huddled against the cold stone walls, head on his knees, and tried to remind himself that marrying Rusty was what he'd dreamed of.

It took a long time to make himself believe it again.

When Quentin heard the front door close, he was still sitting on the bathroom floor, trying to resist tasting Ted's spend. The energy would have mostly dissipated by now, as it had cooled from body temperature. Surely he'd be forgiven for a taste if it didn't *feed* him. It wasn't stealing. It had been Ted's idea after all. *But he doesn't know what it means.* His hand shook as he fought not to bring it to his mouth, certain that allowing even a drop onto his tongue would be the most transcendent, yet catastrophic, thing he could ever do.

Has it really been that long since I've had an orgasm that I've forgotten how it feels? What it makes me want?

Because even as he'd shot over Ted's hand, he hadn't been emptied—he'd been *filled.* So fast and hard and absolutely that he was surprised shafts of pure energy hadn't shot out of his skin—yet Ted hadn't seemed diminished at all. *I touched him and didn't hurt him. Maybe David's right and this is what control feels like when I'm not medicated.*

If that was true, it was *glorious.* Ted's essence—his spirit, his *heart*—was so strong, so pure, so sweet that Quentin was drunk on it, floating, high as the proverbial kite. And like any lapsed addict, he wanted more.

Lips parted, panting as if he'd run a mile, he raised his hand. *A taste. Just a taste.*

He scrambled to his feet and shoved his hand under the faucet, turning the water on full force. He scrubbed his hand and his chest until his skin was red and tender. *I can't give in to temptation. It isn't right. Not for him. Not for me either, if I want to keep my sanity.*

He sighed and got dressed once more in his Stuff 'n' Things couture. The thermal shirt collar was tight against his throat and he tugged at it irritably. Over two weeks trapped here with the most delectable man he'd ever met. *A man who belongs to someone else in spirit, if not in legal fact.*

Two weeks from Tuesday, Ted would be released from their inconvenient bond and free to join with his magically selected soul mate. And Quentin would lock himself into a centuries-long commitment to a dead man.

He glanced at the stove as he passed the kitchen, but he wasn't hungry. *Of course you're not hungry. You just gorged on Ted.*

The memory of it made his jeans feel too tight around the waist, and as he fumbled to undo the top button of his fly, he was startled by a brisk knock at the door. He stared at it, momentarily nonplussed. It couldn't be Ted. He wouldn't knock, even though Quentin had undoubtedly made him feel unwelcome in his own home. The lake wasn't exactly in a population center, and he hadn't heard a vehicle approach. Furthermore, he could sense no energy signature on the other side of the door.

A ghost? Ted hadn't mentioned that the lake was haunted. If he—

"Quentin? It's Dr. Kendrick. Alun."

Oh. The contained fae. No wonder Quentin couldn't detect him. He opened the door, smiling at Alun with what he hoped was welcome. "I'm sorry. I wasn't expecting anyone. Please come in. I'm afraid Ted isn't here right now."

"Yes, I know. He asked me to stop by to see you."

Alun strode into the cabin, nearly as tall as Ted, his exceptional figure outlined by a well-cut suit. Bespoke if Quentin was any judge—and he was. Only a bespoke suit could fit *that* figure *that* well. Yet despite Alun's incredible fae beauty —dark hair in crisp waves, luminous hazel eyes, and perfect classical features—Quentin felt not the slightest attraction. He found himself wondering what Alun would look like with a little more padding around the middle.

Quentin gestured toward the kitchen. "May I offer you some coffee? Tea? I'm sure Ted has other things as well. I've never seen a more completely stocked pantry. Although if you want brandy, I'm afraid that's one thing I can't offer you."

Alun grinned, a rakish expression completely at odds with his conservative tailoring. "Ted never was one for top-shelf liquor. Microbrews are more his passion. However, this isn't a purely social visit. May I see your cell phone?"

"My phone?"

"I want to bespell it so you can use the same communications protocol that Ted uses to contact me. It will allow you to use your phone while you're somewhere with no normal reception."

"Really?" Quentin collected his phone from the solar charger, unlocked the home screen, and handed it to Alun. "So it's a spell, not an actual app?"

Alun accepted the phone and held it in the palm of his hand. "A little of both. One moment please." He closed his eyes, murmuring something in a different language—Welsh, perhaps?—then touched the screen. A new icon bloomed under his fingertip. "There. My brother's boyfriend, Bryce, is a druid, although he's only lately become aware of it. Consequently, he couches much of his magic in the framework of the Outer World. So even though this isn't technology at all, but rather a combination of fae and druid magic, he's crafted it as an app."

Quentin accepted the phone, noting that the icon looked no different from the others. "That's very clever. I know a number of people"—most of them related to him—"who would be very interested in obtaining this."

"Ordinarily, the normal service providers are adequate. But occasionally, a supe could find himself in a remote location unexpectedly. And if human first responder services would compromise the Secrecy Pact . . . well, we wanted an alternative. One that would address the safety of the individual as well as our community as a whole. This is in beta right now. Very limited rollout, but Ted is a friend as well as a client, and since he asked . . ."

"Thank you. I appreciate it. Is there a charge? Because I can pay, of course."

"No. This isn't a paid service. We only accept members with proven need and trustworthiness."

Interesting. Something his family couldn't buy their way into. Because they'd want to do it, of course. A supe-only communication tool? They'd want to control it the same way they controlled every other aspect of their lives.

"Do you need any instructions on how to use it?"

"No. I used Ted's phone the other day. Although I have to ask —why is the incantation to activate the spell 'please and thank you'? That seems a bit . . . odd."

"Ah." Alun's cheeks flushed. "It's something of a family joke. David and Bryce claim that supes, particularly my brothers and me, never remember to ask for permission and are incapable of accepting help gracefully. I think it amuses them to force us to be polite to our phones."

Quentin chuckled. "I see. Well, in any case, you needn't worry about me. I'm fine."

Alun studied him, his head tilted to one side. "Yes. You are. You are much more recovered than I'd have expected in so short a time. You've regained some lost flesh. Ted must be feeding you well."

"Yes." Quentin cleared his throat. "Yes. He is." *More than you know.*

"Good. David is convinced that the 'cubi place far too much emphasis on life essence when simply increasing their caloric intake would supplement many of their nutritional needs."

Quentin smiled wanly. "A revolutionary, is he?"

"A force of nature, at any rate, and one with definite opinions." Alun squeezed the back of his neck, looking as uncomfortable as a six-and-a-half-foot fae could. "However, this isn't the only reason I stopped by. Have you spoken to your grandmother?"

"My—" Quentin swallowed. "No."

"I want to respect your desire for privacy and to manage your own affairs, but please contact your grandmother and let her know you're well. I have personal experience in how poorly concealing critical relationship information can go."

"I understand. But you may not realize how determined my grandmother is to control my life."

"Don't I?" His lips quirked. "In my psychology practice, I treat supes from all races, and one of them is the dragon queen herself."

Quentin closed his eyes and sighed. "My grandmother's best friend."

"So I understand. In fact, it's at her instigation—based on her conversations with your grandmother—that I'm here. I'm aware that your dynasty carries dragon shifter DNA, so the hoarding tendencies are there. Your grandmother hoards her power and connections as well as her money."

"Then you can understand why I might want to escape that."

"Perhaps. As long as you don't attempt your own hoard. One that wouldn't be . . . appropriate in these circumstances."

He knows. He knows that I'm drawn to Ted. "I, ah, take your point. But you needn't worry. And now that I have the means —" he brandished his phone "—I promise to call my grandmother. Thank you."

"You're welcome. I'm sorry to rush, but I have an appointment shortly, and if I'm not back to greet my client, my office manager will have words for me." From the way Alun's eyes glinted, he looked forward to those words.

That's right. His office manager is David. His husband. Imagine being so in tune with your lover that you even relished their ire, if only because it meant you had more time with them.

Quentin saw Alun to the door. "Thank you again. I won't abuse the privilege."

Alun lifted an eyebrow. "Abuse it all you like, as long as you *call your grandmother.*"

Quentin laughed. "Yes. I've gotten that message."

He waited until Alun had nearly disappeared into the trees before he shut the door.

No point delaying the inevitable. He sat down on the sofa, opened the new app, and initiated a video call with his grandmother.

Her face appeared on the screen almost immediately, her cap of silver hair sleek and perfect as usual, her skin almost as smooth as a girl's—which told Quentin that she'd fed recently. She could have altered her hair color if she wished, but she'd told him once that the color gave her stature and authority in the community.

"Quentin! My dear, I've been so worried."

"I'm sorry, Grandmother. I didn't expect you to discover I was gone so soon. You weren't scheduled to return to Boston until after the solstice."

"So you *intended* to hide your whereabouts from me? It wasn't a simple oversight?"

Quentin winced. "No. I apologize."

"Where in blazes are you?"

"I— I'm afraid I can't tell you yet."

"Quentin." Her voice reverberated with the contained wrath of a millennia-old succubus.

"I'm perfectly well, I assure you. I simply have things to take care of."

"'Things'? What sort of things?"

"I can't discuss it now. I'll be out of touch for a couple of weeks, but I'll call you when I can."

"Are you at least feeding? You look marginally better than at our last cocktail party. You barely spoke to anyone at all that night, let alone got close enough to absorb any spark."

"No. But I've started a new ... treatment regimen." *No suppressant and a boost from an* achubydd. *Not exactly in the standard 'cubi pharmacopeia.* "You needn't worry. I promise. But now I really must go. I'll call you."

"Quentin—"

He cut the connection.

Afterward, he tried to settle down on the sofa with his e-reader, but he was too restless to concentrate. He wanted to be up and *doing. You want to be doing* Ted *is what you want.* But with that option now permanently off the table, he needed something else to occupy himself.

Since the cabin was starting to feel simultaneously claustrophobic and empty (without Ted in it), Quentin shrugged into his parka and stepped out onto the porch. It was that liminal time that could occur in the mountains. He'd experienced it at his grandmother's vacation home in Vermont. The sun had dipped below the hills but not beneath the horizon, so while shadows gathered under the trees, the sky was still blue and cloudless.

He struck off along the path to the lodge. When it came into view as he skirted the lake, he studied the shape of the building —its bones, its angles, the way it conformed to its setting. The martens had selected their location well, and the lodge itself was actually quite graceful. When he had first seen it, in his distress and suppressant-induced stupor, he'd termed it derelict. But it wasn't. It was simply unfinished.

He circled the clearing where the lodge stood, observing it from every angle. The clearing itself was lovely too, even in its bedraggled late-autumn state. The way the lake shore curved, it held the lodge as if in a cupped hand, so the lake would be visible from rooms on two sides. One remaining side faced the forest with a mountaintop rising above it, and the other a broad meadow sloping down to a stand of fir and some kind of bare deciduous trees. Some had peeling white bark—birch, or perhaps aspen? If the others were maple, the foliage would be stunning in the early fall.

Quentin walked up to the porch slowly, savoring the peace. A squirrel chittered at him from the bare branches. "Shut up, you. Where were you when we needed your fleas? Keep them away from me now."

He slipped inside. The plywood subfloor creaked under his feet, but didn't give. It was sturdy, like the rest of the building. He wandered through the echoing space. The central lobby was vaulted, roughly three stories high. A temporary staircase led to the upper floors and down into a basement. Using the flashlight on his phone, Quentin went downstairs.

The basement had the same vast footprint as the first floor. He sniffed experimentally and didn't detect the telltale dankness of poor waterproofing.

This could be turned into vampire suites. The ceiling was at least nine feet high and the walls had long narrow windows that admitted some daylight but would be easy to shutter.

He climbed back upstairs slowly, an idea beginning to take shape. He climbed the next flight to the second floor. When he got to the top of the stairs, he caught movement out of a forest-facing window.

There. Just beyond the tree line, screened by fir branches and underbrush, was a shape. A familiar shape: a bear, huge and brown and shaggy. *Ted.* Quentin crept to the window, standing to the side so he wouldn't be readily visible if Ted should look up. His bear form was so beautiful. Strong. Powerful. Still under the trees, he stood on his back legs, and the shimmer of magic swirled around him, lighting him up until Quentin had to shield his eyes.

When he opened them again, Ted was striding toward the lodge. Naked. And Quentin immediately wanted what he couldn't have.

Devil take it, I will not endanger him. But the notion of never seeing Ted again after two weeks was suddenly unacceptable. The idea that had been percolating in his brain bloomed, fully formed—a way he could help Ted. A way that they could still be connected even after they were divorced.

You say you just want to help him like he helped you, because he's a good guy and deserves a break. But really you don't want to completely lose him.

Well, so what if that was true? It wasn't as if Quentin would break his wedding vows or entice Ted to do the same. They couldn't, even if they wanted to, since they'd be magically prevented from ever meeting face-to-face. But there were other methods of remaining in contact, particularly with a legitimate, nonsleazy reason for doing so. Surely they could email. Text. Speak on the phone. Quentin would at least know that Ted was well and thriving. *With somebody else.*

The back door opened and shut. Quentin crept through the forest of bare studs—*toward another bare stud? Stop it!*—giving Ted time to at least get his pants on. He descended the stairs slowly, but even so, one of the plywood treads creaked under his foot.

"Is someone there?" Ted called, his tone laced with both fear and aggression.

"It's just me." Quentin trotted the rest of the way and met Ted in the middle of the big empty lobby. "I was snooping. I hope that's acceptable."

Ted finished buttoning his flannel shirt. "Sure. Not much to see, but I guess it makes a change of scenery from the cabin."

"I think you're wrong."

Ted's hands froze on the last button. "It's not a change of scenery? I know the cabin's rustic, but—"

"The cabin is lovely. What I meant was that there's a lot to see. A lot to admire. What are your plans for this building?"

"Nothing too fancy. I figure the only customers we'd get up here are folks like me who don't mind roughing it. Maybe when supe kids do their outdoor school they could come up here. I thought I'd turn this into the mess hall. Maybe a meeting room or two. But the rest?" He shrugged. "I figure I'll just leave it. Weatherproof it, of course, but that's about it. The martens were planning to fix it up so their huge families could visit, but that never happened."

"While your plans are perfectly reasonable, I don't think you're giving the lodge and this spot enough credit." Quentin took Ted's elbow, intending to lead him to the window, but dropped it when that seductive golden energy sent tendrils into his fingers. He strode to the window and pointed at the lake. "This place is beautiful. The lake. The mountains. The trees. You've got the bones here, the beginnings of a high-end destination venue."

Ted scrunched up his face. "I can't do that. Maybe with Rusty's help, if he wants it, but it would take years."

"Perhaps you could hire the carpenter who built the cabinetry in the owner's cabin to come back and assist."

"Oh, that was me."

"You built those cabinets? The bookshelves? The bed frame?"

"Yeah. I wanted to get the place ready for you. Well, not you, but . . . you."

Quentin's heart bounded sideways. *I wish.* "I get it."

Ted nodded unhappily. "I didn't finish because I got distracted by other stuff, and then—"

"Then I showed up. Luckily, I *don't* get distracted. And don't you think it would be a better wedding gift for Rusty if he arrived to discover he didn't have to do all the work?"

Ted scratched the back of his head. "When you put it that way . . ."

"You'll still finish up the cabin, at least the parts you're building just for Rusty, because that's quite romantic and he'll love it."

"You think so?"

"Of course. I mean, *I* would, and I'm an unsentimental incubus. But as for the rest, we'll get some help for that."

"I should tell you, Q . . ." Ted's shoulders inched toward his ears and he wouldn't meet Quentin's gaze. "I, um, don't exactly have the money for that."

"But I do. Or at least I will, and until then, there's credit." He shrugged. "I don't even have to be discreet about using it anymore, since Grandmother knows I've slipped the familial chain."

"But—"

"There's no point in protesting, Ted. I'm investing, even if I'm nothing but a silent partner who never visits the site after . . . well . . . you know." *Damn witches anyway.* Quentin forced a smile. "And because I believe in protecting my investments, be prepared to work your ass off. Starting tomorrow."

Chapter Fifteen

Apparently they were going to act like the handjob never happened. It had been four days, and Quentin hadn't so much as mentioned it. Ted could be cool with that if Quentin wouldn't keep *looking* at him that way—like he was a giant triple-decker waffle cone and it was the hottest day in July.

Sure, Quentin *tried* to cover it up—by turning away, or by writing up yet *another* list of stuff for Ted to do, or by calling a bunch of local construction companies to line up work crews.

But Ted caught him often enough to *know*. It hadn't only been awesome for Ted. Quentin had felt it too. *Wonder if it's because we're technically married now. Maybe the spell boosts our feelings or pleasure or something.*

While Quentin was on his phone, pacing back and forth across the shell of the lodge kitchen, and bitching at Larry about delivering something or other, Ted snuck out to the porch and used Dr. Kendrick's app to start a video chat with Supernatural Selection.

Zeke's face appeared on the screen. "Good morning, Supernatu—" His eyes widened. "Mr. F-F-Farnsworth. To what do I owe the pleasure?" His voice squeaked a bit on the last word. Ted tried not to take it personally. Yeah, he was big, but he wasn't standing in front of the guy, for crying out loud.

"Hey, Zeke. I had a question about the contract spell."

"If it's about the escape clause—"

"No, no. We've got that covered. I was just wondering . . ." Ted scratched his beard. *How the heck do I put this?* "Does the spell, you know, make you *feel* things more? Like more intense?"

Zeke eyebrows drew together. "What kind of things?"

"You know. *Things.*"

"If you're referring to affection, then no. Absolutely not. Despite rumors to the contrary, love spells are *not* a thing. We can't make you fall in love with your contracted spouse. Or vice versa."

Hmmm. Guess he's answered that question a time or two. "That's not what I mean. I don't mean feelings like *feelings*. I mean feelings like, well, *feelings*."

Zeke's expression turned wary. "I'm not sure I know what you— Oh! Do you mean sexual sensation?"

Ted blotted his forehead with the back of his hand. "Yeah. That."

"No. I'm afraid that's another rumor. There's no magical replacement for sexual chemistry. If there were—" he smiled ruefully "—we'd be out of business."

"Ah. Okay. Sorry to bother you."

"It was no trouble." Zeke bit his lip. "I'm really sorry for the mix-up in your contract, by the way. I still have no idea how it could have happened. I'm glad you and Mr. Bertrand-Harrington have amassed the necessary ingredients for the escape clause."

"Yeah. We've amassed all right," Ted muttered.

"Excellent. We'll see you a week from Tuesday, then. Have a nice day."

Ted tucked his phone in his pocket and stomped back inside the lodge. Right. A nice day. Not likely, with Quentin switching back and forth between a hard-nosed taskmaster and the lead in a slow-burn porno.

Ted wasn't sure which one was hotter, but it was a damned pain in the ass to build a staircase while sporting a semi that grew every time Quentin gave him one of those *looks*.

Like now. *Shit.*

"Something up, Q-Bert?"

Quentin jerked like he'd been startled awake. He blinked those big dark eyes a couple of times. "No. Nothing. The generator will be delivered next Wednesday. The electricians will be here to install the wiring beginning—" he swiped his finger across his tablet "—tomorrow at eight. We were lucky. Most of the crews in the area were already booked. Apparently this is a busy time for them, with so much of the exterior work having been completed during the warm months."

"Yeah. Rusty and I could have gotten hitched in August, but he still had a lot of projects going on. So we decided to wait." Ted buckled on his tool belt. "Guess it would have been better for you if we had, huh? Then we wouldn't have gotten all screwed up this way."

"Yes. I suppose."

Ted glanced up at the weird tone of Quentin's voice. He almost sounded sad. Or maybe mad. It was hard to tell when he sliced off the ends of his words that way. "You got any more calls to make?"

"Not today. I've done all the damage I can for the moment."

Ted grinned. "Oh, I don't know about that." He picked up a hammer and held it out, handle first. "Time to get your hands dirty."

Quentin stared at the hammer like he'd never seen one in his life. "What?"

"You told me I could put you to work on unskilled labor. Now's the time. You can help me with the staircase."

Quentin put his hands behind his back, shaking his head a little wildly. "Oh no. I couldn't. You're doing such beautiful work. I wouldn't want to screw it up."

"They're just nails, Q-Bert, and the treads are oak. Not much you can do to hurt them." Ted waggled the handle. "Come on. It'll help you work off some steam. Seems like you could use it after hollering at Larry for a solid half hour."

Quentin gave him a sour look, then took the hammer. "Working off steam might be a good idea after all."

Ted led Quentin over to the main staircase—the real one, which would replace the rickety temporary one that the martens had used for access to the upper stories. He took one of the pre-cut treads off the stack and laid it over the first notch in the stringers. "Here. You position it like this, and drive the nails in here, here, and here." He took a nail out of the tool belt at his waist and knocked it in. "Like that. I'll do this side and the middle, and you can do that side."

Quentin was staring at him again—not with *that look* exactly, but close.

"What?"

He pointed at Ted with his hammer. "It only took you two strokes to sink that nail. How do I even . . ." He threw up his other hand and walked away a few paces, then returned. "Seriously?"

"It's not a contest, Q. Besides, that's why I'm doing two sets and you're doing one." He pulled a handful of nails out of the pouch—carefully!—and laid them on the floor. "Get cracking."

"Fine." He picked up a nail.

Ted tried not to watch Quentin fumbling while he sank all six of his own nails, but the way Quentin was holding his hammer? Finally Ted couldn't stand it anymore and burst out laughing.

"It's not a dick, Q-Bert. Hold it down near the end of the handle. If you choke up on it that way, you don't get any force out of the swing. You'll be pounding the same nail for a week and never get anywhere."

"Sounds like my sex life," he muttered.

Quentin did as Ted suggested, but his aim was so bad that he nearly smashed his thumb.

"Careful there, John Henry. Here. Let me show you."

Ted grabbed a piece of wood from the scrap pile. Using the pencil from behind his ear, he drew several circles about the same size as the nail heads. "We'll use this for target practice. So you can get the feel of the swing."

"Anything that saves my fingers is fine with me."

"All righty, then." Ted positioned the board on the nearby plywood worktable. "Come here." Quentin approached warily, and Ted manhandled him into position. "Grab the hammer." Quentin picked it up. "Not like that. What did I just say?" He snatched the hammer and took Quentin's wrist in the other. "You hold it here, at the base. Pretend you're trying to keep from shooting too soon."

"I'd really rather not equate the tool with my—"

"Tool?" Ted waggled his eyebrows.

"Very funny." But Quentin gripped the handle when Ted nudged his palm with it.

Ted put his hand over Quentin's. "Now, get used to the weight, the feel of its momentum." He guided Quentin's swing, the hammer head swishing through the air. "Feel that?"

"Y-y-yes."

The toasted marshmallow smell wafted up from Quentin's skin, distracting Ted and going straight to his cock. He let go and stepped back before Quentin could feel Ted's own tool trying to get in on the action.

By this point, though, he knew what that aroma meant— incubus on the rise. *Screw it. We've been dancing around this for days.*

"Q-Bert, I've been thinking."

"A dangerous pastime," Quentin murmured.

"What?"

"Never mind. You were thinking. Carry on."

"I don't think handjobs qualify."

The hammer slipped out of Quentin's grip, narrowly missing his foot. "As—as what, precisely?"

"Consummation, of course. If you ask me, consummation requires an exchange of more than skin. It needs an exchange of fluids."

"I'm not sure Merriam-Webster would agree."

"Why? Is Merriam some kind of witch arbiter?"

Quentin laughed breathlessly. "It's not a person. It's a dictionary."

"Then who cares?" Ted didn't. He didn't care about much of anything right now except getting his hands—and his mouth—on Quentin's dick. Finding out if he tasted as much like marshmallows as he smelled. "Do you really want to show up next week and find out we're disqualified on a technicality?"

"No." Quentin drew out the word. "I suppose that would be bad." His pulse beat wildly in his throat, and Ted wanted to sooth it with his lips. *But that's not part of this deal.*

"Then PBJ."

"You want to eat a sandwich *now*?"

"Not peanut butter and jelly, you dork. Preemptive blowjobs. What do you say? We don't want the fine print to come back and bite us in the ass."

Quentin nibbled on his lower lip. "But, Ted, if I hurt you—"

"Hey. You can do anything you want, Quentin, and if you don't want to hurt me, you won't. End of story." Ted dropped to his knees, even though the plywood subflooring wasn't the softest. "I'll go first. In fact, you don't have to go at all if you don't want to. My mouth, your dick—I think that counts as doing it together."

"Oh trust me," Quentin said breathlessly as Ted opened his fly and took out that lovely cock. "I am absolutely doing it too."

The marshmallow scent intensified as Ted pumped Quentin's shaft twice, then licked slow and dirty, from base to tip, with an extra lap at the slit. "Oh man. What I wouldn't give for some melted chocolate right now."

"Wh-what?"

"You, Q-Bert—" Ted sucked in the head, then let it go with a pop "—are like the world's biggest and best s'more."

I should stop him. I should back away. I should be strong.

But when Ted hummed around Quentin's cock, he could do nothing, heat building in his core, pushing out, infusing his blood, his skin, his bones, and very possibly completely imploding his brain.

"Ted." He strained to get more than one word out, but that seemed to be the only one left in his vocabulary.

Ted pulled off and grinned up at him. "You need something, Q-Bert?"

Quentin nodded, running trembling fingers through Ted's hair, pushing that one wayward lock back. "But I shouldn't—"

"Enough. You've fed me that line before, Q, and I don't want to hear it. I'll say again—a hundred times, if I have to. I. Trust. You." Ted's eyes, so dark and deep, made Quentin's cock throb. "And I want you, no point in lying about it. From how you've been looking at me, I think you want me too."

"But Ted . . ." Devil take it, it was hard to think with his cock bobbing inches from Ted's mouth, Ted's energy enveloping him like a velvet cocoon. "I'm—"

"An incubus. I get that. And you know what I say? So fucking what?"

"You wouldn't say that if you were lying withered in a hospital bed, fighting for your next breath."

"Not gonna happen."

"How do you know? It happened before. I can't—" Quentin fumbled with his fly, trying to stuff his eager cock back into his underwear. "I can't let that happen to you."

Ted stood and circled Quentin's wrists gently with his huge hands. "Then don't. You're not evil. You're not selfish. And you're not controlled by your instincts any more than I am. Let go for once in your life, Quentin. Let go and trust that I'm strong enough to catch you before you fall."

He cradled Quentin's jaw, his palms callused but his touch gentle. Quentin imagined that if he could possibly open his eyes, he would see gold light shooting from Ted's fingertips, bathing Quentin's face.

Then Ted's mouth touched his own, Ted's beard soft and springy against Quentin's skin. Quentin inhaled sharply, lips parting, but Ted didn't take advantage and invade with his tongue. He kept the kiss chaste and soft and devastatingly sweet. Time spun out during that kiss. Had it just begun, or had it lasted for Quentin's entire life?

Maybe I didn't have a life until now.

Then Ted drew away, straightening up, and Quentin swayed forward, chasing that precious heat.

"Damn, Q-Bert. If there's one thing I'd change about you, I'd wish you were a tad taller so your mouth wasn't so far away."

"Sorry," Quentin whispered, still dizzy.

"Don't be. I'll just have to adjust my angle, that's all." He dropped to his knees again. "This is a good one. But I need a little more skin." He tucked his thumbs under Quentin's loose waistband and glanced up. "This okay?"

Quentin didn't reply. Couldn't. Instead, he shoved his pants and underwear down to his thighs, baring cock, balls, and ass.

"*That's* what I'm talking about. Now, just stand there and look at the lake."

"Lake?" Quentin stroked Ted's hair. "What lake?"

Ted grinned once more, then engulfed the head of Quentin's cock, and Quentin threw back his head, fighting a scream. *I can't . . . I shouldn't . . . I ought to pull out before I come, before I take too much, before I—*

Ted grabbed Quentin's ass in both hands and tugged him forward, swallowing around his cock, and it was too late.

Quentin came, and with each pulse, another burst of Ted's glorious golden energy—his enormous, gentle, generous essence—filled Quentin like the beat of a dragon's heart.

After Quentin's last spurt, Ted let go with a gasp and toppled backward onto the floor.

Terror spiked in Quentin's chest, nearly canceling his euphoria. "Ted! No!" He dropped onto his knees, hampered by his pants still bunched at his thighs and heedless of his bare ass hanging out in the chilly air.

Ted's body started to convulse. *No no no. I knew I shouldn't have allowed it. Haven't I learned anything from my own pathetic past? I—*

Then Ted grabbed his arm and hauled him down until he was lying across Ted's heaving chest and staring into Ted's laughing face.

"You're—you're not having a seizure?"

Ted laughed harder. "A seizure? Hell no, unless you call coming so hard in my pants that I saw stars a seizure. Hot *damn*, Q-Bert. Is that what sex with an incubus is like?"

Quentin pushed himself onto his knees. "Well obviously."

"Whoa. I bet 'cubi who aren't as uptight as you have no trouble getting dates. For a minute, it felt like my whole body was one giant dick."

Quentin shot him a disgusted look and stood, yanking his pants up to his waist again. "Unsurprising, since now you're acting like one."

"Hey." Ted sat up and took one of Quentin's hands in his. "I didn't mean that the way it came out. Seriously, you're amazing. *That* was amazing. And no matter what happens, I'll never regret that, for a while, you were my accidental husband."

I'll make absolutely sure you don't regret it. Quentin smiled tightly as he withdrew his hands. *I'm keeping you safe from me from now on. Restraint, damn it. I can do it. Even if it kills me.*

Chapter Sixteen

Quentin was hiding something. Ted was sure of it, but couldn't figure out what it might be. In the days since the epic blowjob—or EBJ, as Ted liked to think of it—Quentin hadn't been as weird about occasional contact between them. They hadn't had a repeat of either the handjob or the EBJ, more's the pity, but Quentin no longer sat scrunched at the far end of the couch when the two of them relaxed after dinner to watch a DVD or just chat. Of course he didn't get close enough to cuddle either, but Ted no longer felt as if Quentin were putting an imaginary wall between them.

I'm probably overthinking this. He'd only known Quentin for a few weeks. Maybe he always acted like he was hiding a giant secret. After all, every supe in the world hid a big honking secret from humans every day of their life. *Except when they violate the pact by pretending to be Sasquatch.* Although maybe that was technically a secret too.

Ted sighed and checked the biscuits in the oven. Almost done. He gave the home fries another stir on the stove top as the bacon spit in its pan. Tonight was the full moon. Tonight, he and Quentin would head into Portland to execute the escape clause ritual. They'd be officially ex-husbands and never see each other again.

Damn it.

Who'd have thought, when that little goateed dude had peeked around the lodge, staring at Ted's naked ass with such horror, that they'd end up actually *liking* each other.

More than liking, if Ted wanted to be honest, at least on his part. But there was no point thinking about that. Quentin had his life mapped out and so did Ted. They'd both made commitments to other people, and Ted had learned enough about Quentin in the last couple of weeks to know he'd honor his word, same as Ted would. They had that in common.

They had a lot in common. Damn damn *damn* it!

"Do I smell bacon?"

Ted turned at the sound of Quentin's voice. He was standing at the end of the counter, wearing one of the thermal shirts he'd bought at Stuff 'n' Things, and holy smokes! The buttons on his fly were undone. Ted swallowed. Did that mean—

"Ted?"

"Huh?" Ted finally tore his gaze away from Quentin's underwear and looked at his face. "Wait. You shaved off your goatee."

Quentin rubbed his smooth jaw. "Yes. After being in close proximity to a beard as prodigious as yours for the last nineteen days, it started to seem rather affected and anemic."

One part of Ted's brain said, *He counted the days?* while the other part was torn between how beautiful Quentin was with no goatee and his open fly. *Maybe he doesn't realize he forgot to close up?* "You . . . uh . . ." Ted jerked his chin in the general direction of Quentin's groin. "Left the barn door open."

Quentin glanced down and chuckled. "I know. It's embarrassing, but I can't button the blasted things anymore. Too much of your cooking, I fear."

He had been eating better, especially since he and Ted were helping out the construction crews whenever they were allowed to. A glow warmed Ted's chest as he noticed that Quentin was filling out his thermal shirt a lot better now.

Whoa. A *whole* lot better.

"Ted?" Quentin's voice held a note of worry. "Are you all right?"

Ted snapped himself out of his stare-fest, shaking himself as if he were in bear form. "Yeah. Sorry."

"I don't suppose you have a pair of pants that might fit me? Maybe a thirty-two?"

"Some of the jeans I wear in early spring might work. I'm at my skinniest then."

Quentin walked toward the stove, making his open fly gape and close as if it were winking at Ted. "You go check. I'll keep an eye on the bacon." He grinned, and without the goatee, the expression emphasized his pointed chin and . . . *Gah! Dimples!* "You've taught me enough about cooking that I can manage not to let it burn."

Ted held out the tongs. "Don't sell yourself short. You've gotten really good."

"At least I can read a recipe with the best of them." When Quentin took the tongs, their fingers brushed—one of hundreds of random touches since the EBJ—and Quentin's breath hitched, just like it always did.

What was it about that little half-hiccup that turned Ted's crank? He had no idea, only that it made his chest swell with some kind of stupid caveman pride because a big awkward guy like him could still affect a high-class guy like Quentin, even if they never went any further.

"I'll be right back."

Ted strode out of the kitchen and practically sprinted up the stairs so Quentin wouldn't notice the hard-on straining his jeans. *Stupid, stupid, stupid.* He couldn't fall for Quentin. He *couldn't.* Nothing about Quentin fit with Ted's plans or lifestyle. And then there was Rusty. He couldn't exactly leave him at the altar, even if Quentin was willing.

I need to be sensible. Quentin could never be happy stuck up here in the middle of nowhere. Yeah, Quentin had been doing okay for the last couple of weeks, but that was because this was temporary. Most people could endure anything when the end was in sight, but Ted had *seen* those suits when Quentin had hung them in the spare closet. He had *three fricking tuxes.* Who needed three tuxes? Who needed *one?*

Obviously a guy who wears tuxes as often as I wear jeans. Could that kind of guy be happy here forever? *And could I be happy somewhere else?* Ted tried to imagine himself fitting into Quentin's life and couldn't. For one thing, if he was forced to eat that microscopic food, or whatever it was called, he'd starve for sure.

And what about hibernation season? That hit right about the time Quentin's fancy events kicked into high gear. So yeah. Him and Quentin? Never gonna happen. *Just find the damn jeans and get through this day.*

He could do it. He was a bear shifter. If he was good for nothing else, he was good at enduring. Cold, hunger, hardship. *Heartbreak.* Yeah. He could do it.

In a pig's fucking eye.

He sighed and grabbed a pair of jeans from the stack he'd shoved to the back of the shelf once his belly had started expanding after the equinox, then stomped back downstairs.

Quentin was just pulling the biscuits out of the oven, and had already plated the potatoes and bacon. "You've made enough for an army again." He shot a cheeky grin over his shoulder. "Or a bear shifter heading into solstice, am I right?"

"Yeah." Ted held out the pants. "Here you go."

Quentin snatched them with another tiny brush of fingers— and another sharp little inhale. "Excellent. I couldn't really face the crew today with my briefs on display."

"Uh-huh. How do you want your eggs?"

"Eggs too? Pulling out all the stops for—" his smile wavered "—our last breakfast together?"

That was enough to deflate the semi caused by all of Quentin's little breath hitches. "Something like that."

Quentin cleared his throat, dropping his gaze to the jeans he was twisting in his hands. "Over easy then, please. Thank you." He hurried down the hall.

Ted transferred the biscuits to a cooling rack, then did his best to concentrate on cooking eggs. He broke the yolk on the first one—he put that on his own plate—but the second one was perfect. Fit for Quentin's last breakfast.

Quentin returned, jeans buttoned securely, although he'd rolled the cuffs up. "These are great except for the length. But then, I could hardly expect my ideal inseam, Mr. Bear Giant." He sat down at the counter on Ted's right, which was weird. He always sat at Ted's left after they'd endured too many elbow crashes from Quentin's left-handedness. "This looks great." He took a sip of his coffee, and his arm brushed Ted's as Ted reached for his own cup. Another little hitch in his breath, and Quentin's cup wobbled a little. "Sorry."

"No problem." Ted would take every touch he could get. Too bad he couldn't hold on to them. He'd store them next to his heart. *But they won't get used up come spring. They'll never get used up. I'll hold on to them forever.*

My secret.

Quentin was weak. He could admit it. After their encounter in the lodge, he hadn't been able to resist stealing little touches, little sips, of Ted ever since. Although he'd drawn the line at any bare skin other than hands. That was just tempting fate, and Quentin's resolve wasn't *that* strong.

It helped that they'd been so busy in the following days. Quentin had used the full force of his advocate-trained and grandmother-honed negotiating skills to get work crews up to the lodge. It helped that everyone within a fifty-mile radius liked Ted and was happy to help him.

Well, everyone except Larry, who was due to deliver something special today that had nothing to do with the lodge construction. Although Larry's animosity might be directed at Quentin personally rather than at Ted, Quentin wasn't inclined to cut him any slack. Larry had tried to put this delivery off, but Quentin had refused, pulling out the big guns—the threat to tell Shirl that Larry had been blowing her off.

Ted was eating the last of the biscuits—did that make eight? —as Quentin washed the breakfast dishes. The man could definitely put away the food. Quentin smiled at him, no doubt with a completely besotted expression. Devil take it, it was their last day and he was tired of hiding his feelings. Although based on the way Ted smirked at him while licking a smear of raspberry jam off his thumb, Quentin hadn't been entirely successful in his stealth anyway.

He put away the last plate. "What's on your agenda for today?"

"You tell me. You're the one with a different mile-long honey-do list every day."

Quentin shrugged at Ted's casual use of *honey*—he didn't mean it literally. "It's dealer's choice today. The only absolute is our appointment at Supernatural Selection at 10:45."

"Ah. Okay." He set the biscuit down half-finished. "What about you?"

"There are several deliveries arriving today, and I have a call with an interior designer at nine thirty."

Ted's brows rose. "Interior designer? I'm not sure what I'd do with one of those. Besides, shouldn't you wait until we have an actual interior?"

Quentin snorted and flicked the dish towel at Ted before he hung it on the stove handle. "It's never too early. We want— *You* want someone to get a feel for the place now, so they can consult on some of the finish materials. Flooring, appliances, tile, window treatments that might require carpentry. That sort of thing."

"That makes sense, I guess." Ted's voice held a giant helping of doubt.

"Besides, this is an investment for me, remember?" He stuck his nose in the air. "I want it to live up to my extremely high standards. I expect to recoup my investment *tenfold*."

Ted chuckled, a warm burr that always went straight to Quentin's cock. "Only ten?"

"Well, ten at a minimum."

Ted stood up, taking a last sip of his coffee. "Since you'll be tied up, then, I think I'll help out the drywall crew. They're installing the Sheetrock in the second-floor suites today."

"Good." That would keep Ted out of the cabin and busy while Quentin staged his surprise. "See you at lunchtime?"

"You know it. And maybe . . ." He glanced down at his feet. "I mean, if you don't mind, maybe we could head into town early. Go out for dinner or drinks or something before our appointment. You know. A little celebration."

Quentin's heart stuttered. "Celebrating your lucky release, you mean?"

Ted scowled. "No, you doofus. Our friendship. Our mutual investment, if you like. Because you won't just disappear on me, will you, Q-Bert? I mean, I know we can't hang out together because of the escape spell and all, but we'll still be friends, won't we?"

Maybe it's a good thing we won't be able to meet face-to-face, because I don't know if I can stand to see you with someone else, someone who can make you happier than I ever could. So he lied. "Of course. Now shoo. I've got deliveries to wrangle, and unless I miss my guess, the drywall crew just arrived." He tilted his head. "Their trucks sound like a herd of marauding dinosaurs."

Ted chuckled again. "I'll be sure to let them know." He hesitated, his dark gaze riveted on Quentin's face, making him shiver. For a moment, Quentin was certain Ted was going to close the distance between them and kiss him—something he'd only done that one glorious, disastrous time.

But instead, his lips quirked in a smile. "I like the new look. Although the goatee wasn't anemic *or* affected, just so you know." He turned and strode across the cabin, grabbing his coat before he lifted one hand in farewell and disappeared out the door.

Quentin heaved an enormous sigh and leaned his forehead against the refrigerator. "What the devil am I *doing*? I'm an *incubus*. 'Cubi don't *moon* over people." His cousins would mock him for *decades* if they ever found out he'd fallen so hard for someone.

They'll never find out. Because after today he'd never see Ted in person again. He'd keep any future communications brief, businesslike, and totally impersonal. *Right. That's as likely as the angelic host inviting the demon hordes for tea and crumpets.* Scowling, he pulled out his phone and dialed his least favorite driver.

"Larry. I trust you'll be here at eleven."

"That's not a very good time for me."

"Nevertheless, I expect to see you then. And by the way, Shirl has a few packages for me too. I'll give her a call and let her know you'll be stopping by to pick them up on your way at, shall we say, ten thirty?"

"Fine," Larry growled, and hung up.

Quentin laughed evilly. "Suck it up, you asshole. If you ever try to victimize Ted again, I'll—"

He'd what? Permanently separated from Ted, it wasn't as if he would be here to see it. Somehow, though, he'd keep an eye on Dewton and its inhabitants, because no matter how odd it was for a 'cubi to become invested in anything outside their families, this place *mattered*.

Chapter
Seventeen

Later that morning, while Quentin was in a meeting with the crew foreman, Ted took a break to head back to the cabin. He'd been running on autopilot since breakfast, which luckily wasn't too bad since he was just following the orders of the drywall guys. But the whole time, he'd been racking his brains, trying to figure out what to do.

His last day with Quentin. Sure, Quentin said they'd still be friends, but they'd both be married to other people. And since they could never meet face-to-face again, Quentin could never give Ted *that look*. Or if he did—in a video call or a selfie or just by tone of voice, because Ted knew how *that look* sounded too—neither one of them could do anything about it.

He burst into the cabin, slamming the door behind him, and ran up the stairs. The fancy folder from Supernatural Selection wasn't where he thought it was—on the shelf next to his T-shirts. *Oh, right. It's in Quentin's room.* He winced. Not Quentin's room. *Rusty's* room. He'd put it on the shelf in there the first day Quentin had showed up, when they were both trying to figure out how to pull their asses out of the mutual fire.

He galumphed downstairs again. The folder was right where he'd tossed it after taking it out of his backpack. He crossed the room to the shelf, trying to ignore Quentin's packed suitcases sitting by the door. He opened the folder and pawed through the contents, scattering papers across the shelf.

Dr. Kendrick was right. I shouldn't put my happiness in somebody else's hands. I should find it myself, work for it, earn it. His gaze snagged on Rusty's dossier. He picked it up, studying the picture on the first page. Rusty was a big guy, almost as tall and wide as Ted, although his waist was narrower than Ted's was at the moment. In his picture, he was smiling, but he looked sad. How would he feel if he found out his perfect match was trying to find a way to dump him?

But if we do get married, what happens if I can't love him?

Ted set the dossier down on the shelf carefully, as if dropping it might cause Rusty pain somehow. He dug his phone out of his pocket and pulled up the Supernatural Selection messaging app with all the texts between him and Rusty that he had never deleted before the enforced radio silence. Those little awkward conversations, and the anticipation they'd sparked of new adventures on the horizon, used to warm Ted like a fire in the woodstove. But now? Not so much. He shut down the app and tucked his phone away.

I never expected love in the first place, at least not right off. I only wanted a companion. A guard against loneliness. Someone to share my life with. Supernatural Selection didn't guarantee love. They only guaranteed a perfect match.

What the hell did that mean, anyway? He looked at Rusty's picture again. Rusty had a beard. Not as full as Ted's, and it was kind of reddish while the hair on his head was brown, which was kinda weird. *What would he look like clean-shaven?* Because Rusty's size, his facial hair, his activities—no wonder he'd been picked as a match for Ted. They might as well be the same person.

Why would I want another version of me? Isn't one enough? But a month ago, he hadn't questioned it. Had been thrilled about it, in fact. The day he'd visited Dr. Kendrick's office, he'd been crowing about his luck. Guess luck could turn on you faster than a rattler, and bite just as deep.

They don't guarantee love, but I found it anyway. Too bad it was with the wrong person.

He sighed and trudged out of the cabin and down the path to the lodge clearing. Quentin had apparently finished with his meeting, because he was trying to haul a bag of Portland cement off a stack some idiot delivery guy—probably Larry—had left in the middle of the clearing. If it rained on that shit—well, it wouldn't be good.

Ted trotted over and took the bag off Quentin's shoulder. "Hey, Q-Bert. Let me handle that. Wouldn't want you to hurt yourself."

Quentin tossed him an eye roll. "I was doing just fine. But you can help. Let's get this up on the porch." He lifted another of the sixty-pound bags without so much as a grunt.

"Whoa, Q-Bert. Where'd you pick up those muscles? Pretty sure Shirl doesn't carry 'em at Stuff 'n' Things."

"Shut up." Quentin's mouth twitched. "I'm stronger than I look. Let's get this taken care of. I have another delivery scheduled in fifteen minutes and the foreman would like you back on drywall duty."

"Sure thing."

They carted the rest of the bags to the porch, and Ted started through the door to join the crew when Quentin caught his arm.

"Ted? I told the crews they could cut out early today. They're quitting at one."

"Okay."

"I thought—" Quentin swallowed, glancing down at his feet and then up at Ted from under his lashes "—maybe we could have a late lunch and spend a little time together before we have to hit the road to Portland."

Ted smiled, but it hurt like he'd been knifed in the gut. "Yeah. Good plan. I'll see you at one."

Ever since Larry had left, Quentin's nerves had been on edge —and it wasn't just because of proximity to the man's revolting energy. No, it was anticipation, pure and simple.

Because he was going to do this.

Yes, he'd seen the picture of Rusty laid out on the shelf in the bedroom—Rusty's bedroom—so he knew perfectly well that Ted was anticipating finally joining with his true partner, his perfect match.

And maybe it made Quentin a selfish SOB, as selfish as any of his 'cubi relatives, but he *didn't care.* Until 10:45 tonight they were still married to each other, and after that, they'd never be able to meet each other face-to-face again. This was their last opportunity—their *only* opportunity—for intimacy, and Quentin intended to take it, whether it damned him forever or not.

Quentin cleared away all the trash from his preparations, just as the front door opened.

"Q-Bert? You here?"

"Just a second." He stuffed the trash in the closet to deal with later. He smoothed his hair and stepped into the hallway, pulling the door closed behind him. "Hey."

Ted's answering grin warmed Quentin from his toes to his scalp. *I am so gone.* Ted's gaze slid away from Quentin's, his eyes widening. "Whoa. You made lunch."

"Yes, Ted. I can be taught."

"Never doubted that for a minute. You're the smartest guy I know."

"Surely not," Quentin protested, but he was secretly thrilled at Ted's approval.

Ted walked over to the counter where Quentin had set out the food. "Where did you get fresh fish?"

"I had Larry bring it up for me when he delivered . . . other things. Hungry?"

"I'll say. Let me wash my hands and then let's eat."

Despite the lovely flavor of the swordfish steaks—and Quentin had to admit he'd done a stellar job on them—he found himself toying with his food instead of eating it.

At first, with Ted's usual focus on his meals, he didn't seem to notice Quentin's distracted state. But after he'd eaten barely half his fish and rice pilaf, he set his fork down. "Okay, Q-Bert. Out with it. What's wrong?"

"It's not that there's anything *wrong*, precisely. But I want to show you something."

Ted pushed his stool back. "Okay, then. Show me."

"You can finish eating first."

"Not if it means you *don't* eat. Come on. Spill."

Quentin took a deep breath. "All right. This way." He stood up and led Ted down the hall to Rusty's bedroom door. He turned to face Ted, who was regarding him with a tiny smile, his head tilted to one side. Quentin pushed the door open. "Surprise."

Ted took one step into the room and froze, taking in his beautiful bed frame now crowned with a top-of-the-line king-sized mattress and bedding in brown, russet, and navy. "Where'd you— I can't believe—" He turned to Quentin, his throat working and eyes suspiciously bright. "Why'd you do this?"

"Because I wanted it to be ready for your dreams, Ted. You deserve that."

Suddenly Quentin was enveloped in Ted's embrace, Ted's beard soft against his neck, as he whispered in Quentin's ear. "Thank you."

The energy rolling off Ted, the greater skin contact that Quentin had tried to avoid for so long, overwhelmed him for a moment. He wanted to sink down on the floor and revel in it. *But this is Rusty's room. Not mine. So we'll go upstairs to his room. Soon.* He pulled back—reluctantly—and smiled up at Ted. "You're welcome. Shall we finish our lunch?"

Ted looked as if he were about to say something else, but he nodded, sniffing a bit, and returned to the counter.

Quentin tried to eat then. After all, the big reveal was over. *That's not the big reveal and you know it.* He managed to choke down a green bean or two before sighing into his iced tea.

Ted chuckled and set his fork down again. "Now what?"

One time. One time and never again. If he's in distress, I'll stop. For him, I can stop.

"I've been thinking."

"That's nothing new. You think all the time. I'm surprised your brain has any treads left with all the mileage you put on it." He pushed his plate away, even though he was only three-quarters done, and picked up his iced tea. "About what?"

Quentin traced circles on the counter, unable to meet Ted's eyes. "I'm not sure blowjobs qualify as complete consummation."

Ted choked on his tea, spraying it over the counter. "Say what?"

"I think—" Quentin cleared his throat as he mopped up the tea spit-take with his napkin "—additional penetration might be required."

"P-p-penetration?"

"Yes. In fact, I think that's the standard definition of 'consummate.'"

"Let me get this straight. You want me to fuck you?"

Quentin stuck his nose in the air. "Maybe *I* want to fuck *you*."

Ted grinned. "I could go for that."

"Or maybe both. I mean, we wouldn't want to get there tonight and—"

"Get disqualified on a technicality," they said simultaneously.

Chapter Eighteen

Ted knocked his stool over in his eagerness to get this show on the road. He couldn't stop grinning like a fool, because this was finally happening. A tiny niggle of *something*—sadness? Regret?—wormed its way into his chest. *The last time. The only time.* He pushed it away, because at least it would happen *once.* He wouldn't live his entire life without having sex with someone he loved.

Quentin righted the stool, smiling at him indulgently. "Eager, are we, Mr. Farnsworth?"

Ted froze, his grin fading. "Aren't you?"

Quentin darted forward and placed his hands on Ted's chest. "I am. Of course I am." He rose on his toes and pressed a soft kiss to Ted's lips—which somehow now had a laser-beam connection to Ted's cock. Ted would have been happy to stand there making out all afternoon—or at least most of it—with that lovely toasted marshmallow smell drifting around him, but Quentin drew back. "And we don't have much time, so . . ." He lifted his eyebrow like a question mark.

Yeah. Not much time. And Ted wanted all the time he could get. "Lead the way."

Quentin's hands drifted over Ted's chest as he walked by, like a trail of liquid fire. *If that's what his hands feel like on top of my clothes, what will they feel like on my skin?* The handjob seemed so far away now, and it had been great, phenomenal even, but it had nothing on the brush of Quentin's fingertips along the sleeve of his flannel shirt, the promise of what was about to happen. *Things are different now. I'm different. He's different.* Ted was pretty sure Quentin had way more than a teasing touch in mind right now, and Ted was absolutely on board with that. One hundred and ten percent.

Quentin took a fold of the sleeve between two fingers and drew Ted down the hallway, and the smile he tossed over his shoulder? *Ursa give me strength.* He'd never imagined anyone— especially someone as classy as Quentin—would look at him like that.

When Quentin started up the stairs, Ted put out a paw and took his hand. "Not up there. That bed's not good enough for you." He backed up two steps and pushed open the door to the bedroom. "In here."

Quentin's eyes widened. "But—but that's Rusty's room."

"You said you'd fixed it up for my dreams." He drew Quentin close, capturing their joined hands between their chests. "Turns out my dream is you."

Quentin's face crumpled. "Ted—"

"Shhh. It's okay. I know this is a one-time deal. I know we'll never see each other again after tonight." He smiled crookedly. "Dreams never last long anyway, right? Everyone has to wake up eventually. But at least they're something to remember." He dipped his head and kissed Quentin again, soft and sweet. "Come on. Let's get naked."

Quentin's laugh caught on one of those little half-hiccups. "I thought you'd never ask."

But when they stumbled into the room, shedding clothes in their wake, and finally faced that perfect bed, Ted realized he didn't want to rush. Well, except for the naked part. That was a given. For everything else though? They might not have a lot of time—although Ted would be willing to push their dinner in Portland back an hour or three—but they'd damn well make it count.

He gazed at Quentin as he kicked his pants away. *Ursa's bones.* The last time he'd seen Quentin completely naked—the day of the handjob—either he hadn't paid attention or Quentin had *really* buffed up with regular meals and all the work they'd been doing. Ted remembered him being a little scrawny, with narrow shoulders and a hollow chest and an almost concave belly, although with gorgeous skin. Not anymore.

Well, the skin was still gorgeous—and holy smokes, the *smell.* Without his clothes, the toasted marshmallow aroma was even stronger. Ted wanted to lick every inch of that skin. And there was way more of it to lick now.

Quentin's shoulders had widened, his pecs had definition—not crazy gym-rat definition, but just enough—and *whoa.* Stomach muscles. Not a six-pack maybe, but who wanted one of those anyway?

And then there was that dick.

"Wow, Q-Bert. Just . . . wow."

Quentin ducked his head and peeked at Ted from under his lashes, sending Ted's cock bobbing against his belly. "You're not so bad yourself."

"Pfft. Big ol' plodding bear shifter. Nothing to write home about."

"Trust me, writing is the last thing I want to do right now. And you'll have to allow me to disagree with you about your appearance. You—" he stepped forward and slid his hands over Ted's chest "—are incredibly sexy. I thought so when I first I saw you." His mouth quirked in a sly smile. "Maybe it was the outfit you were wearing at the time. Very stylish." He pressed a kiss between Ted's pecs, causing Ted's breath to hitch for a change. "And I do love the way it fits."

"Yeah?" His voice was hoarse. "I don't know. I think you may need to check the measurements. All of 'em."

Quentin chuckled. "It would be my pleasure." He opened his mouth over Ted's nipple, flicking it with his tongue, and when he sucked, teasing the nub with his teeth, Ted threw back his head and roared.

With Rory, it had never been like this, like the two of them completed a perfect circuit, an unbroken circle of golden fire. Quentin could *see* it, flowing from his hands into Ted and back again with every brush of Ted's fingers, every stroke of his tongue, every press of his lips. Gold and fire and heat, filling him, filling them both. Surely without the walls of the cabin, the glow would be visible for miles, possibly from space.

Seated astride Ted's thighs, Quentin sucked Ted's finger into his mouth, swirling his tongue to activate the glands in his cheeks, and when he pulled off, Ted's finger was coated in 'cubi slick.

"What the—" Ted dabbed his finger with his thumb. "You can make your own lube?"

Quentin grinned, leaning forward and swiveling his hips to slide their erections together. "It's antiseptic too. No condoms necessary, regardless of our partner's nature."

Ted's eyebrows rose. "You're kidding."

"What can I say? We sex demons are *always* prepared."

Ted sniffed his finger, and his grin could have lit up the sky. "It smells like toasted marshmallows."

"Please. I prefer to think of it as—"

"The burnt sugar crust on crème brûlée," they said together.

"Whatever you call it, I'm putting it inside you." He cupped the back of Quentin's neck with his other hand and pulled him down until their lips were a breath apart, Quentin's ass at a convenient angle for Ted's finger to tease his hole. "And then I'm putting *me* inside you."

Quentin shuddered as Ted's finger breached him, lighting him up, making him gasp. *You're already there.*

He sealed his mouth over Ted's, their kiss escalating far beyond soft and sweet. When Ted's finger hit his gland, they both moaned, as if the pleasure that fountained up through Quentin's core burst over them both in heat and glory.

Ted ripped his mouth away, dropping his head back on the pillow. "Now," he gasped. "I need to be in you now or I might actually die."

No, you won't. I won't let you. But mother of fire, I might. Quentin gulped in one desperate breath after another until he could croak, "Just a minute."

Ted raised his head, his expression mingled with pain and disbelief. "You want to *wait*? What the—"

"Trust me," Quentin panted. "You'll like this."

He scooted down the bed until he was face to single eye with Ted's glorious cock. His heart thundered in his ears. How long had it been since he'd done this? How long had it been since he'd allowed himself to even *think* about it? *Too long.*

Ted trailed his fingers down Quentin's spine. "I think I'm starting to like it already."

Just you wait. And Quentin engulfed Ted's enormous cock, taking it *all* the way down with zero hesitation in true 'cubi fashion.

"Ursa's fucking *teeth*," Ted shouted, his fingers grasping Quentin's hip. Then, as Quentin hollowed his cheeks, activating his glands again and pulling up and down and up and down, Ted's back bowed and his legs trembled as if he were ready to shoot.

Luckily, 'cubi slick included an orgasm retardant too. Ted wouldn't come until Quentin was ready. *Until we're both ready.*

Shivering in delicious anticipation, he pulled off, leaving Ted's cock lubed and glistening, and Ted himself panting on the pillow, his eyes dark and smoldering. Keeping their gazes locked, Quentin straddled Ted's groin. "Put it in me. Put it in me now, just like you promised."

Ted's smile was wicked. He grabbed Quentin's hip with one hand and his cock with the other and guided the tip to Quentin's hole. Quentin gasped, eyelids fluttering. *So long. It's been so long I'd almost forgotten what pre-come feels like down there.* But he hadn't forgotten what came next. Between the preparation with Ted's finger and the 'cubi ability to *relaaax,* Ted slid in with no resistance in one smooth glide.

When Ted was fully seated—and Quentin was fully seated as well, his ass on Ted's pelvis—Quentin couldn't move, alive and full and *complete* for the first time in his three hundred years. He might have sat there forever, if Ted hadn't grasped his hips and lifted him, holding him suspended as he pumped into Quentin, first with long, slow strokes and then with short, sharp thrusts. Long and slow again, followed by short and sharp.

Quentin closed his eyes, head tilted back, lips parted. *His rhythm. It's like us. Ted, tall and steady. Me, small and abrupt.* And together, the pattern sent Quentin flying as he hadn't done since he'd lost his wings.

Ted was grunting now with effort—even a man as strong as him couldn't hold Quentin up indefinitely. *And even sex demons can't hold out forever.* Quentin opened his eyes. Sweat matted Ted's forehead, that wayward lock of hair plastered to his skin.

"Let me," Quentin murmured. He loosed Ted's hands off his own hips and laced their fingers together instead. Then, with his weight supported on their joined hands and his knees, he began to rock in opposition to Ted's thrusts, matching his cadence before speeding up, heading for the tipping point, that place where the heat building between them, inside them, could erupt, flying outward.

Ted grimaced, his neck muscles straining as he began to pulse, and at the first spill of his semen *inside, right there,* Quentin cried out his own release, ropes of white lacing Ted's chest hair and—just slightly—his beard.

Ted jerked one last time, triggering another burst of gold in Quentin's chest, then drew Quentin down to nestle against his side.

He kissed the top of Quentin's head, and Quentin nearly purred, snuggling closer, head on Ted's chest, reveling in the beat of his heart. *Thump thump thump.* Strong and steady, no faltering. Rory's staggering heartbeat was the first clue Quentin had gotten that something was wrong.

But it's only one time. Once won't hurt him. He's fine. More than fine. He's spectacular.

Ted chuckled, bouncing Quentin's head and sending the usual *zing* to his balls. Quentin raised his head to see Ted smirking. "What?"

"Guess they can't say we didn't consummate, eh?"

Ted's words sent a wash of cold surging over Quentin, extinguishing his golden afterglow. Supernatural Selection. The escape clause. *Rusty.* Apparently Ted's dreams could be conveniently replaced as necessary. *And my dreams? They're impossible anyway. Because for us, "forever" is less than a year, even if we don't go through with the ritual.*

Quentin rolled away and sat up on the edge of the bed.

"Q-Bert? What's wrong?"

"Nothing. But we should get ready to go."

"Now?" Ted propped himself up on one elbow. "It'll only take us a couple of hours to get to town and we don't need to be there until late. What's the rush?"

"We have dinner reservations."

"Yeah, at seven. It's barely three. Besides, we can always cancel and make dinner here." He leaned over and kissed the base of Quentin's spine, which, devil take it, made him shiver. "I'm sure we can find plenty of ways to pass the time. I think you might have mentioned a little turnabout?"

Quentin launched himself off the bed, snatching his briefs off the floor. "*No!* I don't think that's a good idea. We should start distancing ourselves. For our own good."

Ted grabbed some tissues out of the box on the bedside table. "That'll come soon enough. Why rush it?"

"Because." He pulled on his briefs and picked up his pants. "Just because."

"That's the worst reason in the history of ever. You know that, right?" Ted stood up and circled the bed. "Can't I kiss you? I really want to kiss you." Ted waggled his eyebrows. "Your kisses are addictive."

Quentin froze. "Don't say that."

"Why not? You're a good kisser. A good everything."

I shouldn't. But they had so little time left. *And we've already established that I'm weak.* So Quentin went into his arms and lifted his chin for a kiss. The stroke of Ted's tongue against his sent another spike of *gold-heat-want* down his spine to pool in his balls. *Devil take it, stand down.*

Ted started chuckling in the middle of the kiss, and Quentin pulled away, a little offended if truth be told. "What's so funny?"

"Nothing. It's not as awkward to kiss you anymore."

Quentin jerked away. "Glad to hear it." He thrust his legs into his pants.

"Aw, Q-Bert. Don't get in a snit." Ted pulled on his own jeans. "It's just that . . . Heh."

"Now what?"

"It's funny, but— Nothing, I guess." He shook his head and pointed at Quentin's ankles. "You expecting a flood?"

Quentin glanced down. The cuffs he'd rolled on the pant legs were at least three inches above his ankles now instead of resting on the top of his instep. Ice balled in his belly. *Not awkward to kiss me—because I'm five inches taller than I was half an hour ago.*

He looked up, fists clenched in horror, to see Ted peering down at his stomach with a bemused expression. "You know, I must have been working harder than I thought this week." He glanced up at Quentin. "Check it out? My belly's gone. I don't have a six-pack, but hey. Flat is good, right?"

No no no. Flat is not good. Flat on you plus height on me means I'm draining you, just like I drained Rory.

Panic burned through his veins like acid, and he backed up until he ran into the wall. "Stay away. Get away. Get *out!*"

"What the fuck, Q? I know it's not technically my bedroom, but why should I leave?"

"Because I can't be near you now."

Ted's face turned stormy. "Really? Suddenly I repulse you? Afraid when your clan rep sees me tonight that I'll *embarrass* you?"

"That's not it. Damn it, I thought it would be okay. I thought once wouldn't hurt. I thought I could control myself. But I was wrong. *I did this to you!* You need to get away from me. Far away."

"That'll be a trick, considering we'll be sitting within three feet of one another for two hours in my truck. If you—"

"Devil take it, you stupid bear, will you just fucking *leave!*"

Ted jerked back as if Quentin had struck him. *I'm sorry, I'm sorry. I don't mean it. You know I don't mean it.* But if it kept Ted away, kept him safe from Quentin's parasitic urges, it was worth it. Better hurt feelings than dead any day. *Better that he lives without me than dies with me.*

"Fine. I need to get some different fucking pants anyway." He stalked toward the door.

Quentin slid down the wall, huddling there with his arms around his knees, as far as possible from Ted's enticing energy. He put his head down so he couldn't see Ted walk out.

Chapter Nineteen

Damn it, damn it, *damn it.*

Ted tromped up the stairs, holding his pants up around his waist. *What the hell is Quentin's problem?* He stalked over to his shelves and dug around until he found another pair of his "spring" pants, then switched the current pair for them. He had a strong urge to flop down on his bed and brood, because weren't the two of them going to be separated soon enough? For *eternity*, for fuck's sake?

But if Quentin insisted that Ted leave, then *fine.* He'd leave. Not just the room, but the whole fucking cabin, no matter how much his body—and, let's face it, his heart—screamed for him to go back down and take Quentin in his arms again, find out what was upsetting him, soothe him, kiss him, lick him—

No!

Ted knew way too much about the awkward consequences of overstaying his welcome. It was the story of his fucking *life*—not to mention the story of his life fucking. *Damn isolationist bear shifters.* That was one of the upsides of Supernatural Selection—his perfect match was guaranteed to want him, at least enough to commit.

Well, Quentin isn't my perfect match, is he? He'd made that super clear just now. Man, nothing killed afterglow like a guy kicking you out of the bedroom.

He pulled on a tee, a flannel shirt, and a clean pair of socks and stomped downstairs, then stared at his stockinged feet. *Shit.*

His boots were in the bedroom with Quentin. No way was he going back in there to face that look of horror on Quentin's face. He kept a battered pair of cross-trainers in the hall closet, so he shoved his feet into them and grabbed his coat off the hook. He paused with his hand on the door, straining his ears for any sounds of distress coming from the bedroom, but the place was silent except for the crackle of the fire and his own heart pounding in his ears.

He stepped outside into the afternoon sun. A distant laugh and the slam of a car door made him jerk his head toward the lodge. Apparently the crew hadn't all knocked off early, which meant Ted couldn't shift to get away, damn it. Even if he stripped off inside the woods, he couldn't swear he'd be completely out of sight, and the last thing he needed right now was the council on his ass about Secrecy Pact violations.

But he wanted nothing more than to escape, maybe hole up in his cave until it was time to head into town and end this whole fricking farce, but he couldn't get there and back in time without shifting. Instead, he shoved his hands in his pockets and took off down the trail behind the cabin, the one that led to his favorite fishing spot. He'd sit on the outcropping overlooking the stream that fed into the lake and . . . and what? Mope? Brood? Mourn?

Yeah, that's what it feels like. Mourning something that he wouldn't have again, that apparently he'd *never* had, even though for a while this afternoon, gazing into Quentin's eyes, he thought he'd finally found home. *Stupid. I knew it had to be temporary. What part of "no face-to-face contact for all eternity" didn't I get?*

He smacked a fir branch out of his way and glared at a squirrel that stood on its haunches at the side of the path. "What are you looking at? Get out of here!" He broke out of the trees next to the creek and scooped up a small stone, winding up to send it into the water.

"Ted?"

He dropped the pebble and whirled. Matt was sitting on the flat rock, fishing pole in his hand, staring at Ted with wide, startled eyes from under the brim of his Mariners ball cap. "Matt. Sorry. Didn't know anyone was here."

Matt pretended to wipe sweat off his brow. "Whew! For a minute I thought you were yelling at me to scram."

"What? Oh that. No, I was just talking to a squirrel." That didn't sound crazy or pathetic at all. "Didn't mean to disturb you. I'll just . . ." What? Go somewhere else where he wasn't wanted?

"Hey, it's your property. I'm just an invited squatter."

"Doesn't mean you don't have the right to your privacy." *Wait. Quentin has a right to privacy too.* It wasn't like he had anywhere else to go. *Maybe I should stop acting like a big baby and get over myself.* Ted sighed. "Mind if I join you?"

Matt patted a spot next to him. "Like I said, it's your property. I've got an extra pole if you want to try your luck."

Ted stepped up and sat down next to Matt, his legs dangling over the water. "Catch anything?"

"Nah. But that's not always the point, is it? Fishing is more a process than a product-driven activity."

Ted huffed a laugh. "Yeah. Going by my success rate, anyway." He frowned down at the water. Maybe that was true of relationships too. He'd been looking at his marriage as a *thing*, like a machine that would be whole and perfect and functional right off the bat, as soon as he said "I do." But if his temporary marriage was any example, it wasn't like that at all. It was two people working things out every day, some good, some bad. It wasn't something you could *have*. It was something you *did*. Something you continued to do, if you expected the machine to keep running. It was never going to be *done*. *Unless your husband kicks you out. Or unless you had the wrong husband to begin with.* He sighed.

"Thinking deep thoughts?" Matt held out his spare pole.

"Yeah, I guess." Ted took the pole and cast into the stream.

"Care to share?"

"I dunno. Love. Life. The universe and everything. I have no fucking clue what I'm doing."

Matt cast his line into the water again. "Join the crowd, bro. Join the crowd."

Quentin huddled in the corner, rocking back and forth, while Ted stomped around the cabin. *At least he's ambulatory. I haven't sucked all the life out of him.* Because despite Ted's confidence that Quentin could control himself, monitor his own behavior, corral his incubus instincts, Quentin hadn't thought of that at all while they were making love. His entire focus had been on the way they fit together, the way the energy flowed between them, how it made him feel alive and vital and strong for the first time since before Rory.

Of course I felt strong—I was stealing his strength.

He didn't know how long the cabin had been silent when he raised his head, but gooseflesh crept along his arms in the chill. *The fire must be dying.* But when he staggered into the living area, pulling his thermal shirt over his head, the fire was still crackling merrily in the woodstove, oblivious to the fact that Quentin's whole life had upended in the space of an hour.

Wait. If the fire isn't dead, if the cabin is still warm, why am I chilled? His belly tumbled to his feet. *The rush from sex is dissipating. I'm coming down, crashing.*

And if Quentin was crashing, Ted must be too. What if his vigor as he left was nothing but the artificial high that any 'cubi's partner felt in the afterglow? Quentin should have prepared a hot drink, a protein-rich snack, made Ted take a nap. Something to replenish his energy. But he'd sent him away because Quentin was a coward, afraid he'd lose control, afraid his desire for another round of sex to feed his incubus appetites would overwhelm his concern for Ted's welfare.

Where the fuck is my phone? Ted was out there somewhere with no idea what the aftermath of incubus sex was like. What if he lost consciousness? What if he fell into the lake? Or hit his head? Or passed out somewhere and got attacked by a mountain lion? *Anything* could happen!

He found the phone exactly where he'd left it—in his messenger bag, charged and ready for the trip to Portland. He pulled up the fae communications app that Alun had installed, and closed his eyes with a brief and heartfelt *thank you* when Alun's number was already registered. He chose the audio option—he wasn't ready for Alun to see him right now. He was certainly thinking like a maniac, so he probably looked like one too. 'Cubi—any demons, really—could turn damn scary when under severe emotional stress.

He recited the invocation and pushed Connect. "Come on, come on. Please be there. Please—"

"Dr. Kendrick's office. This is David. How may I help you?"

"David, this is Quentin Bertrand-Harrington. Is Alun available?"

"Oh, hello, Mr. Bertrand-Harrington. No, I'm afraid not. He's at a council meeting. Is there anything I can do? If you don't mind my saying so, you sound a bit flustered."

Quentin clutched his hair, pacing back and forth across the room. "No. I really need—" Wait. David was an *achubydd*. If Ted was ill, suffering from incubus energy drain, maybe David could cure him. "Actually, yes. I'm afraid there's something wrong with Ted. Could you come out here and check on him, please?"

"Mr. Farnsworth is ill?" David's cheerful voice took a turn for the pragmatic. "What are his symptoms?"

"I don't know what they are right this minute."

"Can you check on him? I'll hold."

"No. He's not here. That's the problem. He left. Well, I kicked him out really, but that was because I didn't want to kill him."

"I . . . see. Is there a particular reason why you wanted to murder Mr. Farnsworth?"

Quentin ground his molars together. "I didn't *want* to kill him, but I'm afraid I might have. Inadvertently. From . . . from . . . gah!"

"Oh. Was there perhaps hot incubus sex involved?"

"Yes!" Quentin wailed.

"What happened? And no, I don't want *those* details. I mean what makes you think Mr. Farnsworth was adversely affected?"

"He's lost flesh."

"So he was emaciated? Shriveled?"

"No. Actually, he had a six-pack instead of his—" Quentin rested his hand on his middle "—hibernation belly."

"Well, from what I've learned since we met, 'cubi thrall desiccation can't occur from a single encounter. The worst effects are caused by prolonged exposure. I know bear shifters start sleeping more at this time of year, but has he been sleeping longer than you consider normal? Had difficulty rousing in the morning? Seemed to be losing stamina?"

"N-n-no. In fact, he's been getting up earlier than usual to help the construction crews. He's been eating a lot, of course. We both have. But that's normal for this time of year, isn't it?"

"Yes." Quentin heard a rhythmic tapping, as if David were drumming a pencil against his desk. "Forgive me for questioning your concerns, but it doesn't sound as if he's suffering at all."

"You don't understand. I've been in this situation before. I can't— If something happened to Ted because of me, I'd never forgive myself. Can't you come out here? Check him out yourself?"

"I would if I could, but I can't gate through Faerie on my own. I need Alun to take me."

"Please. He's out in the woods. What if he's incapacitated? Even if the sex aftermath doesn't kill him, he might become disoriented and injure himself."

"Hmmm." More tapping. "Let me call my brother-in-law. I expect I can talk him into bringing me."

"Thank you."

"Hold tight. I'll be there as soon as I can."

Quentin sank down on the sofa, letting the phone slide out of his hand onto the cushions. He felt as if he were suffocating, the collar of his thermal too tight around his throat. He tugged at it, but it didn't help. *Fuck it.* He ripped the damn thing from collar to hem.

Wha— I can't do things like that.

He stared at his hands—his claws were extended on all ten fingers. *No wonder the damn shirt ripped.* He glanced down at his bare chest. *Holy mother of fire.* His height wasn't the only thing that had increased. His chest wasn't as broad as Ted's, but it was damned close.

No no no. I've stolen all this from him. What if his body, his big, beautiful body, is as frail and useless now as mine used to be?

"Please, David. Please get here quickly," he murmured. *Gah! Not exactly dressed to receive visitors.* He ran down the hall and up the stairs to Ted's room and took a long-sleeved T-shirt from a neatly folded pile. His momentary post-sex chill had passed, and now he felt too hot even in Ted's cooler quarters, so he didn't bother to borrow any flannel.

Before he could put on the shirt, he heard a knock at the door. He raced back downstairs, the shirt flapping in his hand, and flung the door open. David was standing there with a tall, dark-haired fae in motorcycle leathers behind him.

David's eyes widened and his mouth dropped open. "Quentin?"

"Yes. Come in, come in."

"Holy cats. The last time I saw you, you looked like Justin Long. How the heck have you morphed into Joe Manganiello?"

Quentin flung up his hands in exasperation. "That's what I'm talking about. I've stolen this—" he gestured to his body "—from Ted. And you have to figure out how I can give it back."

"It's none of my business, mate," David's companion said, "but if I were Ted, I'd want you to keep it." He flashed a grin, his dark-blue eyes twinkling. "Looking damn fine there."

David elbowed him in the ribs, which didn't seem to faze him at all. "This is my brother-in-law, Mal Kendrick." He glared at Mal. "Maybe you could find somewhere else to wait, so Mr. Bertrand-Harrington and I can speak privately?"

"Privacy is irrelevant." Quentin yanked the shirt over his head. "Ted is the priority."

"I understand. But first, I'd like to check you out."

Mal chuckled. "I'll tell Alun you said that, boyo."

David cast a sidelong glance at Mal. "You're not helping, Mal."

"Do what you need to do, but do it quickly." Quentin thrust his hands out, his fingertips tingling with the urge to extend his claws. "We don't have much time."

Nodding, David took Quentin's hands. His eyes lost focus as the now-familiar trickle of *achubydd* power threaded along Quentin's nerves.

"Wow."

"Is that a good wow or a bad wow?"

"It's just a wow-wow. Your DNA is completely repaired."

Quentin dropped David's hands like they were nuclear. "I knew it. I stole his life essence for my own benefit. I can't be here. I need the suppressant. I have to—"

"Calm down, Mr. Bert— May I call you Quentin? If I have to say your name every time, we'll be here all night." Quentin jerked a nod. "Now, simply because you've overcome the effects of the drugs and are the picture of health, it doesn't necessarily mean that Mr. Farnsworth isn't perfectly well. Given the way his energy signature is twined with your own—"

"Mother of fire, save me the empty consolation. I don't *care* about my condition except as it's the result of Ted's damage."

"Yes. That's what—"

"We have to *find him*. Immediately."

"Okay. Do you know where he went?" David's tone was so reasonable that Quentin wanted to scream.

"If I knew," Quentin said through clenched teeth, "then *finding* him wouldn't be necessary."

"Hold on, mate. Take this." Mal took something out of his pocket and tossed it to Quentin, who caught it reflexively— another thing he wouldn't have been able to do when he'd arrived. "That's a druid-made locating spell."

"A druid potion? Won't that—"

"Hurt? Nah. My bloke doesn't believe in that kind of shite."

Quentin turned the little glass tube in his hand. "How do you happen to conveniently have this potion on you?"

"I always carry a couple. I use them in my work. This is left over from the last job. Just hold something that represents what you're searching for, and it'll let you find it in a hot-and-cold kind of searching way."

"Hide the Thimble," Quentin murmured. He shook off a pang at the memory. "This is his shirt. Will that suffice?"

Mal shot him a thumbs-up. "Aces."

"Good." Quentin unstopped the vial and tossed back the potion. It was tart, vaguely vinegary, but not as revolting as most druid potions he'd encountered in the past. "It's not working— Oh." He felt the pull, the *awareness* of Ted, someplace to the north of the cabin. He tore open the door and launched himself off the porch.

"Quentin!" David's voice faded as Quentin crashed through the first line of trees. "Wait!"

Not likely. Quentin had no time to wait, because Ted might have even less.

Chapter
Twenty

"Ted?" Matt's soft question jerked Ted out of his Quentin-mourning-and-fishing trance. "Can I ask you something?"

Ted flicked his fishing line. "Sure."

"Why aren't you wearing your ring? You were so happy about your wedding when we drove back from Portland."

Ted glanced down at his hand. He always took the ring off before he shifted, and for some reason, he hadn't put it back on after the flea-hunting incident. He hadn't even worn it long enough to get a tan line. "Kind of a change in plans, I guess."

"Wanna talk about it?"

"Not really."

"Okay." Matt adjusted his own rod and didn't say anything. That was the great thing about Matt. He didn't push.

Which weirdly made Ted want to spill his guts. "Did I tell you that I found my husband through a matchmaking service?"

"You . . . ah . . . may have mentioned something about it."

I did? Jeez, Dr. Kendrick is right. I need to watch my mouth. "I thought I'd be okay with committing to someone I hadn't met before, but turns out my therapist was right. It's better to meet someone and get to know them. Pick them out yourself, even if they weren't the best match on paper."

"So the matchmaking service didn't give you the perfect guy, huh?"

"They did. Sort of." Rusty probably would have been nearly perfect, and Ted would have been perfectly happy with him, if he hadn't met Quentin.

"Are you in love with somebody else?" Matt's tone was gentle, understanding. "Somebody who's not your husband?"

Technically, Ted *was* in love with his husband—the one he had now—but that would change tonight at 10:45. *And after that, I can never see him again.* "You could say that." Because even after he married Rusty, he couldn't imagine not loving Quentin. Even though Quentin had kicked him out, the same as every other lover he'd ever had. "It's . . . complicated."

"I get it, Ted."

"You do? I never knew you were married."

"I'm not, but I'm in love with someone who's not my husband."

"Then you should say something." Ted set down his pole because he wasn't catching anything. *Probably because I'm obsessing over the one that got away.* "Maybe it'll work out, maybe it won't, but if you do nothing, you'll never know, you know? And then you'll regret it."

"Same goes for you."

"What?" Ted turned at the odd tone of Matt's voice. "What goes for me?"

"If you don't say something, you'll regret it. And who knows?" He shifted on the rock, bumping Ted's shoulder as he switched his pole to his other hand. "Maybe the other guy feels the same way."

"I kinda doubt it. I'm not his type." *I'm alive, which is apparently a problem for him.* "He's made that pretty clear."

"I wouldn't be so sure about that."

This time, the sultry burr in Matt's voice was unmistakable. Ted turned to find Matt's face inches from his. "Uh . . . Matt? What are you doing?"

"You don't have to worry, Ted. The feeling is definitely mutual." He leaned closer and nuzzled Ted's beard.

Ted reared back, sending his fishing pole spinning off the rock. "Matt! What the hell?"

Matt scooted closer. "No worries, Ted. You don't have to say it in so many words. I could tell you've been working up to something for a while now, same as I have. I was going to make my move on the way back from Portland, but you had that damn ring on your finger. Since that didn't work out, though—"

"*Don't touch him!*" The roar echoed over the water, bouncing off the creek banks and probably scaring every fish from here to Astoria.

Ted's arms slipped out from under him and he fell backward, banging his head on the rock. Matt toppled onto him, his ball cap knocked to the ground and his face planted in Ted's crotch.

A figure loomed over them, and Ted tried to make sense of it from this wonky perspective. *Tall, built, dark hair, jeans, shredded T-shirt, and—* Ted's mouth fell open. Wings! Enormous black ones with a wingspan at least twice Ted's height.

The guy glared at Matt. "I said *don't touch him*. Get off him. Now."

Whoa. "Q-Bert?" If it weren't for the fact that Ted recognized his own jeans and T-shirt—well, the front of it anyway; the back was toast because, holy smokes, *wings!*—he wouldn't have recognized him. Quentin's normally smooth hair was writhing around his head like angry black snakes, his eyes were glinting red, and his bared teeth seemed extra-pointy, almost vampire-sharp.

Quentin advanced on Matt with a snarl. Matt pushed himself off Ted and crab-walked backward, knocking his fishing pole into the stream, his eyes popped wide and mouth open in a silent scream.

Ted sat up just as Matt scrambled to his feet and took off into the woods as if the devil were on his tail. Which, considering Quentin's transformation, wasn't too far off the mark.

Quentin stared down the trail after Matt, his wings—*wings!*—quivering as his shoulders rose and fell. He whipped around—

and how he didn't get those things tangled in the trees, Ted had no idea. He stalked forward, his lips still lifted in a snarl. Quentin had never hurt Ted, at least not physically. He hadn't been strong enough. But the way he was now? Ted closed his eyes and braced himself for a blow.

It didn't come.

When he finally cracked one eyelid and peeked, Quentin was standing a couple of feet away, staring at his feet, his wing tips trailing on the ground.

"Q-Bert," Ted murmured. "You've got wings."

Quentin chuckled weakly, but didn't meet Ted's eyes. "What can I say? It's an incubus thing."

"I like 'em. But what's the deal scaring Matt out of his britches?"

Quentin lifted his head, and though his hair wasn't doing the snake dance anymore, his eyes still sparked red. "He was hitting on you."

Ted rubbed the back of his neck, wishing he dared to trace the bones under Quentin's shimmering black wing membrane. "Yeah, I think I figured that out."

"I didn't like it."

"I figured that out too. But why? It's not like you and me have a future together. By now it's probably six hours, tops, and you booted me out like you couldn't stand to spend that time together."

Quentin's expression—exasperation combined with affection—was familiar even on the stronger-featured face. "Maybe because I didn't want to kill you. Look at me, Ted. Look at my wings."

Ted waggled his eyebrows. "Yeah. Sexy."

"No, you idiot. I'm *bigger*. I've got my wings back for the first time in over forty years. My claws extend again." Holding a hand up between their faces, he flexed his fingers—and his nails were replaced by glossy brown claws. He relaxed his hand and they disappeared.

"Okay, now that's kind of Wolverine scary."

"'Cubi *are* scary. And dangerous, never more so than to their lovers. I'm bigger, Ted, and you're smaller." He extended a finger, sans claw, and pointed to Ted's middle. "What I gained, you lost. That's the way 'cubi work. We consume life energy from our sexual partners, and if we take too much, those partners die."

"But I'm not dead. In fact, was feeling pretty damn incredible until you, you know, *kicked me out.*"

Quentin rolled his eyes. "Focus, Ted. That feeling of well-being is an illusion. Partners *always* experience it at first. That's how we keep them coming back for more. It's called thrall."

"I don't think—"

"Uh, guys?"

Ted whipped around at the sound of the familiar voice. "David? What are you doing here?"

Dr. Kendrick's husband crept out of the trees, his big-eyed gaze focused on Quentin's wings. *Can't blame him for that.* "Quentin called me because he was worried about you."

"He didn't need to be. I'm fine."

"He's not. He's lost flesh."

"Not flesh, Q-Bert." Ted patted his newly flat belly. "Padding. But I lose that over the winter anyway, once I stop the pre-hibernation-period binge eating."

David smiled. "You certainly appear a picture of health."

Quentin's face turned stormy. "Appearances can deceive. Rory looked the *picture of health* too, almost ethereal, but then his muscles atrophied, his systems started to fail, his heart— his heart *stopped.* We got to the ICU with minutes, maybe *seconds* to spare . . ." He stepped back and turned away. He furled his wings, tucking them against his back, and they were sucked into his shoulder blades, sort of the same way Ted's fur was absorbed into his skin.

"That's what those scars were!" They didn't look like scars anymore. More like a skin pocket. *Heh. Wing foreskin.*

Quentin shrugged one shoulder. "Yes. I didn't think I'd ever — Well. Anyway. I'll let you get on with it." He shuffled toward the trees.

"Wait." Ted lurched toward him, but David shook his head and touched Ted's arm. "I'll, uh, see you at the cabin?"

Quentin glanced over his shoulder but didn't answer. Instead, he locked gazes with David. "Please. Fix him." Then he disappeared into the woods.

"Quentin!" Ted's chest ached like he'd taken a punch in a shifter fight pen. *If I follow him, if I can hold him again, it'll be better. I know it.*

"Mr. Farnsworth. Ted." David looked up at him, his eyes impossibly kind. "I think it might be better to give him a little space, don't you?"

"Q-Bert never does well with space. It gives him too much chance to *think* about things, and that gets him in trouble. Gets us *both* in trouble." *Except when it gets us into bed.* But apparently *that* caused trouble too.

"Nevertheless, I think we should honor his wishes. May I examine you now?"

Ted peered into the trees but couldn't see any trace of Quentin. "Whatever." He sighed and turned his palms up. "Examine away. It's not like I've got anything better to do."

By the time Quentin staggered up the porch steps, Ted's shredded shirt balled in his fist, his skin was striped and stinging from collisions with tree branches and brambles. As recently as this morning he would have been able to negotiate the path untouched. *But this morning I was smaller — and wasn't half naked into the bargain.*

He burst into the cabin only to come face-to-face with Mal Kendrick, crouched in a battle stance in the middle of the room with a beer in his hand.

"Shite, mate." Mal stood and downed the rest of his beer. "Give a bloke a warning, can't you?"

"Sorry." Quentin gestured helplessly with the ruined shirt. "I'll just . . . get changed."

Mal squinted at him, his head tilted to the side. "You might want to put something on those slashes. You look like you've been jousting with the forest."

Quentin choked on a startled laugh. "That's not far from the truth." *Although I've been jousting with my heart for days—and just lost the fight.* "But I'll be fine. 'Cubi heal quickly." *Especially when they're juiced up on energy stolen from a partner.*

"If you say so." Mal frowned at the door. "Where's my brother-in-law? Did you lose him in the woods?" His frown morphed into a wicked grin. "Don't tell me the druid potion didn't work. I won't half take the mickey out of Bryce if—"

"No, no. It worked perfectly. David's with Ted. I just—" Quentin took a deep breath and reminded himself that he was three centuries old and a trained advocate to boot—he ought to be able to string several coherent sentences together and make a fucking *plan*. "Do you think— That is, would you object to taking me to Portland now?"

"Now?" Mal's eyebrows lowered. "Without David and Ted?"

"I know it's an inconvenience. But I'd count it as an immense favor." He glanced at the door, half-afraid that Ted would walk through and destroy Quentin's resolution. "I—"

"Say no more." Mal saluted Quentin with his empty bottle. "Awkward relationship business. Trust me, I get it." He jerked his chin at Quentin's bare chest. "Soon as you're covered, I'm at your service."

"Thank you." Quentin fled down the hall, but when he got to the bedroom—*Rusty's bedroom*—he couldn't go in. *None of my clothes will fit me now anyway.*

Instead, he hurried upstairs and grabbed another of Ted's long-sleeved T-shirts at random. As he pulled it on, he got distracted for an instant, freezing with it tangled around his ears

—*Ted's scent.* He ordered himself not to whimper, and yanked the damn thing down over his chest.

A plan. I need a plan. He had a way to get to Portland, but what then? It was hours before the ritual appointment. He'd need— *Fuck!* The ritual. He had the ingredients, but he'd forgotten the *other* thing he needed—a representative of his clan. *Time to swallow the remaining shreds of my pride.*

He pulled out his cell phone and opened the fae communications app, then forced himself to sit down cross-legged on Ted's mattress, steeling himself against the *Ted* scent that arose from the bedding.

Then he initiated a video call—with his grandmother.

She answered immediately, making him feel guilty for not keeping her informed of his progress. "Quentin?" She took in his appearance, and a relieved smile spread over her face. "My dear, you've *fed!*" Her gaze flicked up and down, obviously studying his image on her screen. Her smile faded, horror gradually replacing relief. "Please tell me your recovery is the result of brief yet satisfying liaisons with—" her gaze flicked north and south again "—a minimum of a dozen human hosts."

He choked out a laugh. "No. There was only one."

"Ah." She straightened her shoulders and clutched her pearls. *I thought that was only a metaphor.* "You need help with the . . . disposal?"

"Grandmother! No! He's alive and perfectly healthy." *At least I hope he is.* "Where are you now?"

She waved one elegant hand dismissively. "At council headquarters, but that doesn't matter. How can a human be perfectly healthy when you've clearly . . ." Her eyes widened. "Quentin, *please* tell me you haven't fed from a *supe!*"

"I'm sorry, but I can't tell you that. He is in fact a supe. A bear shifter."

"A *bear?*" she shrieked—or rather it would have been a shriek in anyone less controlled and refined.

"Why?" Spots danced before Quentin's eyes. "Are bears more susceptible? Have I—"

"No, of course not. Not any more than any other supe. But *bears*? They're so . . . so . . ."

"So *what*, Grandmother?" Quentin's teeth ached from clenching them. "Rough? Rustic? *Low-class*?"

"I was going to say unassuming. Simple in their tastes. Unsuited to the demands of a lifestyle such as ours."

"The lifestyle of a parasite?"

Her nostrils flared, and she became every inch the intimidating matriarch of the world's oldest dynastic 'cubi clan. "A life that trades on power and influence and the responsibilities that come with wealth. A *social* life. A *public* life. A life where solitude is not an option, particularly in gala season."

"Oddly, I don't think he'd be intimidated by that at all. He'd probably like it." Quentin chuckled softly, remembering how Ted had described himself once. "He's not really your average bear."

"That's beside the point."

"What *is* the point, Grandmother?"

"He's a supe. 'Cubi don't feed from other supes. Ever. It's forbidden."

"That can't be—" Quentin blinked, then rubbed his eyes under his glasses. "If that's true, then why didn't I *know* that?"

"Quentin, *all* 'cubi know it. It's covered in detail during the Change March."

"Not that I recall." He'd blocked most of his Change March from his memory, but surely he'd have remembered something that fundamental. "Couldn't you have mentioned it, say, once or twice, in the *centuries* since then?"

"Really, Quentin. As if we'd discuss anything so indelicate. Besides, it's *obvious*. Have any of our little host parties *ever* included a nonhuman?"

"No, but—"

"Have they *ever* included anyone who wasn't part of our social sphere, anyone not fully aware of the rewards and . . . challenges of affiliating themselves with our family?"

"No, but—"

"Have I *ever* presented anyone to you as a potential partner who wasn't human?"

"No, and *that nearly got Rory killed!*"

She huffed. "Rory's condition was his own fault. If he—"

"Grandmother. Do not go there. I won't listen to victim-blaming, not even from you. I—" A sound from downstairs startled Quentin out of his anger and reminded him that he was trying to make a plan. *Damn it.* "In any case, you won't have to worry about my liaison with a bear shifter. That's why I called. I need you to meet me at the Portland offices of Supernatural Selection. I— I'm getting divorced, and the ritual requires a clan representative."

"I see." Her eyes narrowed, the faint shimmer of the vision spell glinting on her spectacle lenses. "I'm not certain— Never mind. We can discuss it when I see you. What time?"

"The appointment is at 10:45, but I'll be in town within the next half hour. I'm . . ." He scrubbed his hand through his hair. "I'm not sure where I'll go between now and then."

"Really, Quentin, you couldn't have given me a trifle more notice?" She sighed. "However, the witches who run Supernatural Selection maintain a transportation portal, so I can be there quite soon. The Governor Hotel is within walking distance. I'll arrange a suite and meet you there."

He nodded, a lump forming in his throat. "Thank you, Grandmother."

"Nonsense, my dear. You're my grandson. I would do anything for your well-being and happiness."

"I appreciate it." And while Pauline Bertrand-Harrington in full battle mode could vanquish a boardroom full of corporate sharks, quash the pretensions of a dozen social upstarts at once, or pull off the event of the season with one manicured hand behind her back, he feared she hadn't the power to mend a simple thing like his broken heart.

Chapter Twenty-One

As they stepped out of the woods into the cabin clearing, Ted lifted a fir bough out of David's way so he wouldn't get smacked in the face. "So you're sure I'm okay? I mean, I *feel* okay, but Q-Be—Quentin was so freaked out, like my instant abs were gonna give me a heart attack or something."

David ducked under Ted's arm. "Absolutely. Your heart is in perfect condition. If there were a better-than-perfect condition, your heart would be a poster child for it."

"If you say so," Ted muttered, rubbing his chest because it still ached.

"In fact, everything about you is in tip-top shape." When David's steps slowed, Ted glanced down and caught the *considering* look on his face.

"What?"

"It's just . . . I'd love to examine the two of you together, because there's an interesting pattern in your energy in a few places, like it's looking for an outlet. I've never seen anything like it before."

"What places?"

"Your hands. Your heart. Your—" David's glance flicked to Ted's groin, and he blushed. "Never mind. I'm sure it's nothing to worry about."

"Yeah, right." Ted led the way up the porch steps and held the door open for David to enter first.

"Mal? Quentin? We're back," David called. He turned in a slow circle. "Mal?"

His heart creeping toward his throat, Ted strode down the hall and peered into the bedroom. Quentin's luggage was still there, and he was able to breathe again, because surely Quentin wouldn't leave without his fancy suits, not to mention his three tuxes.

His three tuxes that don't fit him anymore.

He sagged against the doorframe. *He wanted to ditch me so bad that he couldn't stand to ride in my truck?* Ted pinched the bridge of his nose, *hard*, but tears pricked his eyes anyway.

His cell buzzed against his hip. *Quentin!* He pawed at his pocket and managed to pull the phone out without dropping it. He swiped at the screen with a trembling finger. But it wasn't a text from Quentin.

It was on the Supernatural Selection message app. From Rusty. *But I'm still married to Quentin.* Maybe the app activated on the date of the contract termination, even if the termination hadn't . . . well . . . terminated yet.

Hey. Looking forward to tonight. New life FTW, am I right?

Ted typed out a response, deleted it, then tried again.

You bet. Can't wait.

He stared at the screen for a couple of minutes, but Rusty didn't text again. Before he could weaken and send some pathetic message to Quentin, he shoved the damn phone back in his pocket.

"Ted?" At David's murmur, Ted brushed his cheeks with his knuckles and turned, forcing a smile.

"Yeah?"

"Mal's waiting outside. He . . . he took Quentin into town through the Faerie portal."

Ted drew in a shaky breath. "Oh."

"Apparently Quentin's meeting his grandmother before your appointment, otherwise I'm sure he'd have waited."

"It's nice of you to try to make me feel better about this, but you don't need to." Ted shoved his hands in his pockets. "Quentin left. We're gonna be divorced by the end of the day anyway."

"Yes, but— Dang it, I can tell you're upset. Do you want—"

"It's okay, David. Really." *No, it's not, but there's not a lot I can do about it.* "Thanks for checking me over. Now if you don't mind, I've got to get cleaned up so I can make it to Portland in time."

"Mal could take you through Faerie if you want. You could maybe talk to Quentin before your appointment?"

"Nah. He made it pretty clear that he's moving on. I am too, so you know, it's all good."

"Okay." David's voice was loaded with doubt. "If you say so. But call if you need *anything*, all right?"

"Sure." He saw David out of the cabin, waved to Mal on the porch, then closed the door and leaned his head against it.

Pull it together, Farnsworth, and get the place cleaned up. You're welcoming your "real" husband home tonight.

He trudged down the hall to strip the bed in Quentin's—in *Rusty's* room. As he stood there with his arms full of sheets that still smelled of toasted marshmallows, he was afraid—no, he was certain—that no matter how many years he and Rusty lived here, without Quentin, the cabin would feel empty forever.

Quentin was huddled in the chair by the window when his grandmother sailed through the hotel room door.

"Darling!" She glided over to him, perfectly groomed in her burgundy raw silk suit and pearls, her hands outstretched. He stood to meet her, leaning down to kiss her smooth cheek. "I'm so sorry I'm late. Woodward called at the last minute to complain about his portfolio's performance. I *told* the ridiculous man not to invest in mandrake futures until after the equinox, but does he listen to me? No, of course he doesn't."

"It's all right." He gestured to the tea tray he'd ordered. "May I pour for you? We still have some time before we have to report to Supernatural Selection."

She quirked one silver brow. "Bertrand-Harringtons never *report* to anyone. We graciously allow them to attend on our pleasure."

"Grandmother . . ."

She patted his hand. "I'm only teasing you, my dear. For the most part. Lemon, please. No sugar."

"Yes, I know." He prepared her cup and handed it to her. "Thank you for coming."

"Of course. Although if I'd known you'd be dressed like *that*, I'd have made a push to locate more appropriate clothing for you." She took a sip of her tea. "Now perhaps you can explain to me why you felt it necessary to contract with a matchmaking agency—and so far away—when I've got any number of perfectly eligible mates for you at home."

"All of them are human."

"Exactly. As they should be."

"I don't understand. Rory was human and he nearly died. All of your partners, all of Woodward's partners, all of *everybody's* partners fade far too soon."

She tilted her head and regarded him over the rim of her teacup. "'Too soon'? How long do you imagine most human marriages last?"

"I don't know. Seventy or eighty years?"

"Quentin. How could you have gotten through your Change March and still be so naive? What was the master *thinking*?"

"I couldn't say. I avoided him whenever possible."

"My dear, our contracts with our human hosts are only for a limited time precisely because we don't want to stress their systems as they age, or jeopardize the Secrecy Pact by raising questions about mismatched partners." She set her cup and saucer down. "We can't risk too many May-December pairings or we call attention to ourselves. In fact, May-September is skating on the edge of exposure, which is also why we're careful to stagger our contracts so *all* of us don't appear far younger than our mates at once."

"But Rory—"

She held up one hand. "Stop. I know you don't want to hear anything against the man, but he was warned that introducing emotion into a transaction that should have been strictly nutritional was dangerous. Yet he persisted in attaching himself to you, knowing that you would be incapable of forming the connection with him that he wanted."

Quentin curled his hand around the china cup to try to infuse warmth into his fingers. "In-incapable? Are you saying I c-c-can't fall in love?" *But I can. I do. I have.*

"You're not attending, Quentin. 'Cubi can become sincerely fond of our host partners."

"'Sincerely fond' is not love, Grandmother."

"It's what passes for love between 'cubi and humans. With your unfortunate empathic tendencies, *you* are at greater risk—"

He set down his cup with a clatter. "Of what? Of getting my heart broken? I don't believe that. Other than Rory"—*and Ted*—"I've never felt anything approaching fondness, sincere or otherwise."

She fixed him with the look that froze corporate drones in their tracks. "The risk is not to *you*. It's to your host. You think you're sparing their feelings by allowing them to be with you, that you're preventing them from feeling rejected or unloved. But that's counterproductive. It's not healthy. *For them.* That's what happened with Rory. He couldn't keep a proper distance, and you wouldn't send him away."

Quentin sat back in his chair, tangling his fingers together in his lap until his knuckles whitened. "Oddly, Grandmother, this isn't making me feel any less guilty."

"Guilt, or lack of it, is not my point. Did you believe yourself in love with Rory?"

"I—" He squeezed his fingers tighter, tempted to say yes even though it wasn't true. "No. But I was . . . sincerely fond of him."

"And you could never have been more. Because he was human and you are not."

"But—"

"When all is said and done, my dear, and despite eons of careful breeding with humans, dynastic 'cubi are demons at heart. Demons were created to *manipulate* humans, and for that we need to maintain a certain objectivity. Our affection can go only so far without compromising our nature. Our center, our *calon*—" she touched the middle of her abdomen, just below her breasts "—inhibits it as a survival mechanism too. For if we become too attached to a human host, who are short-lived by supe standards, we risk grief and misery from which we might never recover. Which"—her voice resumed its usual tartness—"you would know if your Change March master had been even marginally competent."

He sighed and looked down at his hands. He forced them to unclench, flattening them against his thighs. "I see."

"Do you? Do you doubt that I love you?"

His gaze shot back to her face. "Of course not!"

"That's because our *calon* does not inhibit love between supes." She sat back with a frown. "I wish it did, because *calon*-enabled connections are far more dangerous when severed unexpectedly."

"How . . . how dangerous?"

"Our first ancestor *died* when her dragon shifter mate was killed by a stray crossbow bolt in some ridiculous internecine war."

"From grief? That seems a bit extreme, even for those times."

"Not from grief, although that didn't help. No, she *starved to death* because their connection was so strong that she wasn't able to feed from anyone else."

He blinked. "Oh. Why didn't I—"

She placed two fingers against her forehead, closing her eyes. "Let me guess. You didn't hear *that* story on your Change March either. Mother of fire, Quentin, you spent twenty-two years on that blasted march. What *did* you learn?"

He smiled wryly. "How to braid a flogger tail." And how to dodge the master—which apparently hadn't always been the right choice.

"In any case, I hope you understand now why I was so dismayed to learn you'd registered with a supe matchmaking agency—and why this divorce is the best thing for you. You can come home with me and choose from one of the human hosts —"

"No, I can't. Once this marriage is . . . is terminated, I'm obligated to enter into the contract I should have signed originally. With Casimir Moreau."

Her brows drew together. "Moreau. The rebel vampire?"

He's a rebel? From his dossier—which, since they were to be married in two hours, Quentin should be reviewing now instead of mooning over someone he couldn't have—Casimir had a few issues with the vampire council, but a rebel? "He's a vampire, yes. I thought that would be best, since I couldn't kill somebody who was already dead."

"Darling." She held out a hand, and he took it. "*He* is not the one who would be in danger. If you were to fall in love with him, and he should meet the sun through carelessness or council command—"

"Don't worry, Grandmother. I can safely promise you I won't fall in love with Casimir." *Because I've already fallen in love with somebody else.*

"And I can safely promise *you*, my dear, that you'll have no obligation to Casimir or Supernatural Selection whatsoever. Because as I've told you from your cradle, contracts—" she smiled with a hint of 'cubi fang "—are made to be broken."

Chapter Twenty-Two

The drive to Portland had never seemed this long. *Would it have seemed shorter if Quentin had been with me?* Ted snorted. *Nah. If Q-Bert had been here, he'd probably have been sitting almost on top of the door handle and wouldn't have spoken to me for the whole two hours.*

After twenty minutes of circling the Pearl District streets, Ted finally found an on-street parking spot across from Little Big Burger. *Closed now. So what?* He supposed he should have stopped on the way into town to grab a bite to eat, since he'd canceled the reservations for his dinner with Quentin, but he'd passed every one of his usual joints without pause. Somehow, he didn't have much of an appetite.

He trudged the six blocks to the Supernatural Selection offices, his hands shoved in the pockets of his tweed blazer, the closest thing he had to a suit. He should at least *try* to spruce up for his first meeting with his future husband, right? The jacket was kinda old, and didn't fit very well because it was sized for his winter body. *I left that behind in bed this morning.* But at least it was more formal than what he'd been wearing when he'd met Quentin the first time.

Supernatural Selection was located on the top three floors of a four-story multiuse building, above a falafel restaurant, a Pilates studio, and a New Age bookstore owned by the same witches' collective that ran the matchmaking agency. He suspected that they didn't sell many books—most of their business was conducted out of the back room, where they kept the arcane supplies.

Bet we could have gotten the silver-bladed knife here. Heck, probably the fleas too. I wouldn't put it past them to breed the damn things.

He pushed through the glass doors that led to the building's lobby and took the stairs up to the second floor. He froze on the top step, his hand tightening around the rail.

Quentin was standing outside the Supernatural Selection entrance next to a silver-haired woman in one of those ladies' suits that looked simple but probably cost more than Ted's truck.

Quentin, on the other hand, was still wearing a pair of Ted's "spring" jeans. *And that's my Bad Robot T-shirt.* His hair was tousled and his eyes were wide behind the glimmer of his spectacle lenses.

Ursa's teeth, he's so beautiful. But then, Ted had thought he was beautiful from the beginning, even when he was smaller, thinner, and—let's face it—pissy.

Ted forced himself to take the last step onto the landing. "Hey, Quentin." *Please don't let Rusty be waiting inside. I don't know if I can fake it in front of him. Not now. Maybe not ever.* "Ready to do this thing?"

"Um . . . of course." He turned to the woman at his side. "Ted, this is my grandmother, Pauline Bertrand-Harrington. Grandmother, Ted Farnsworth."

Ted wiped his hand on his pants, then held it out. "Nice to meet you, Ms. Bertrand-Harrington." *Wait. She's a succubus. Maybe shaking hands is not a thing?* Quentin sure got all weird about it. He dropped his hand to his side before things got awkward.

She inclined her head and greeted him with what his mom would have called a company smile. "Please. Call me Pauline." But then her smile wavered, a pucker growing between her brows. She glanced briefly over her shoulder at Quentin. "Perhaps we should chat for a few minutes before—"

"Hello!" Zeke stepped out of the Supernatural Selection reception room, one of those shiny folders clutched to his chest and a flickering golden pillar at his back. "We'll be proceeding to the ritual chamber momentarily, but first, there's someone here to see you, Mr. Farnsworth."

Ted gulped. *Not Rusty. Please not Rusty. Not yet.* But when Zeke stood aside, a familiar figure in flannel and denim, with a beard bushier than Ted's, shuffled into the hallway.

"Ben?" Ted rushed his brother and grabbed him in a fierce hug. "What are you doing here?"

Ben pounded Ted on the back with his usual perfunctory force and stepped back. "You asked me to show up, remember? Sent me that email a few weeks ago."

"Oh. Right. I forgot about that."

"'S a good thing I didn't. Demon there says you need a witness or something, otherwise the fucking sky will fall."

Zeke clutched his folder tighter. "I didn't—"

"Don't mind my brother." Ted patted Zeke's shoulder. "He doesn't get out much." He bobbed his head at Pauline. "Sorry about the language, ma'am."

She arched a brow. "I've heard worse, but I appreciate the courtesy. Now, if you don't mind, I'd like to speak to Ted and my grandson privately."

Zeke smiled apologetically. "I'm sorry, but we're a bit pressed for time."

"Surely you can spare me five minutes."

The golden pillar flicked out and then reappeared in front of Zeke, flaring brighter so that Ted could just make out the towering figure inside. By the way Zeke's eyes popped wide, this wasn't a good thing.

"I'm, um, afraid not. If the witnesses could please accompany the AI to the observation room?"

Pauline pursed her lips, and if the AI had balls, the look she gave it should have shriveled them to nothing. Seemed it was made of sterner stuff than Ted, though, because it grew taller and wider.

She sniffed and murmured something that sounded like, "Arrogant, pretentious asshole." But Ted figured he hadn't heard correctly. She looked much too refined to say anything like that. She made him feel as clumsy as a bull shifter in a china shop just by standing there.

Ben must have felt the same way, because he shot Ted a wide-eyed glance as he lumbered off behind her and the AI.

Zeke blew out a breath. "Good. Gentlemen, if you could come with me please?"

As they followed Zeke down the hall in the opposite direction, Quentin murmured, "Are you okay? Did David fix whatever I did?"

Ted hunched his shoulders, increasing his pace when Zeke disappeared around a corner. "There's nothing wrong with me." *Nothing that can be fixed anyway. Not with us about to be separated for eternity and married to other people.*

"That can't be."

Ted stopped, reaching out for Quentin who—big surprise—flinched away. "Look, Q-Bert. You need to chill the heck out. I feel fine. David said I'm fine. Say it with me—*I'm fine.* We both know we've got to do this. We made promises to other people and they're depending on us. But don't make this about you saving me from yourself, okay?"

"But—"

"You went into a tailspin out of guilt before. You don't need to do it again."

Quentin opened his mouth, probably to argue because that was what he did. But then he shut it and nodded. "You're right. And since I won't be touching you again—"

"That's *not* why. You don't need to guilt yourself into starvation because you didn't do anything wrong. I'll prove it."

Ted reached for Quentin's hand, but he snatched it behind his back.

"Please, Ted." Quentin blinked rapidly, his eyes shiny behind his glasses. "I'm not strong enough for this. Even if it's true, even if I didn't hurt you, touching you again now, when I know I can't even *see* you after today, would hurt *me*. I don't know if I could bear it."

Ted's chest pinched, right under his heart. *How can I say no to that?* So he did what he always did, what everyone expected him to do—the wrong thing. "'Bear' it. Good one, Q-Bert." But he couldn't make himself chuckle.

That was expecting too much—even for him.

Quentin couldn't tear his gaze from Ted's dear face. *Trust him to take the burden on himself.* "I lo—"

Zeke peeked around the corner. "Mr. Farnsworth? Mr. Bertrand-Harrington? The officials are waiting." He smiled with obvious forced brightness, a sheen of sweat on his forehead. "If you'll all come this way?"

For a demon to sweat took some serious terror. *I wonder what will happen to him as a result of this clusterfuck?* If the lords of Sheol were involved, it wouldn't be pretty. However, if the witches were annoyed? Quentin shuddered and hurried down the hall. Zeke held the door for them to enter the windowless chamber.

The floor, the same blue-gray slate as the walls, was inscribed with the required pentagram-within-a-circle. Three witches in formal robes stood at the north side, representing Maiden, Mother, and Crone.

Zeke pointed to the left. "Mr. Farnsworth, if you could take your place in the green-chalked circle by the west wall. Mr. Bertrand-Harrington, the red-chalked circle by the east wall."

They all took their places, Quentin meeting Ted's gaze across the inscriptions. *Why does he seem so far away?* After the ritual, he'd be completely out of reach. *Don't fool yourself. He was out of reach from the moment you met him.*

Zeke glanced between them. "May I have the required artifacts, please?"

Ted's eye widened. "Shit. I forgot all about them."

"Don't worry." Quentin offered him a tight smile. "I have them here." He pulled a linen-wrapped bundle from his jeans pocket and handed it to Zeke.

Zeke unwrapped the bundle almost reverently, presenting the bound hair to the Maiden, the coins to the Mother, and the vials containing the fleas to the Crone. She handed them back.

"Sorry," Zeke murmured. Then he unstopped the vials and dumped the now-deceased fleas into her palm.

One by one, each of them paced forward and placed their items in the center of the pentagram. Zeke extracted a set of papers from one of his files and set them at the point of the pentagram closest to Ted. *His contract, I presume. The one with my name on it.* Zeke laid the contents of the other folder on the point closest to Quentin, then scooted over to the south wall next to the door under the baleful stares of the witches.

They waited several beats, just long enough to be awkward and uncomfortable, before they spoke.

"*Finita,*" said the Maiden.

"*Consummatum,*" said the Mother.

When the Crone said, "*Contritum,*" fire streaked around the circle and down the lines of the pentagram, setting the papers ablaze.

As the items Ted and Quentin had so painstakingly gathered erupted into green witch-fire, burning pain exploded below Quentin's sternum, and he doubled over, trapping a groan behind his teeth.

"Ursa's fucking *teeth!*" Ted shouted.

Guess I'm not the only one to feel it. He panted and wheezed as the agony flared in sync with the green flames that he could see out of his watering eyes. Through ringing ears, he could still make out Ted's growls and whimpers.

The three witches, however, paid no attention to either of them. They gazed straight ahead and marched across the circle, out of Quentin's sight lines and—judging by the swish and click of the closing door—out of the room. *Apparently aftercare isn't part of their services.*

But it's part of mine—at least where Ted is concerned, even if we're not still married.

So Quentin forced his breathing back to normal, ignoring the pain that had subsided but not died, and stood up. He took one more deep breath and blew it out, focusing on the rough slate wall to center himself, then faced Ted.

Or tried to.

He had only turned halfway around before he hit an invisible wall with his shoulder. He tried to turn his head. No good. The most he could manage was to catch a fleeting glimpse of Ted's back out of the corner of his eye.

"Congratulations to you both!" Zeke said with far too much cheer. "Your contract is severed."

"Q-Bert?" Ted's voice was shaky. "I . . . I can't turn around."

Mother of bloody fire. For a group so steeped in symbolism, witches could be so fucking *literal.* "I think that's because the escape clause spell prevents us from meeting face to face for, you know, eternity."

Ted's fierce mutter was unintelligible, but judging by Zeke's horrified gasp, Quentin suspected it was highly unflattering to the witches.

Gingerly, Quentin backed across the room. *Even if I can't look at him, maybe I can touch him once more.* Surely one last fleeting touch wouldn't hurt Ted. *Although it might just eviscerate me.*

"Mr. Bertrand-Harrington! What are you doing?" Zeke suddenly appeared in front of Quentin, and the AI was back, flickering at his shoulder. "You can't—"

"I can't face him. I know. But can't we have a few minutes alone? We never had a chance to say goodbye properly."

"It's really not done." Zeke glanced at the AI. "I mean, *I've* never witnessed this ritual personally, but as I understand it, the *intent* is that you aren't allowed any contact."

"Screw that," Ted said. "It said we can't meet face-to-face. That doesn't mean we can't call each other. Text. Heck, maybe even Skype."

Zeke shifted from foot to foot. "I, um, suspect *virtual* face time is prohibited as well as *actual*."

"Well, I'm willing to give it a shot if you are, Q-Bert. Except . . ." Ted heaved a giant sigh. "I suppose it's not such a great idea. We shouldn't go into our next marriages half-assed, you know? I mean, Rusty was my perfect match once."

"And Casimir was mine." *If I hadn't excluded the living, would the results have been any different?*

"So he's waiting for you, and Rusty's waiting for me."

"That's right," Zeke said. "Upstairs in altar room three and conference room seven." He shrugged apologetically. "Sorry about the conference room, but we thought it would be insensitive to put all four of you in the same ritual space. Although if you're in a rush and don't mind sharing the altar, we could conduct both ceremonies simultaneously."

Watch Ted marry someone else? I'd rather emigrate to Sheol. "You go ahead. I'll wait until you and Rusty are . . . are done." Although his lips were trembling, he attempted to add a smile to his voice since Ted couldn't see his face—and he wasn't particularly concerned what Zeke or the smug flicker of the AI thought. "I doubt my grandmother would appreciate attending my wedding in a conference room. She has her standards."

"You could take the altar room. I bet Rusty wouldn't mind."

"No. Please. Go ahead." *Before I lose it completely.* "You deserve to start your life together without compromising on something so significant. For that matter, we all deserve that, don't you think?"

"Yeah. I guess." Ted's tone was heavy. "But before I go, I just want you to know. I'm not sorry, Q-Bert. *Quentin.* Not sorry you were my husband. I only wish— Well, never mind."

"I know, Ted," Quentin said around the enormous lump in his throat. "I'm not sorry either."

Zeke frowned, picking at the corner of the folder he was holding against his chest. "But you're both happy, aren't you? This is what you wanted."

"Yeah. Sure." Ted sighed, and Quentin had never wanted anything more than he wanted to hug Ted right now. "Let's get on with it." His footsteps dragged across the slate, moving away from Quentin, out of his life for good.

Tears welled in Quentin's eyes, and through their blur he caught an out-of-focus glimpse of a face inside the AI's golden pillar: wide noble brow, large deep-set eyes, sculpted cheekbones—and a mouth twisted in a triumphant sneer.

But when Quentin blinked, the vision was gone, the AI nothing more than a tall column of shimmering light.

"Mr. Bertrand-Harrington? Your grandmother is waiting for you in the observation room."

"If you don't mind, Zeke, I'd like a few minutes alone first."

"Certainly." He couldn't have sounded more uncertain if he'd tried. "But I'll need to cleanse the chamber before the next scheduled ritual. You could use the reflection room if you—"

"Just ten minutes. Is that too much to ask?"

Something far too like pity flickered across Zeke's face. "No. Of course not. I'll let your grandmother know you're delayed." He left, shutting the door behind him.

Quentin huddled in the corner, legs tucked against his chest, the slate rough and cold against his back, and let his forehead drop to his knees.

Goodbye, my love.

Chapter
Twenty-Three

Why the hell did I ever agree to that stupid escape clause? If only he'd waited, even for another week, he'd have known that Quentin was his *real* match. They'd have stayed married and everything would have been fine.

Except I'd never fit into his fancy-ass lifestyle. And why would he want to give it up for a tux-less life in the wilderness?

This was better. This was what should have happened in the first place.

But as he trudged up the stairs in Zeke's wake, guilt crawled up his back like one of those stupid fleas. What if Rusty was expecting a husband who'd love him? How was it fair to him to stick him with a guy who'd always be wishing for somebody else?

I'll just have to try twice as hard to make him feel welcome, that's all. They had a ton in common. But already Ted was feeling closed in again, the very thing that made him kick over the traces and do something really stupid—like phoning in another Sasquatch sighting to Matt. *At least* somebody *would be happy then.* Even if it wasn't Ted. Or Rusty, come to think of it.

Crap. This knot was way beyond Ted's ability to unravel. He needed Q-Bert here to talk him through this. To even him out. To tell him he wasn't a screwup.

To love him.

Nope. Nope. Nope. Wasn't gonna happen. *Couldn't* happen. Ted needed to get over it and move on.

Zeke stopped outside a closed door halfway down the long, curved hallway. "Here we are," he said brightly, although his eyes darted left and right, like a rabbit who was trying to decide which way to bolt. "Mr. Johnson is *very* excited about meeting you."

"Really?" Ted's stomach sank another six inches.

"Oh yes. When he arrived this evening, he said . . ." Zeke blinked. "I mean, I'm sure he's looking forward to beginning your life together."

Ted snorted. "What'd he say? 'Let's get this over with'? 'It's about time?' 'Beats a poke in the eye with a sharp stick'?"

Zeke hugged his folder until it buckled in the middle. "Nothing like that. I'm sure he— Well, anyway . . ." He fumbled for the handle and shoved the door wide, plastering a desperate-looking smile on his face. "Here's Mr. Farnsworth!" His smile faded as he crept into the room, peering right and left and even behind the door. "Mr. Johnson?"

Ted followed him inside. It was a lot more welcoming than the ritual chamber, with polished oak floors and walls painted sky blue. The altar was draped with a dark-green cloth and topped with a big vase of yellow and orange chrysanthemums. Candles flared in the wall sconces, and the sideboard had a little white-frosted cake with bear and beaver cake toppers.

What the room *didn't* have was the other groom.

"Say, Zeke? I'm not by any chance being left at the altar, am I?"

"No, no. I'm sure Mr. Johnson is just in the restroom, or perhaps getting a cup of coffee or a snack. He's been waiting for quite a while." He opened his abused folder as the AI drifted into the room. "In the meantime, we can take care of your paperwork. Here's the new contract for you and Mr. Johns—" He frowned at the folder. "This isn't right," he muttered.

"What?" Ted edged closer and looked over Zeke's shoulder. "Party of the first part, Ted Farnsworth. That's me, all right. Party of the second part—" He jerked back, a growl fighting to escape his throat. *Party of the second part, Quentin Bertrand-Harrington.* "That's not fucking funny."

"I assure you, it's not intended—" Zeke slapped the folder shut. "I'll be right back." He rushed out, past the pulsing golden AI, which flared orange for an instant before following him.

"Great. Just great." Ted shoved his hands into his jacket pockets. He glanced at the altar again, and the cake. *No way am I hanging out in here by myself.*

He stepped outside and paced down the corridor, which seemed a lot longer and had more side passages than were possible in a building this size. And when Zeke was suddenly hurrying *toward* him even though Ted had gone in the opposite direction? Weird. *Whole place must be built in an interdimensional pocket.*

"There you are, Mr. Farnsworth. I've got the corrected contracts." Zeke waved a sheaf of papers in the air, then slapped them against the wall. "Now if you'll just— Wait." He frowned at the papers, then crumpled them in both fists. "Fire and damnation, what is going on?"

Ted rocked from his heels to his toes. "Let me guess. Names wrong again?"

"I'm truly sorry. I'm not *trying* to annoy you." He scrubbed a hand through his curly hair. "I don't understand what's happening. I suppose it's a good thing that Mr. Johnson is missing."

"Is he? Missing?"

"That's not what I— I meant missing from the *altar room.* I'm sure he'll return momentarily." He huffed out a breath and set his jaw. "Don't worry. I'll get these contracts right if I have to write the entire things out by hand with a blood quill."

He marched off down the hall with the AI at his heels. Jeez, didn't that thing *ever* leave the poor guy alone? It was as bad as being tagged.

Ted sighed and resumed pacing, purposely not glancing inside the altar room when he passed. Was there another festively decorated room behind one of the other doors, this one holding a cake with a vampire and an incubus on top? For that matter, did one of the rooms hold an actual vampire? Rusty might have run out on Ted—and why didn't that bother him more?—but that didn't mean Casimir wasn't anxiously awaiting Quentin.

He'd be an idiot if he wasn't. Because only an idiot wouldn't thank his lucky stars to have Quentin for a husband. *Too bad I didn't figure that out in time.*

He made another circuit of the hall—without having to turn any corners—and was approaching the room again when an invisible force shoved at his shoulder, spinning him around to face the other direction. He tried to turn, but no dice. Which could only mean—

"Q-Bert? Is that you?"

"Ted?" Quentin laughed a little breathlessly. "I'm assuming you're there since I just got spun around and nearly fell on my ass."

"Yeah. I'm here."

"Hold on. I'm walking backward, toward your voice, and . . . ah . . . here's an open door."

Shit. The only open door was *that* door, and the last thing Ted wanted was for Quentin to see the room decked out for Ted's wedding to another guy. *Those damn cake toppers.* "Not there."

"No, it's okay. I've got this idea, see? If I duck in here and lean against the wall, you can stand outside. As long as we're not face-to-fa— Oh."

"Q-Bert?"

"Have you"—his voice was rough and a little choked up— "gotten married already?"

"Nah." Ted was able to turn sideways and scoot down the hall. He flattened himself against the wall outside the open door. "Still waiting for Rusty to show." *And now that you're here, he can take his own sweet time.*

"I left the ritual chamber just as Zeke rushed by as if the Grand Inquisitor was on his tail, followed by the AI—which, I don't mind telling you, seems to be enjoying all the drama far too much for an entity that's supposed to be pure of heart."

Ted chuckled, warmth swirling in his chest because it was so fricking *good* to hear that edge of snark in Quentin's voice. "Yeah. I guess when you hide out inside a pillar of light, you can be as smug as you want and nobody'll be the wiser."

"Was Zeke off to fetch Rusty?"

"Nope. He's having trouble getting the contracts right."

"Again?"

"I know, right?" Ted let his head rest against the wall and hooked his fingers around the edge of the doorjamb. *He's so close.* "Seems like that famous perfect match spell should help a little more with the paperwork."

"That's a very good point. Zeke is just one demon with an overzealous AI watchdog. It's not as though he's got the magical power to override an entire coven of witches."

"Yeah. Poor guy can't seem to get the contracts to print with the right names. When you saw him, that was the second time they were wrong."

"Really? Whose names were on them?"

Uh-oh. I shouldn't have mentioned that. "Nobody you'd know."

"Ted," Quentin said in his you're-not-getting-away-with-*that* voice. "Whose names are on the contracts?"

"Weeellll. Mine of course."

"Yes, yes. And?"

"And . . . well . . . yours."

Quentin managed to tear his gaze away from the tiny wedding cake. "M-m-mine? Are you sure?"

"Yeah. I saw it. Well, I saw it the first time, but they were wrong the second time too, and I don't imagine there are *that* many people who are interested in me."

You have no idea. But something niggled at the back of his brain. Something about the matchmaking spells. *There. Got it.* And suddenly, the day wasn't nearly as bleak, despite that stupid cake. "Ted. Remember the day we met?"

The warm burr of Ted's chuckle sent tiny shock waves of joy along Quentin's nerves. "Hard to forget. I wasn't sure whether you were gonna run screaming down the mountain or stab me with the nearest tree branch."

"As I recall, you didn't look too cheerful either. Aren't you the one that *did* run screaming down the mountain?"

"Hey, bears don't scream. We're tougher than that."

This time, Quentin joined in the chuckle because he'd figured it out. "I know a silent scream when I see one, but never mind. After you ran, screaming—"

"Q-Bert."

"—I called Zeke. He told me that the spells that govern the matchmaking protocols are global and in fact *should* have prevented clerical errors."

"So?"

"So . . . tell me this. Do you want to be with me? If I asked you to marry me right now, would you say yes?"

"Q-Bert," Ted groaned. "Don't do this to me. You know I can't. *We* can't. We promised."

"But those promises are based on the wrong assumptions. That you're Rusty's perfect match. That I'm Casimir's. How can we be their perfect matches if we want each other?"

"It doesn't matter. They want *us.* Or at least they're supposed to, even though neither of them is on time for their own fricking wedding."

"Just don't sign anything, Ted, okay? *Especially* not in blood."

"Q-Bert—"

"*Please*, Ted. Promise *me* this time."

"All right. Fine. But I don't know what difference it'll make."

"Just trust me." *And hope I'm right and that I can pull this off.* He scooted closer to the edge of the door, then flipped, pressing his belly against the wall. He reached around the doorjamb as heavy footsteps thudded down the hall.

"Bunch of people coming, Q-Bert. You expecting a crowd?"

"No. Don't pay any attention to them." He waved his hand up and down, and Ted caught on, lacing their fingers together. The energy that surged into Quentin soothed the residual ache from the escape ritual, and eased the feeling of being trapped and bottled up that had plagued him since he'd left Ted at the stream. *It's only our hands. Not sex. He'll be fine. But oh how I've missed his touch.*

On the other side of the wall, Ted sighed, deep and contented.

"Ted Farnsworth." The deep, resonant voice was vaguely familiar.

Unfortunately, it made Ted release Quentin's hand. "Hey, Dr. Kendrick, David. What are you doing here? If you came for my wedding, there may be a slight delay. Besides, I, uh, don't think those trolls'll fit in the room."

"That's not why I'm here."

"Alun." David's voice held an edge of urgency. "Wait a minute. There's something I need to check."

"I'm afraid that will have to wait, Dafydd. Ted Farnsworth, for gross negligence with respect to the Secrecy Pact, I arrest you in the council's name."

"What?" Quentin outraged shout was masked by Ted's.

"But I haven't done anything. Not lately. Who says—"

"We have evidence—photographic evidence—that you're still consorting with the tabloid photographer, Matthew Steinitz, and as a result have exposed the supernatural community to discovery."

"What, just by having dinner with him at the diner? Fishing with him?"

"Look at these."

Quentin pressed himself against the wall, wishing desperately that he dared rush into the corridor. But what would that accomplish? It'd only force Ted into awkward gyrations as they jockeyed to avoid facing one another.

He didn't dare breathe in case the sound of air sawing into his lungs blocked Ted's response. But Ted was quiet for a long time. Was that a hitch in his breath? Quentin couldn't tell.

"I . . . see." Ted's voice was defeated. "Okay. Let's go."

There were sounds of movement as the group in the hall rearranged themselves. David shuffled into Quentin's sightline. He met Quentin's gaze, his eyes wide and stricken.

"These guards will escort you," Dr. Kendrick said. "I have to collect Mr. Steinitz."

"You're arresting Matt too? But—"

"Ted." Dr. Kendrick heaved a heavy sigh. "He's sold pictures of your Bigfoot impersonations to three different publications. He's a party to nearly blinding a vampire fledgling—then had the gall to capture the moment and sell *that* image to three different papers. And now he's threatened us with *these*. He can't be allowed to distribute these photographs. You know that."

"Yeah, but . . . Shit."

No no no. Don't go with them. Not now. Not without me.

"Ted." Quentin's croak was drowned by the heavy march of feet. As soon as they faded down the hallway, Quentin rushed out of the room.

Dr. Kendrick—Alun—stepped back, his hand going to the hilt of his sword. "Quentin. What are you doing here?"

"I just got divorced and I was supposed to be getting married." He glared at Alun. "It seems to me that I'm the only one presently in this corridor who has a legitimate reason to be here."

Alun scowled, although he released his sword hilt. "I'm here on council business."

Quentin folded his arms across his chest. He was nearly Alun's size now, and for the first time he was glad of it. "That business sounds remarkably specious to me. May I see this alleged evidence?"

"I don't see what business it is of yours."

"Alun." David put a hand on his husband's arm. "Show him the pictures. Please."

Alun looked down into David's face, fondness and exasperation vying for ascendance in his expression. "Oh very well."

He extracted several photographs from inside his jerkin and handed them to Quentin.

The first was a grainy photograph of Quentin himself, his fingers buried in Ted's grizzly fur. *Hunting for fleas.* "The only thing it proves is that I might have an unfortunate death wish or a close personal friendship with a bear."

"Except there are no grizzlies in this part of Oregon."

"Regardless, Matt wasn't present that day." Although . . . there was that point where Quentin thought he'd heard something in the underbrush. He wasn't mentioning that to Alun, however.

He shuffled it to the bottom of the stack. The second picture was far more damning—but not to Ted. It was a picture of Quentin, his wings fully extended, his mouth twisted in a snarl. Since Matt's presence had been what prompted Quentin to lose control so completely, he could scarcely deny the man had been there.

Quentin scared up some bravado. "The Bertrand-Harringtons and the other dynastic 'cubi families have protocols in place for dealing with this sort of . . . accidental breach. I can contact my lawyers immediately and put things in motion. There's no need —"

Alun's expression turned wooden. "Are you sure it was accidental?"

"Are you serious? Ted had no idea I'd manifest in full incubus mode. *I* didn't even know I could do it."

"That's not what I mean. Both incidents occurred on Ted's property. How did Steinitz know to show up at that time and in those locations? How did he get his information?"

Heat prickled along Quentin's scalp and across his shoulder blades. *Now is not a good time to lose control.* "Are you insinuating that Ted set me up?"

"*I'm* not insinuating anything, but the council is interpreting it exactly that way. You're being characterized as a victim, which is why I haven't been ordered to arrest you too."

"But that makes no sense. *I'm* the one who committed the infraction. You're arresting Ted yet letting me off scot-free?"

Alun rubbed the back of his neck. "Not entirely scot-free. You're being fined for failure to control."

"Fined? How much?"

Alun glanced down at his shoes, but David grimaced and said, "Two hundred dollars."

Quentin's shoulders twitched and burned, his wings ready to burst free. He clenched his teeth and attempted to dial back his outrage. "Two hundred dollars for the person who committed the infraction versus an arrest and trial for someone who was merely present at the time? How is that fair?"

"It's not. But when the council considers Secrecy Pact violations, they fall squarely on the pragmatic side rather than the philosophical." Alun smiled rather grimly. "As you said, your family, with their money and influence, is in a position to suppress the images and minimize exposure. Ted . . . is not."

"That's—that's *monstrous.*"

"Quentin—"

"If you believe for one minute that these ridiculous charges are grounds for arrest, you—"

"*Quentin!* Look at the last picture."

Quentin growled under his breath, snapping the picture of himself to the bottom of the stack. But the last picture sent a wave of ice through him, shutting down his anger.

The photo showed a line of children, probably between the ages of six and ten, filing into a brick building at the edge of a forest.

"What's this?"

"The local school for shifter kids. The message is clear, the threat obvious, even without the ransom demand that the head of the bear council received not two hours ago. This person is targeting the entire supe community, including our most vulnerable members, our children."

"But Ted wouldn't— He's not the kind of man who'd endanger children."

Alun sighed. "Not deliberately, perhaps. But he doesn't always think before he speaks, and his continued association with Steinitz is a known security risk. He's been warned to cut the connection—more than once—and he hasn't. This is the result."

"Look, Alun, I'm not exactly a fan of Mr. Steinitz, but just because he took an unflattering picture of me, I don't see him as the sort who would ransom children's safety. When he ran off this morning, he... Wait a minute." Quentin shuffled the picture of him with his wings extended. He tapped it with one finger, not really caring that his claw was half-extended. "He couldn't have taken this picture. He didn't have a camera and he was flat on his face"—*in Ted's crotch*—"at the time."

"Is that so?" Alun held out his hand, and Quentin passed over the photographs. "In that case, I hope Mr. Steinitz has explanations for the others—and proof that he couldn't have taken them too." He tucked the photographs away and leaned over to kiss David. "I'll bring him to headquarters for questioning." He nodded at Quentin. "Don't worry. I won't let the council railroad Ted." He took off down the hallway.

And neither will I. Ted needed somebody to speak for him, and Quentin was a trained advocate.

With a very personal agenda.

"I've got to get to that hearing." But how could he get there in time? Alun could gate through Faerie to supe headquarters, but Quentin didn't have that option.

"I think we should both go," David said, nodding decisively.

"How do you suggest we do so? Can you call your brother-in-law again?"

David flashed a grin. "Oh we don't need to do that. There's a translocation door on the fourth floor next to the vending machines. But before we go—"

"Later, David, please."

He caught Quentin's sleeve. "It's important. Besides, Alun can't possibly apprehend Mr. Steinitz so quickly, and the proceedings can't start until he's there."

"Fine. But let's not waste time. I don't want to take chances with Ted's fate."

"You left so quickly this morning that I didn't get to tell you about the results of my evaluation of Ted's health."

Quentin waved his words away. "He told me that he was fine, but I can't really believe it."

"You should. But the thing is—" David bit his lip, extending his hands to Quentin. "May I?"

"Oh why the hell not?" Quentin muttered with something less than grace. He thrust out his hands, and David took them, the telltale thread of *achubydd* power skating immediately along Quentin's nerves.

His eyes half-lidded, David hummed tunelessly to himself. After a minute or so, he released Quentin and smiled up at him.

"It's just what I thought."

"What is?"

"When I examined Ted, I noticed that there were several places where his energy was tangled. Sort of—" he cupped both hands and brought them together as if packing a snowball "—backed up. Looking for an outlet. You have that same condition."

"I do?" Quentin stared at his hands. "Where?"

Pink infused David's cheeks. "Um . . . a few places. That's not relevant. The important thing is that when we came down the hall, I saw you holding hands with Ted."

It was Quentin's turn to blush. "I didn't think it would hurt him. Just holding hands. You said the desiccation required prolonged exposure—"

"Don't worry. Nothing's wrong. In fact, I think I found out what Ted's energy snarls were looking for." He pointed at Quentin. "You. And yours are tuned to him. I saw the exchange from way back there. It was pretty hard to miss."

"But—but that can't be. If I'm taking energy—"

"Excuse me, who's the *achubydd* here?" David propped his fists on his hips. "Despite what you believe, I've learned in the last months that energy is not a zero-sum game." He squinted at the ceiling. "Think of it like those hybrid cars, where the kinetic energy from the brakes recharges the electric batteries. It works that way with *achubydd* healing. And it looks like it works that way with you and Ted. You're completing a circuit, feeding each other energy. Ted, as a bear shifter, can store a boatload of energy with his prehibernation eating patterns, which means you're consuming those reserves, not his life force. And as a by-product, you're . . . well . . . transmogrifying it and feeding it back as a sort of antisnooze discharge. So he's not only svelter— he's not sleepy." He cast a critical glance at Quentin, and Quentin could swear he looked right through him. "When you're separated, though, the circuit is broken, and I don't think it's good for either of you."

Quentin stared at him, hope warring with his near-panic at Ted's arrest. *I could be with him. We could be together.* So they couldn't ever look each other in the face again. They could at least be together. They could touch. *It's enough. It has to be.*

But first he had to keep the council from throwing Ted in jail or whatever medieval punishment they were cooking up.

"Come on. Fourth floor you said?"

They raced down the hallway, but at the head of the stairs, they encountered Zeke, the tip of each finger swaddled in a Band-Aid, another damn contract in his hands. "Mr. Bertrand-Harrington. Has Mr. Moreau returned?"

Quentin shared a sidelong glance with David. "Casimir is missing too?"

"Yes. I mean, of course not. That is, I'm sure he's only momentarily detained." He peered around the hall while the AI pulsed as if with silent laughter at his shoulder. "Where's Mr. Farnsworth?"

"He's been detained too, and not so momentarily. They've taken him to supe headquarters."

"But—but the ceremonies. The celebrants are already booked and they—they—"

"Turn very noncelebratory if they're stood up?" Quentin said dryly.

"No. But everything's *prepared*."

"Too bad." Quentin narrowed his eyes, focusing on the contracts. "In fact—" He snatched the papers out of Zeke's hands.

"Hey! Those aren't yours!"

As Quentin peered at the rusty cursive writing on the first page, his own name formed under Party of the Second Part, in the loops and whorls of formal script. A laugh bubbled up from somewhere nearly forgotten. "As a matter of fact, they are." He grabbed Zeke's wrist. "Come on. We've got a date with a drumhead court."

Chapter Twenty-Four

Magical handcuffs sucked.

The two enormous troll guards in metal studded-leather had slapped them on Ted the instant they were out of sight of Dr. Kendrick. They prevented him from rubbing his chest, which ached twice as bad now that he'd had a chance to touch Quentin again.

The guards had hauled him up the stairs, past the soda machine, and through a door that led straight to council headquarters. *Handy.* Although he could have wished for a little more time. Everything was happening too fast. He needed a chance to *process*, damn it.

From the look on the guards' faces, though, they wouldn't be open to a little time-out. They marched him through a warren of narrow hallways, each holding one of his elbows in a bruising grip, their other hands on their sword hilts. *What the heck do they think I can pull in the middle of council territory?* He couldn't even shift with these cuffs on. If he tried, he'd cut his own paws off.

The trolls stopped in front of a massive door, reinforced with metal strapping that glowed with eldritch fire. It looked like something out of a medieval dungeon. *Guess the council likes to mix it up with their interior decoration.*

The guards opened the door, and it swung inward with a very theatrical creak. "In here. You'll be summoned when the council's ready for you."

"Do you know when that might be?"

"When they're ready. I said get in!" One guard shoved Ted in the middle of the back, forcing him to stumble inside the cell. The door *thunked* closed behind him, followed by the key grating in the lock and what sounded like a bar being dropped into brackets as well. *Overkill much, guys? I'm a bear shifter, not a demon necromancer.*

He glanced around. As cells went, it wasn't bad. Even though the door looked like something out of the Spanish Inquisition, the interior was modern, with an oversized cot, a sink, a toilet, and a low shelf with several battered paperbacks.

He sat on the cot, his back to the wall, trying to control the trembling in his hands—which were still cuffed. The cell didn't have a clock or a window, so Ted had no idea how to mark the passage of time. How would his trial go? Who would be there? *I wish I could see Quentin again.* Oh right. He couldn't *see* Quentin again for all eternity, give or take. *But maybe I could touch him. Hold his hand again.*

Ted closed his eyes and leaned his head against the rough stone wall. He might have dropped off for a while—when one of the troll guards banged the cell door open, it could have been an hour, six hours, or maybe only minutes later.

It hardly mattered. He'd gone beyond numb at this point.

He let the guard haul him up the stairs and down a narrow, stone-walled hall that twisted in a way that made no sense. *Huh. Another interdimensional pocket.* It would have to be, now that Ted thought of it, since it needed to be accessible to all supes regardless of where they called home.

They reached the end of the corridor and crossed a room that looked like the lobby at the Jetsons' dentist's office. At the far side, beyond the unoccupied space-age desk, was a huge set of double doors, carved all over with tiny figures. Ted caught a glimpse of wolves, bears, demons, and dragons before the doors opened and his guard prodded him inside.

Ted had been on a jury a couple of times—one Outer World and one supe—and this room looked pretty much like those courtrooms, with a jury box on one side, and a few rows of seats that held a handful of spectators on either side of a center aisle.

But that was where the familiarity ended. He'd only seen a single judge or arbiter on the bench before, but this time there were three.

Wait. Three? Only capital offenses—the ones that could result in execution or form-locking—were presided over by three arbiters. Ted swallowed against a surge of bile. *I knew it was bad, but not* this *bad.*

The one in the middle, in the chief arbiter's throne, was a tiny elderly woman with a sky-blue headscarf and the sharpest black eyes Ted had ever seen. Her nameplate read *Elder Bowen*, and he didn't need its acorn motif or her title to know she was a druid. The two others, though—*Holy shit, they're not screwing around.* Because the other two were queens. On the right, the dragon queen herself, Teresa Tomlinson with her famous pearls and an emerald ring the size of a walnut. On the left, the *fricking Queen of Faerie*, red-haired, green-eyed, as beautiful as the day, and as remote as the moon.

In a way, Ted was glad that the council was taking his case seriously. On the other hand, his belly wanted to drop through the floor because the council was taking his case *seriously.* A druid elder and two queens? Ted's belly did a barrel roll. *Ursa's claws, I'm going to die.*

Then he saw who was in the jury box and decided a preemptive death might be an option. Because not only was Bruno Killingsworth, the chief of the bear council, sitting there with his arms crossed over his prehibernation paunch and a scowl that could sour milk, but somehow Ted's brother, Ben, had gotten whisked here from Supernatural Selection, as had Quentin's grandmother. Ben was slouched in his chair, not meeting Ted's eyes or even acknowledging his presence. Pauline, however, gave him a faint smile before directing her attention to the bench.

There were other people there—a werewolf alpha, a slender man so pale he had to be a vampire, a guy in horn-rimmed glasses who looked like his tie was about to strangle him, a witch in about a ton of blue-green draperies—but Ted's gaze was riveted on his brother. *I never thought they'd bring him here or I would have asked them not to.* Not that anyone had paid much attention to his wishes so far.

Elder Bowen rapped on the bench. "The combined supe tribunal is called to order with Cassandra Bowen, Eldest of the North American Druids, and their Majesties Teresa Tomlinson of the Dragons and Caitrìona of Faerie presiding." She struck a tiny brass gong with a mallet, then turned to the people sitting in the jury box. "Our first order of business is the matter of gross violations of the Secrecy Pact on the part of Ted Farnsworth, bear shifter. Representatives, this matter will be decided by the arbiters. You are here as witnesses only, and may be called upon for testimony. Otherwise we ask that you allow the hearing to proceed without comment. Do you understand?"

The people in the box murmured, "Aye."

"Good." Elder Bowen glanced between Ted and the box. "Ordinarily, the head of the accused's shifter council acts as his advocate, but in this case the head of the bear council is the complainant. Do you have an advocate of your own, Mr. Farnsworth?"

"I didn't know about this until two minutes before I got thrown in jail, so no. I don't have an advo—"

The doors banged open and a familiar voice called from the hallway, "*I* am Mr. Farnsworth's advocate."

Q-Bert. Despite this whole fucked-up situation, Ted grinned.

"If that is indeed the case," Elder Bowen said, "perhaps you could approach the bench."

"I would like nothing better, Your Honor; however, I have to ask Mr. Farnsworth to face the east wall first."

Elder Bowen raised her thin eyebrows. "That is a very irregular request."

"No, no. I get it." Ted stood up and faced the wall. "Ready when you are, Q-Bert."

Even with Ted facing the wall, Quentin couldn't walk straight down the aisle. The invisible force that kept them from facing one another compelled him to sidestep toward the front of the room.

"Could you face the back wall, please, Ted?"

"Sure thing."

Ted must have complied, because Quentin managed to turn and face the tribunal.

"You are an incubus, are you not, sir?" Elder Bowen asked.

Quentin bowed. "I am."

"I was not aware that 'cubi were quite so casual in their dress. Do you consider this appropriate attire for an advocate in this chamber, Mr. Bertrand-Harrington?"

"Perhaps it's time for supes, including Your Honors—" Quentin kept his voice smooth and neutral "—to cease placing so great an emphasis on how things *appear* and pay closer attention to how things *are.*"

"I see you don't intend to mince words. However, with regard to your client, the photographic evidence—"

"Does not implicate Mr. Farnsworth. Whom it *does* implicate, if I may be so bold—"

"You haven't held back so far," Elder Bowen said dryly.

Quentin acknowledged her with a slight bow. "Whom it *does* implicate, is the council. Instead of focusing on this rather flimsy evidence of Mr. Farnsworth's complicity, I believe the council should be launching a full-scale investigation into the *true* source of this serious external threat to supe security."

"This is a waste of time," a bearded man with a roll around his middle that proclaimed him a bear shifter muttered.

"Really?" Grandmother gave him a *look*. "What exactly is on your busy agenda, Mr. Killingsworth? A nap? Or a cheesesteak and fries?"

Elder Bowen rapped her knuckles on the table. "Representatives, if you please. Mr. Bertrand-Harrington still has the floor." She fixed Quentin with an intense gaze. "Do you have any suggestions about where this threat might originate, Mr. Bertrand-Harrington?"

"With all the magic at the council's disposal—druid, fae, and witch—I believe that now that the breach is acknowledged, you should have no trouble tracing it. It does require *looking*, however, which I don't believe has been attempted before."

"There is no need to dwell on that point, Mr. Bertrand-Harrington."

"Yes, Your Honor." Quentin raised his fist to his mouth to muffle a laugh. "I believe I may be able to assist in the investigation." He nodded at Alun, who was standing at the door with his sword in his hand.

He opened the door, and two other troll guards strode in, one leading Matt, who was looking around him like he'd just landed in Oz, and the other dragging a gibbering Larry.

Aha! I wonder if Matt pointed at Larry or if Alun used one of those druid location potions. However it had been accomplished, it created a veritable uproar among the audience and the representatives as well.

Matt did a double take when he spotted Quentin. "Wait. Don't you have wings? Where—"

"Silence!" Elder Bowen's druid power voice echoed in the chamber. Everybody shut up, and no wonder. Despite being so tiny, she was formidable. "Lord Cynwrig," she said in her normal voice, "would you care to explain to the council why you have brought not only the human we summoned, but another?"

Alun paced up the aisle. He shot Quentin a half smile as he passed. "Mr. Steinitz is the human who was present at Mr.

Bertrand-Harrington's—er—spontaneous transformation. However, Mr. Williams is the person who actually took those photographs."

He did? Good job, Alun.

Quentin picked up the ball for him. "That being the case, Dr. Kendrick very properly brought both these men here because it's supe policy that any human who is exposed to supe existence be subjected to council adjudication for appropriate action, whether treatment for shock and trauma, or . . . suppression." *Suppression. The supe euphemism for execution. Wonderful.* "Isn't the proper order of events to question the witnesses?"

"Yes, yes." Elder Bowen turned to the Faerie Queen. "If you wouldn't mind administering the truth spell?"

She lifted her index finger a fraction of an inch, causing Matt and Larry to jolt. "It is done."

Quentin approached Matt. "Mr. Steinitz, did you take those photographs?"

"No. If it was my work, they wouldn't have been so poorly composed." Matt's eyebrows shot up, as if he hadn't intended to say that.

"Did you, in any of your . . . photographic excursions . . . mean any harm to Mr. Farnsworth?"

"Jesus, no. I didn't want to *hurt* Ted. I wanted to *date* him." Matt winced. "If you're going to kill me, now would be a good time."

Quentin fought a growl. *You're not getting a chance to date him. Not ever.* He tugged on the hem of his shirt, clearing his throat to mask his response since his own jealousy wouldn't help Ted's case. "You're in no danger of that, Mr. Steinitz. One more question. Every published photograph that has seemed to expose the supernatural world, whether actual or false, has been taken by you. Why have you pursued leads about supernatural occurrences so assiduously?"

"Because I *wanted* it to be true. Ever since I was a kid and saw what I thought was a dragon flying over Mount Hood one night, I've wanted it to be true. A promise of something other than the crappy world we live in, something fantastic, something beyond politics. Although—" he scanned the representatives "—it looks like politics is just as fucked up here as in the human world." He slapped his forehead. "Okay, now *really* kill me before I say something else."

"I have no further questions for you." Quentin turned to Larry, who looked more terrified—rightfully so—than when Quentin had confronted him about Ted's truck. "However, for Mr. Williams—" Quentin collected the pictures from Alun's extended hand as if they'd planned it, and advanced on Larry. "Did you take these pictures?" He held them out, but when Larry took them, his hand shook so much that he dropped them.

He clenched his eyes shut. "Yeah."

"How long have you been attempting to expose the supe communities?" Quentin withheld his rage by the tips of his claws, which itched to extend and rake Larry from throat to groin.

"What? I haven't. I didn't. Soups? I don't even know what you're talking about."

"Did you issue the ransom demand?"

Larry's eyes nearly bugged out of his head. "Ransom? No!"

"Then why did you take these photographs?"

"Money. It was the money, okay? Some guy called me and offered me a couple grand for every picture I could deliver."

"How long has this been going on?"

"It's new, I swear." He glared at Quentin with loathing. "The guy told me he wanted pictures from Ted's place, but I wasn't gonna do it until you showed up and started throwing your weight around, dissing me in my own shop. Figured I'd make some dough, and if I could screw you over at the same time, even better." He wiped his forehead with a trembling hand. "I figured you were just some runner, you know? I didn't know you were a fucking *freak*."

"Kindly refrain from the pejorative comments, Mr. Williams," Elder Bowen said.

Quentin took a step toward Larry. He cowered against the troll, who rolled his eyes and pushed him away. "Who was this person?"

"I don't know. I swear. Just a voice on the phone, kinda breathy."

"You said 'guy'—are you sure it was a man?"

"Coulda been a girl, I guess."

"How did you arrange payment?"

"Locker at the Greyhound station in Portland. I'd go to a coffee shop down the street, and an hour later, the money was there. Don't know how they knew I put the stuff in there."

"Thank you." Quentin nodded at Alun. "Lord Cynwrig, you may remove them."

"'Remove'?" Larry's gaze bounced wildly from Quentin to Alun to Elder Bowen. "You don't mean—"

"He means the guards will take you out of this room." Alun gestured to the trolls, who escorted the two men down the aisle. "You're not finished, however. The council will interview you later and determine your fate."

"'Fate'?" Larry squeaked. "What do you mean 'fate'? I know what I mean when I say 'fate.' What do you mean when you say 'fate'? Because I was only doing it for the money. I didn't care about—"

The doors shut on the guards, cutting off Larry's babbling, praise be to all gods and devils.

Quentin turned to the arbiters. "Now, I trust that dispenses with the question of this particular Secrecy Pact infraction. What are the other charges?"

Elder Bowen nodded to Killingsworth.

"He has no ambition. He can't hold on to a job to save his life."

"I'm a bear shifter." Ted's voice echoed oddly since he was facing the wall. "I *can't* hold a regular job. Not all year anyway, which you should know, Bruno, since you've got the same problem. But I help at the diner and the grocery and at Stuff 'n' Things outside of hibernation season."

"I think— That is, it's the opinion of the bear council that Ted's lack of a regular routine leaves him too much time to screw up—I mean transgress." Killingsworth's words took on a stilted cadence that suggested he'd memorized them. "So we request that he be tagged so his activities may be monitored and regulated as necessary. If that should fail, we ask that he be form-locked."

"F-f-form-locked?" Ted's choked whisper tore at Quentin's heart.

The dragon queen leaned forward. "Is that really necessary? Form-locking has severe consequences for the shifter. Few who are locked in human form have remained sane, and as for the ones locked in animal form . . ." She spread her palms with a wince.

Not on my watch, thank you. "Just a moment, Your Honors," Quentin said. "Mr. . . . Killingsworth, is it? Mr. Killingsworth has stated that Mr. Farnsworth has no ambition. While this isn't against the law—either supe or human, and therefore should have no bearing on these proceedings, *particularly* when the proposed penalty is as severe as form-locking—the statement is incorrect."

"Bullshit. He—"

Elder Bowen rapped the dais with her cane. "Mr. Killingsworth, *if* you don't mind." She nodded at Quentin. "Please continue."

"Mr. Farnsworth recently purchased an unfinished resort from the Walton marten shifter clan. He plans to transform the property into a high-end destination resort for both supes and humans."

"Yeah, right," Killingsworth scoffed. "Like *that* will ever happen."

"As a matter of fact," Quentin said coldly, "renovations are already underway and expected to be completed by third quarter."

"They are?" Ted said. "I mean, yeah. They are."

"That sheds a slightly different light on things," Elder Bowen murmured.

"No, it doesn't," Killingsworth growled. "He needs to be tagged."

Quentin glared at him. "On the strength of nothing but photographs that weren't even his fault? What exactly do you have against Mr. Farnsworth?"

Killingsworth deliberately turned his shoulder to Quentin. "You know what kind of shit Ted's got up to in the past, Your Honors. Those Bigfoot scams? I'm sure there were others. Those were just the ones we found out about."

"An interesting deduction," Quentin said. "However, I'm unwilling to accept your certainty as proof of guilt without corroborating evidence."

"Well, think about it. He spends half his time in town, hanging out with the mundanes—"

"The humans, you mean."

He glared at Quentin. "That's what I said. He doesn't behave like a proper bear shifter, always wanting to be *watched*—"

"He doesn't want to be *watched*"—*you pompous asshole*—"he wants to be *seen*."

Killingsworth snorted. "Well, tagging him would take care of *that*."

Quentin took a measured breath because decking the bear council leader would *not* promote Ted's interests. "Not spied upon. Not deprived of his right to privacy. *Recognized*. For who he is. As something other than a bear shifter cliché. As someone who has needs outside your narrow view of acceptable supe behavior." Quentin wanted so badly to see Ted's face, but the best he could manage was a bare glimpse of his back as he stood facing the wall. "You've been treating him as a nuisance, an embarrassment. But in truth, he represents the best of all our communities. He deserves to be appreciated." He turned to face the arbiters. "He deserves to be honored. He does *not* deserve to be prosecuted."

"A fair point," the Faerie Queen murmured.

Quentin bowed to her. "Are you prepared to drop the charges against Mr. Farnsworth?"

Elder Bowen glanced from one queen to the other, both of whom nodded their approval. "Very well."

"Hey!" Killingsworth leaped to his feet. "What about my complaint?"

"What about it?" Elder Bowen fixed him with a stony stare. "Mr. Farnsworth wasn't responsible for the security breach, which frankly was the only issue of concern to the supe council as a whole, regardless of the bear council's views."

Killingsworth's face turned an alarming shade of red. "I demand to be heard."

Elder Bowen frowned irritably. "I'm sure you do. However, we are not required to listen." She turned to the Faerie Queen. "Caitrìona, thank you for your time. Please don't feel obliged to stay."

The Queen rose gracefully, swept the crowd with a regal glance, spared a wintery smile for Ted, then disappeared through the door behind the bench.

Elder Bowen picked up the little brass mallet. "If there is nothing more—"

"Actually, I would like to propose an item of new business," Quentin said. "Something for which I'd appreciate the opinion of the remaining tribunal." If he was going to pull this off, he needed the weight of the arbiters' authority—the dragon queen because she outranked Killingsworth, and Elder Bowen because the druids' most sacred tenet was *balance*. She'd be tough but fair. *It's the best I can hope for.*

"Your request is slightly unusual but not out of line." Elder Bowen glanced at the dragon queen, who nodded graciously. "Pray continue."

"In the matter of Mr. Farnsworth's marriage, I'd like to ask Mr. Zeke Oz to answer a few questions."

"Me?" Zeke squeaked from his seat in the back row.

Elder Bowen beckoned to him. "Come forward please, Mr. Oz."

Zeke scuttled to the front of the chamber and bobbed his head to each of the arbiters.

"Mr. Oz, could you tell the arbiters what happened several weeks ago when Mr. Farnsworth and I signed our mating contracts—" Quentin swept the representatives with a bland stare "—in blood?"

"Ah. Yes. Well. For some reason, the final contracts were . . . incorrect."

A woman in a dress that seemed to consist solely of green and blue chiffon scarves muttered about incompetence.

Elder Bowen raised her eyebrows. "Did you have something to add, Magistra Lenore?"

Magistra? A seriously high-ranking witch.

She stood up. "My collective owns and operates Supernatural Selection, the matchmaking agency that employs Mr. Oz. Mr. Farnsworth is a client and was scheduled to enter a blood mating contract with Mr. Elmer—aka Rusty—Johnson nearly a month ago."

"A good match," the dragon queen said. "Rusty is extraordinarily stable and dependable. He would certainly offset Ted's more volatile nature."

"Unfortunately," Magistra Lenore said, with a narrow-eyed glare at Zeke, "it didn't occur because of clear negligence on the part of Mr. Oz."

"*Alleged* negligence," Quentin countered. *And Rusty is not getting anywhere near Ted.* "Mr. Oz, had that kind of error ever occurred before?"

"Not to my knowledge. Although I haven't been with the agency for long."

"Tell us what happened, please."

"Mr. Farnsworth's contract should have been with Mr. Johnson, and yours with Mr. Casimir Moreau, the vampire. But instead, they were between the two of you."

"So the names on both contracts, executed on opposite sides of the country, were inexplicably altered, when neither Mr. Farnsworth nor I had ever heard of the other?"

"Yes, that's correct." Zeke's gaze darted to Magistra Lenore and he swallowed audibly.

"What happened this evening?"

Zeke's forehead wrinkled. "A lot of things. Which one exactly?"

"Let's say the events at 10:45."

"Oh. You and Mr. Farnsworth participated in the escape clause ritual to break your contract. Which is why you can't—" he gestured between Quentin and Ted "—look at each other. Although I still think the spell's terms are manifesting in a really strange way."

"What happened then?"

"You asked to be alone for a few minutes, and I took Mr. Farnsworth upstairs to meet Mr. Johnson for their wedding. But, ah, Mr. Johnson wasn't there."

Elder Bowen lifted an eyebrow at the dragon queen. "Stable and dependable, is he?" She nodded at Zeke. "Please continue."

"I thought I could have Mr. Farnsworth fill out his paperwork, but the contracts were wrong again. They had Mr. Bertrand-Harrington's name on them."

"Clearly you had an old copy," Magistra Lenore said.

"No, it was fresh. Furthermore, when I generated it again, the same thing happened. So I wrote it out longhand." He held up one hand and waggled his bandaged fingers. "With a blood quill."

"But that didn't work either," Quentin said. "My name replaced Mr. Johnson's on the contract, regardless of Mr. Oz's . . . extraordinary measures." He turned to the arbiters. "When I spoke to Mr. Oz on that first day, he told me that the Supernatural Selection spell for perfect matches is global. That it should *prevent* clerical errors like the one we assumed had occurred."

"'Assumed'?" Elder Bowen said.

"Yes. Assumed. I believe the Supernatural Selection spell is stronger than any of us imagined. The altered names in our contracts—and Mr. Oz's inability to bypass those alterations—are manifestations of the spell's self-correcting power."

"Are you saying," Elder Bowen said, "that *you* are Mr. Farnsworth's perfect match?"

"I am."

"Then why in blazes did you break your contract?"

"We were . . . misinformed. And perhaps slow to shed our own preconceived notions. But this is the truth." Quentin raised his voice so Ted would be sure to hear him. "Even if the escape clause prevents us from ever facing one another again, I would still marry him. I would still live in the same house with him, even if we had to eat every meal back to back and hold hands around corners. I will still love him, still be *in* love with him, even if we can never *make* love again."

"This has gone far enough." His grandmother stood up, tugging the hem of her jacket straight. "Permission to speak."

"It seems you are doing so already," Elder Bowen said. "Continue, by all means, Ms. Bertrand-Harrington."

"My grandson and Mr. Farnsworth have imprinted." Teresa Tomlinson inhaled on a little gasp. "Yes, you know exactly what that means, don't you, Your Majesty?"

She nodded, her pearls *clishing* as if she were trembling. "Your grandson will die if he's not allowed to be with Mr. Farnsworth. I'm not certain what would happen to Mr. Farnsworth. It's never come up."

"So you see, Supernatural Selection, by conducting the escape clause, has condemned my grandson to death." She looked down her nose at Magistra Lenore. "If the Supernatural Selection management refuses to escape the escape, as it were, they will have committed premeditated murder. And I for one would take exception to that. *Extreme* exception."

Magistra Lenore met Grandmother's glare with a scowl of her own. "The terms of the escape ritual were made perfectly clear. Reversing it is simply not done."

"You mean it *hasn't* been done, or you are *incapable* of doing it?"

Magistra Lenore pressed her lips together, nostrils flaring. "Of course I could do it. But it would take some particularly expensive ingredients, and this time *somebody* would absolutely have to sacrifice a body part."

Pauline raised an elegant silver eyebrow. "Perhaps you could volunteer for the sacrifice. Doesn't the doubloon stop with you?"

Quentin held up his hands, palms out, before his grandmother could throw down with the witch. "Your Honors, representatives, please. I believe this situation could be resolved to everyone's benefit." He bowed to the magistra. "Haven't we just proven that your perfect match spell is effective even when your clients have completely different results in mind? Think of this as an opportunity."

Magistra Lenore narrowed her eyes, peering at him with obvious suspicion. "An opportunity?"

"Exactly. Mr. Farnsworth and I aren't a liability. We're the perfect demonstration of the infallibility of your services—an unlikely and *unexpected* match that is nonetheless perfect. Don't you think it would be a better public-relations move to reverse the escape clause voluntarily? Because if you persist in dividing a perfect match by refusing, what does that say about your brand?"

She tapped her chin with one silver-enameled nail. "You have a point. However, it will be tricky. And until I can execute the counterspell, you and Mr. Farnsworth must keep to the spirit of the escape clause as well as the letter."

Quentin inhaled sharply, tempted to shout in triumph. He restricted himself to a bland smile. "Of course." He turned to the arbiters. "Thank you for indulging me, Your Honors. I have nothing further to say."

"Thank you, everyone. We are adjourned." Elder Bowen struck the little gong in front of her. "Please clear the chamber."

Magistra Lenore strode toward Ted, her draperies billowing. Quentin sighed and began crab-walking his way down the aisle.

"Hey, Q-Bert?" Ted called. "Don't worry, I'll take care of this. But before you go? I love you too."

Chapter Twenty-Five

The session with Magistra Lenore was fairly brutal, but at least the counterspell was short and involved zero fleas. Ted hurried out of the chamber, scents of sage and rosemary clinging to his clothes, and ran right into his brother.

"Ben. You're still here?"

"What do you expect, man? First you get divorced, then you're supposed to get married but get left at the altar, then you get *arrested* thanks to that douche canoe Bruno Killingsworth, and now you're getting married *again*? I mean, dude. Seriously?"

Ted rubbed the back of his neck. "Yeah. It's been a night."

"You think?" But then Ben grabbed him and hugged him tight. *A literal bear hug. Heh. Q-Bert would appreciate that notion.* "Congratulations, Ted. I guess."

Ted chuckled as Ben let go and stepped back, reestablishing his preferred personal space. "Thanks, bro. I want this. A lot. I know it's not your idea of heaven—sharing your space with another person forever—but it's all I've ever dreamed of."

A smile quirked Ben's mouth. "I get it. You're not me. Maybe you could . . ." He swallowed, seeming really interested in the floor all of a sudden. "That is, both of you could, well, visit me sometime?"

Ted had to laugh at the mingled hope and horror in Ben's tone. "Even though the thought makes you want to run for the hills and never come back?"

"For you, I'll make an effort. Don't—" He patted Ted's shoulder awkwardly. "Don't be a stranger. Okay?"

"Okay."

Ben lifted a hand and trotted down the stairs.

Ted waited until his brother was out of sight. His nerves were lit up like Independence Day, and he wasn't sure whether he wanted to prolong the suspense, or end it right the fuck now.

Right the fuck now wins. He ran down the endless hallway until he reached the conference room where Zeke had directed him—he had refused to go back to the altar room and risk seeing that stupid cake again. He paused outside the door to steady himself, although he couldn't control the grin that split his face.

He stepped inside. Quentin and his grandmother were sitting at the conference table, Quentin's back to the door. Pauline caught Ted's eye and smiled graciously.

Quentin turned around, and his eyes widened. "Ted?" He pushed himself out of the chair so fast that he tripped over its leg. "I can face you. She did it? It worked?"

"Uh-huh."

Quentin stumbled across the room and launched himself at Ted. Laughing, Ted caught him around the waist, staggering back a few steps. "Whoa, Q-Bert. Have a heart. You're not the lightweight you used to be."

He reared back, searching Ted's face. "Does that bother you?"

"Nah. I like you no matter what size you are."

Quentin grinned, then kissed Ted—but didn't take it too far, thank goodness, because *grandmother*. Jeez.

But when the kiss ended, Pauline was on her phone, so Ted kept his arm around Quentin's waist and led him back to the table.

"Hey. You're not pulling away from me."

Quentin sighed—but it was a happy sigh, not a defeated sigh or a Ted's-being-annoying sigh. "No. Never again. David told me a few things about how our energies work together.

Although—" he turned in Ted's embrace "—you'll have to eat like it's prehibernation season all year. And you probably won't get a hibernation season."

"So this is what—the incubus weight-loss plan?"

"Something like that. Do you mind?"

"Heck no. I'll be the only bear shifter in the history of ever who's not chubby on New Year's Eve. For that matter, I'll be the only bear shifter ever who's *awake* on New Year's Eve."

Quentin leaned into him. "And I'll be the only incubus who eats regular meals. I'm up for it if you are." He sighed again. *Definitely a happy sound.* "I'm so glad to have you back. To be able to see you. Touch you."

"Me too."

"I was getting ready to hunker down and camp out here for a week in case it took the witches some time to work the reversal."

"I think you inspired Magistra Lenore. Or maybe she just wants us out of her hair."

"So it didn't take her long to cook up the counterspell?"

"She didn't have to." Ted held up his left hand and waggled his little finger—now missing its last joint. "I sacrificed a body part."

"What?" Quentin captured Ted's hand, cradling it gently between both of his, even though Ted's finger didn't hurt at all. "Ted, you didn't have to do that. Your beautiful hand—"

"Look. The way I see it, you've been the one making all the concessions, all the sacrifices. Downscale wardrobe. Living in the woods. Pulling my ass out of the fire with the lodge and . . . well—" he gestured to the room around them "—other things. There's not much I wouldn't have been willing to sacrifice for you."

"Is that all—I mean, you didn't have to give them anything else, did you?"

"Nah. Witches may not have much of a sense of humor, but they're really focused on precise measurements. You know those equivalency chart things that Zeke has? Turns out the body part they needed isn't proportional to the person making the sacrifice. It's proportional to the spell they need it for. Since I'm bigger than most?" He shrugged. "What I had to give up wasn't as much of me as it would have been for a smaller guy. At least they let me pick." He waggled his eyebrows. "Because some parts are nonnegotiable."

"So when will Zeke show up with the new contracts?"

"Boys." Pauline tucked her cell phone into her bag and stood, brushing the wrinkles out of her skirt. "You will not be signing any more contracts in this place. Your wedding will take place in Boston, in the Bertrand-Harrington mansion, not in some—" she flicked her fingers "—*office*." She turned to Ted, looking him up and down. "You'll look splendid in a tux, my dear. I'll make an appointment for you with Quentin's tailor." She eyed Quentin's new and improved physique—and his mountain-casual clothing. "I'll make an appointment for both of you."

She offered Ted her hand, and Quentin froze. "Grandmother."

She looked down her nose at him. "You're *imprinted*, Quentin. His energy is attuned to you and you alone." She glanced up at Ted again. "Although I must say, that aura is *remarkable*." She sailed out of the room.

"Q-Bert," Ted whispered out of the corner of his mouth. "Did your grandmother just hit on me?"

Quentin laughed. "No, darling. She just assured me that no 'cubi could hit on you again." The laughter bled from Quentin's face. "Unless . . . unless you don't *want* to marry me."

"Are you kidding?" Ted wrapped both arms around Quentin. "You *fought* for me. You faced down swords and lying mechanics and the whole fricking *council* for me, something nobody has ever done." He kissed Quentin softly. "But most of all, you set me free. I might not be the average bear, but that's okay. I don't have to be ashamed of it anymore."

"You should never have been ashamed of it in the first place. And if anyone tries to make you feel that way *ever again*, I will have *words* for them."

"Words?" Ted smirked. "Is that all?" He lifted Quentin's hand to his lips. "No claws? No . . ." he leaned down—not as far as he used to need to—and whispered in Quentin's ear, ". . . wings?"

"The wings, my darling, are only for you. Now." He took Ted's hand—the one with the missing piece—as if it didn't bother him at all. "Ready to go?"

"And how." They left the room and headed down the stairs.

"Talk about exhausting," Quentin said. "I want nothing more than to be *home* again."

"Back in Boston, you mean?"

Quentin gave him the stink-eye as they reached the bottom of the stairs. "No, you infuriating bear. I mean *our* home. The cabin. The lodge. Dewton. If I remember correctly, we have a full crew showing up bright and early tomorrow morning."

Ted's grin built from the inside out. "Yeah. Yeah, we do."

Quentin craned his neck, scanning the people milling around the place. "Alun," he called. "If we could have a moment of your time?"

Dr. Kendrick strode over, smiling as he held out his hand to Quentin. "Of course. Congratulations on your successful divorce and engagement. In that order." He turned to Ted and shook his hand too. "Ted, I couldn't be happier with this outcome."

Ted grinned in return, but it faded a bit when he remembered Rusty and Casimir. "I feel kinda bad not telling Rusty and Casimir to their faces. You know, after leaving them at the altar and all."

Dr. Kendrick lifted an eyebrow. "If you recall, they left the altar first, and from what I can discover, they haven't returned. So I think you two are off the hook where they're concerned."

Ted heaved a giant sigh. "Thank goodness for that." He locked gazes with Quentin. "Ready for a two-hour drive?"

"About that . . ." Dr. Kendrick's grin made him look exactly like his brother Mal. "I've arranged for someone else to drive your truck home. I'll be taking you through Faerie."

"Really?"

"Yes. I figured that under the circumstances, you'd appreciate a shorter journey. We'll have to take the upstairs door and detour through supe headquarters, but it's still quicker than the highway."

He was right. In fact, Ted barely noticed the trip at all because he was so drunk from holding Quentin's hand—freely, openly, and without attendant incubus freak-outs.

Dr. Kendrick paused by the gate near their cabin. "I'll leave you two here. Don't hesitate to call if you need anything, but I suspect you'll be fine." He raised a hand in farewell and disappeared through the portal.

Ted and Quentin strolled down the path toward the cabin. When they mounted the steps to the porch, Quentin stopped and gazed across the water at the lodge. Ted came up behind him and wrapped his arms around Quentin's waist, nuzzling his neck.

Quentin chuckled. "We're going to make the lodge the most sought-after venue for *any* event, supe or non-supe. They'll be *clamoring* for bookings for years in advance, just you wait and see."

"Don't you think we should finish the place first?"

"That's as good as done." He leaned against Ted's shoulder. "Do you question my organizational prowess?"

"I don't question any of your prowess. Your prowesses all *rock.*"

"Then the lodge— We have to find a name for it. We can't keep calling it 'the lodge.' That name won't generate the kind of buzz we need."

"It already has a name. The martens gave it one."

"Really?" Quentin twisted around in Ted's arms to face him. "What is it?"

"The, uh, Weasel Pit."

They stared at each other for a moment and then burst into laughter. Quentin recovered first. "Well, *that* has to change." He bit his lip, his gaze slipping down until he was staring into Ted's beard instead of his eyes. "Once it's done, though, we won't have as much privacy anymore. Do you think you'll like it? Running a hotel, I mean?"

"Are you kidding? That's why I've always gotten in trouble with the bear council. I love being around other people, and I didn't always make the best choices about how to arrange a meet-up."

Quentin scowled—at Ted's beard. "Yes. Matt. A definite poor choice." He opened the cabin door and stalked inside.

Fear punched Ted in the gut. "Ursa's teeth, *Matt*. Larry." He hurried inside as Quentin was unlacing his boots. "What happened to them? Are they all right? The council wouldn't have done anything to them, would they?"

Quentin looked up as he wrestled the boots off his feet. "Don't worry. They're both okay." His gaze slid sideways. "Mostly."

Ted toed off his trainers. "What's that supposed to mean?"

"I asked Alun about it. Apparently they turned Larry over to the druids, who've worked some kind of selective memory-slash-restraining spell on him. He won't remember anything about the hearing or my transformation or you as a bear—assuming he ever made that connection—but they didn't erase anything to do with his dodgy contact. They're hoping they can use Larry to track the leak."

"And Matt?"

"He's . . . another story."

Ted's belly pitched sideways. "They didn't hurt him, did they? He really didn't do anything bad. This time anyway."

Quentin patted Ted's chest. "They understand that. Actually, he, ah . . ." He scrunched up his face. "Weeellll . . ."

"Q-Bert. Tell me."

"He's working for the council. More or less."

"*What?*"

"He convinced them that knowing supes were real was all he wanted, that he has no desire to *share* that knowledge, and that he's just as outraged as they are about somebody threatening harm and exposure. He's helping to track down the leak too."

Ted blinked. "That's . . . Wow. Is this the first time they've let a human do that?"

"Yes, at least in several centuries. Apparently," Quentin's tone was dry as toast, "he can be *very* persuasive."

"I know." He glanced down to find Quentin scowling. "I mean—"

"As long as he doesn't attempt to persuade you to date him, he can be as persuasive as he wants. Preferably at a distance."

Ted chuckled, then kissed Quentin's forehead. "You don't have to worry about Matt persuading me to do anything other than share a cup of coffee now and then. You're it for me, Q-Bert. Now and forever."

This time, Ted kissed Quentin's lips, so soft and warm, opening for him sweetly with the brush of Ted's tongue, as the toasted marshmallow aroma made its entrance. *Yes!*

Ted pulled back before they took it further, because he didn't want their first time as *real* fiancés to be on the bare floor with Ted's old trainers and Quentin's boots scattered around them. He stroked Quentin's cheek, hardly able to believe that this was real, that Quentin was *his* and he was Quentin's. "You know, I hope the magistra doesn't give Zeke too bad a time."

"You want to talk about him *now?*" Quentin's mock outrage was so dang cute.

"Well, he did us a solid, you've got to admit, and it's not everyone who can get it right by doing everything wrong." He kissed Quentin again. "Supernatural Selection promised us the perfect match, and that's exactly what we got."

"We had to give a little in return. I forgot to tell you. I promised we'd appear in promotional pieces for them. Ads and such. But the way I see it, that's good for us too. Free publicity for the resort."

"You're amazing, you know that?" Ted pulled Quentin close, but the jacket—his own jacket on Quentin's body—got in the way. "Here. Let me help you with this." He slipped it off Quentin's shoulders, but as he turned to hang it up, something hard banged into his hip. He reached into the pocket and pulled out a bag that held some kind of heavy object.

"What's this?"

Quentin took it from him before Ted had a chance to peek inside. "Just something I asked Zeke to pick up for me." Quentin grinned slyly, rattling the bag. "Think I *persuaded* him to do something illicit for me?"

"You could persuade *me* to do all kinds of illicit things. Gimme that." Ted grabbed for the bag, but Quentin snatched it out of his reach, backing away and holding it up like a carnival prize.

"Come and get it, then." He dodged around Ted and darted for the hall.

With a shout, Ted pursued him, catching the tail of his shirt—Ted's shirt, actually—and spinning him into his arms, knocking both of them off-balance. They caromed into the doorframe of Rusty's—no, Quentin's . . . no, their *own* bedroom, staggered across the floor in a graceless embrace, and fell onto the bed, laughing like idiots.

"Okay. I've got you, fair and square. What's in the bag? If it was anybody but you, I'd say that was supplies, but you don't need 'em."

Quentin smirked. "There are supplies and then there are *supplies*." He slowly pulled out a tin of—

"Hot *damn*, is that Ash Grove Confectionery chocolate sauce?"

"Mm-hmmm." Quentin pushed to his knees and pulled his T-shirt over his head. "I warn you though—" he popped the top button on his fly "—I draw the line at graham crackers."

"You remembered." Ted sat up and shed his own shirt, mouth watering. "You really prepared for my stupid fantasy."

Quentin placed a finger over Ted's lips. "Shhh. There are no stupid fantasies." Then he stood up on the bed and shucked his jeans. "And sex demons are *always* prepared."

Ted and Quentin have found their happily ever after with each other, but what happened to Rusty and Casimir, the men they were *supposed* to marry? Find out in *Vampire With Benefits*.

About Vampire with Benefits

Silent film actor Casimir Moreau had imagined that life as a vampire would be freewheeling and glamorous. Instead, he's plunged into a restrictive society whose rules he runs afoul of at every turn. To "rehabilitate" him, the vampire council orders him mated to an incubus with impeccable breeding who'll mold Cas into the upstanding vampire he ought to be. Or else.

As an inactive beaver shifter, construction engineer Rusty Johnson has fought—and overcome—bias and disrespect his entire life. But when his longtime boyfriend leaves him for political reasons, Rusty is ready to call it a day. Next stop? Supernatural Selection and his guaranteed perfect mate, a bear shifter living far away from Rusty's disapproving clan.

But then a spell snafu at Supernatural Selection robs both men of their intended husbands. Rusty can't face returning to his clan, and Cas needs *somebody* on his arm to keep the council happy, so they agree to pretend to be married. Nobody needs to know their relationship is fake—especially since it's starting to feel suspiciously like the real thing.

Are you worried about what happened to poor, lovelorn human Matt after his embarrassing testimony at Ted's trial? Follow his adventures in the supe community, beginning with *Five Dead Herrings*, the first in the Quest Investigations series!

ABOUT

FIVE DEAD HERRINGS

Something's definitely fishy about this case…

On my last stakeout for Quest Investigations, I nearly got clotheslined by a grove of angry dryads. I expected my bosses to reprimand me, but instead they handed me my first solo assignment. Me! Matt Steinitz, the only human on the Quest roster!

Okay, so the mission isn't exactly demanding. Obviously, the bosses wanted to give me something they think I can't screw up. I'm determined to show them what I can do, however, so I dive right in with no complaints.

At first glance, it looks as simple as baiting a hook: A selkie's almost-ex-husband is vandalizing his boat with unwanted deliveries of deceased sea life. All I have to do is document the scene, tell the ex to cease and desist, and present the bill for property damages. *Boom.* Mission accomplished, another Quest success, and as a bonus, I get to keep my job.

But then things get…complicated. Suspicious undercurrents muddy up my oh-so-easy case. Nothing is as clear as it should be. And the biggest complication? My inappropriate attraction to the client, who may not be as blameless as he claims.

Turns out those dead herrings aren't the only things that stink about this situation.

Dammit.

Five Dead Herrings is the first in the Quest Investigations M/ M paranormal mystery series, a spinoff of E.J. Russell's Mythmatched paranormal rom-com story world. It contains no on-page sex or violence, and although there is a romantic subplot, it is not technically a romance.

a message from
♥ *ej*

Dear Reader,

Thank you so much for reading about my scrumptious cinnamon roll, Ted, and his prickly incubus, Quentin. I hope you'll dive into the other Supernatural Selection tales to find out what's going on with those misbehaving spells!

I'm so happy you've taken this journey with me, and I'd be immensely grateful if you'd take a moment to leave a review at your retailer and any other site you use for reviews. Believe me, reviews make an *enormous* difference to the health and well-being of books (and not incidentally, to their associated authors!).

If this is your first taste of my Mythmatched story world, you might want to travel back to the Fae Out of Water trilogy where it all began. Book One, *Cutie and the Beast*, is David and Alun's story, and you wouldn't want to miss out on *those* shenanigans! (Incidentally, Ted makes his first appearance there, a very glancing mention that planted the first plot seed for this book!)

Pop on over to my website, https://ejrussell.com, for all the deets on my books—the rest of my Mythmatched tales, my other paranormal rom-coms and mysteries, my contemporary romances, and my one lone historical. If you're an audio fan, you can find the audio scoop there too. The Supernatural Selection trilogy, for instance, is narrated by the wonderful Greg Boudreaux. (The QR code on the next page will get you there with your smartphone camera or other code reader.)

My newsletter is the place to get the latest dish on new releases, sales, and more. I promise I only send one out when

I've got...well...news. You can subscribe here: https://
ejrussell.com/newsletter.

All my best,
—E

Also by

ej

Paranormal Romance
Mythmatched Universe
Fae Out of Water Trilogy
Cutie and the Beast
The Druid Next Door
Bad Boy's Bard

Supernatural Selection Trilogy
Single White Incubus
Vampire With Benefits
Demon on the Down-Low

Other Mythmatched Romances
Howling on Hold
Possession in Session
Witch Under Wraps
Cursed is the Worst
The Skinny on Djinni
Assassin by Accident (part of Carnival of Mysteries)

Mythmatched Companion Stories
Rusty's Really Bad Day (free to newsletter subscribers)
Second First Date (free to newsletter subscribers)
First Flight (free to newsletter subscribers)

Quest Investigations Mysteries
Five Dead Herrings

The Hound of the Burgervilles
The Lady Under the Lake
Death on Denial

At Odds with the Gods (A Mythmatched / Purgatory Playhouse
crossover)

Art Medium Series
The Artist's Touch
Tested in Fire
Art Medium: The Complete Collection (omnibus edition)

Legend Tripping Series
Stumptown Spirits
Wolf's Clothing

Enchanted Occasions Series
Best Beast
Nudging Fate
Devouring Flame

Royal Powers Series (shared world)
Duking It Out
Duke the Hall
King's Ex

Magic Emporium Series (shared world)
Purgatory Playhouse

Science Fiction
Sun, Moon, and Stars Series
Partnership
Principles

Interdimensional Time Bureau

Monster Till Midnight

Historical Romance
Silent Sin

Contemporary Romance
Camera Shy
Summer Kitchen
The Thomas Flair
Mystic Man
For a Good Time, Call... (A Bluewater Bay novel, with Anne Tenino)

Christmas Kisses (holiday shorts)
The Probability of Mistletoe
An Everyday Hero
A Swants Soiree

Geeklandia Series
The Boyfriend Algorithm (M/F)
Clickbait

Writing as Nelle Heran
(traditional cozy mystery)

Crafty Sleuth Series (with C.K. Eastland)
Die Cut
Mixed Media
Found Objects (*coming soon)*